Brian Krans
2012

A Constant Suicide

A NOVEL
BRIAN KRANS

Rock Town Press, Davenport, IA

ROCK TOWN PRESS, MAY 2007

Book design by Shawn Eldridge.

Author photograph by Meredith Wood.

This novel was written in conjunction with National Novel Writing Month and Q-C November Novelists.

www.aconstantsuicide.com

ISBN - 13
978-0-9793726-0-5

ISBN - 10
0-9793726-0-7

For those at WSU who told me to keep playing.
For Kautza, who told me to keep working.
For Dan, who told me to keep living.
Especially for John, who told me to keep writing.

A CONSTANT SUICIDE

A NOVEL
BRIAN KRANS

Rock Town Press, Davenport, IA

NOTE

This is a work of fiction.

Any and all references to people living or dead, or events in the past or future, unless specifically noted, are purely coincidental or accidental. Any and all references to earlier artistic works, brand names, products or services are not meant to disparage, defame or degrade in any way.

No animals were hurt in the writing of this novel.

ONE

Visions haunt the mind of unforeseen things of the future. Action is of no possibility, but meandering doubts of a stoic nature made real by the mind are persuasive enough to destroy hope.

It's the overly-broad confusion, but not knowing what to be confused about, that is the most perplexing. Whether it is the future, the present or the past, all of the answers will never come. The uncertainty lies not in the answer, but not knowing what question to ask.

Life must have meaning, but God—if there is such a thing—is having too much fun not telling me what that is.

TWO

We create our saviors.

A personal Jesus can be found anywhere if you look hard enough.

These television messiahs, with their dimples, tan skin and designer suits, come at you live every Sunday, standing before a studio audience of Bible-thumping souls that crave salvation. Their image is one we all want them to be. Plucked, exfoliated, moisturized. It's how we see God. They'll heal the sick and give us words of inspiration to carry out our attempt at a Christ-like life.

For all we know, God is a four-hundred-pound slob sitting in His spaghetti sauce-stained armchair. Maybe the closest thing He can offer to salvation is the Salvation Army.

Everyone wants to be God. We manufacture our own worlds, duping ourselves with things to escape the reality we call our lives. Drugs, alcohol, sex, work, school. Bigger houses, newer cars and designer clothes are the universes we invent to exert our god-like rule. We can't control the weather, but it's always a perfect seventy-two degrees in our central-air controlled worlds.

We stay busy so we don't have to admit we don't have all the answers. After long enough with our constant distractions, we end our search for them. And God. Soon enough, we'll all come to realize we can't be God. We'll settle for telling ourselves we can. Or we'll just make one up.

My savior? He's dead.

Where was I when it happened, I'm not sure. But I can tell you where I was when I got the phone call. Something seemed wrong before anything even happened. Two days ago it was seventy degrees out and out of nowhere—snow. Some would call it an omen. I call it the Midwest.

The shifting weather and the thought of upcoming midterms had everyone in a stir, a brewing fever that couldn't go unnoticed. The glimpse of sunshine and warmer weather had us all crawling out of our winter holes and clamoring for real, live, in-your-face human contact. The lawns on campus were filled again between classes with collegians not toting heavy backpacks, but Frisbees and Hacky Sacks. Pale complexions soaked up the sun when it returned.

That really doesn't matter though. What matters is that phone call.

It was early in the morning. Well, early Sunday for me, so that meant it was around ten when I was startled awake. I hadn't set my alarm clock, so the morning interruption was an unwelcome eye-opener.

Rrrr. Rrrr. Rrrr.

The noise was like a jackhammer digging into a ash tree. It bounced off the living room walls, echoing into the hollow emptiness where my wits used to be.

My debilitating hangover turned my cell phone's vibration against the coffee table into a horrific chattering. I was only a few feet away from it on the couch. My slits for eyes opened slightly as I attempted to see my latest enemy.

The night before I didn't even make it to my bed. A bottle of some type of cheap whiskey was next to my phone along with the rest of the contents of my pockets. A few dollar bills, a pack of cigarettes, a Zippo lighter and my fake ID.

Still the noise continued.

Rrrr. Rrrr. Rrrr.

Grudgingly, I rolled off the couch to grab the phone as it hovered across the table's surface with its annoying buzzing. I just wanted to make it shut up. I tried to reach with my right arm, but it wouldn't budge. It was still asleep from being laid on in the most awkward of positions. I reached with my left.

Fumbling to flip the thing open, I muttered something into the phone that resembled "Hello." I didn't even have the energy to sit up.

A panting voice shot back. The depth and tone resembled something motherly. Then again, at this time of the morning and my current mental state, it could have been any woman over the age of forty.

The frantic pace of the voice on the other side of my phone told me this call wasn't good.

"Oh my God! Are you there?"

Smacking my lips together to loosen the white stickiness from the corners of my mouth, I asked who it was. I knew it wasn't my mom.

"He's … gone! Oh my God! He's gone!"

She was screeching, her voice more distant with every breath.
Who? What?
"Ethan. Ethan's gone," she yelled. It must have been his mom. At least I had pieced together that much at that point. Me, and my keen powers of deduction. Chris, detective of the obvious.
"Where, um, did he, uh, go?"
"He ... *sho*t ... himself!" she screamed at me. She was undoubtedly crying.
Then she hung up.
Now I know why.
Her reaction was appropriate considering the circumstances. It wasn't until later that I would learn she had just found her son with a hole in the back of his head that started inside his mouth.
Get that image into your head. A twenty-year-old kid's head after swallowing the end of a Beretta. Is that stuck in your mind yet? I hope so.
Now add in a supposed best friend who answered the phone like he would to a late night, long-forgotten booty call. This friend also failed to grasp the gravity of the situation by asking where this dead kid went. That would put you where Ethan's mom stood right at the moment when she hung up on me.
In my defense, how was I supposed to know I'd be getting a phone call like that on that morning? Moreover, I wasn't supposed to get that phone call ever. Especially about Ethan.
I was the first person she called after finding him.
She called me before the cops.
Before 911.
Before his dad.
She knew Ethan trusted me more than anyone.
She thought I could save him.
I couldn't.
He was the last person I ever figured who needed saving.
That was supposed to be me.

THREE

Ethan was one of those guys who everyone knew. Everyone. He embodied everything about the social sieze-the-day-style of college life.
Most people couldn't remember when or where they first met him, but you'd be hard-pressed to find anyone who'd spent more than a year on

campus, or ten minutes in a house basement, without knowing him. You might not recall his name if you never got a formal introduction, but you'd remember him. Something about him guaranteed everyone did.

Ethan gathered his entourage from the ranks of party revelers, those with the same lousy campus job and the few people who actually went to class. He was the uniting force behind what would be known as First Prentiss, the Revolutionary of Homecoming and the Daddy to Drink Day. These were a few of his better-known accolades.

Everyone knew him. Everyone.

Me? I knew him forever. At least it seems like it.

You could say we grew up together, but that would just be some after-school-special crap you're supposed to say after someone's dead. We didn't live next door as kids or anything, but he did create the person now telling his story. I don't know his favorite color or what his class schedule was, but I can give you a few colorful, amusing anecdotes.

In telling Ethan's story, I can't tell you everything. I can only show you things that might give you an inkling of who Ethan Costello was. I don't even fully understand that myself. More importantly, none of us knew right away why he'd killed himself his sophomore year in college. It was my job to find out.

I can only tell you what I know.

Yes, it was because of him that I ended up inadvertently killing all of the koi in the fish pond in the center of campus. Yes, it was because of him I spent a good chunk of freshman year without any body hair. Yes, we were the ones who streaked campus and then, standing there butt-naked in the freezing cold, had a security guard stop us and ask for ID.

"Where in God's name would I put it, buddy?" Ethan asked the guard, who was probably a freshman, like we were at the time.

Ethan still holds the school record for number of counts against him for drinking in the officially dry dorms. By the school's math, if two people got busted with a sixer, it was three counts each. Ethan's record stands at one hundred and forty-two just by himself. One December he was stuck in the dorms for a few nights by himself while the rest of us had gone home for Christmas break. Actually, in the name of political correctness, it was called Holiday Break. So, Ethan piled up the booze in his fridge to kill the two days until his dad could pick him up. It was the loud music and clanking of too many bottles in his recycling bin that tipped off campus security.

After returning from break, I was his accessory after the fact and owned up to some of the booze to chill the heat from the dorm supervisor, or whatever she was called. Because of that, he was allowed to stay in the dorms for the rest of the year. He never failed to show his gratitude. I would have taken the whole rap for him. I owed him at least that. It was because of him I didn't spend the best year of my life cornered in my room.

Stories. We have a few.

Most revolve around a night of getting soused, doing stupid stuff around campus, and getting busted for said drunken antics. The best nights, or mornings, depending if you were concerned with the time, were when we didn't get caught. But the stories I like to tell are the ones that show Ethan's true self—what he held important. The ones about the constant pursuit of five-dollar freedom, boredom-killing time with friends, and the hunt for beautiful girls.

Now I remember where I was. I was sleeping.

It seemed like Ethan was always a driving force in my life, but the months of our friendship could be counted on my fingers and toes with a few left to spare.

I met the now-deceased Ethan Costello on the first day of college.

My parents had driven me to campus in an attempt to help me settle in. It was a college not far from them, but still far enough that I wouldn't be going home every weekend.

It was a school my parents had almost chosen for me.

My crappy rust-bucket of a car had finally died the last month I lived at home and my parents didn't figure I'd need one in a town this small. I was there to learn, not drive around, or so they said.

My mom made my new bed for me, hung my shirts and ties, and tucked plastic totes away in my closet. Her nervousness to see her baby off was apparent in the way she organized anything that could be given order.

When everything was packed away, all of my stuff in its appropriate place, my parents realized it was time to leave their only child behind so he could start a life of his own. After all, that was the reason I was here.

To my mother, not only would I be gone, but also when her son hit college age it was a sure sign that old age wasn't far off for her. She had mentioned this to me numerous times.

"I can't believe my baby is going to college," she'd said, sighing in that sad way mothers do when they have to release their maternal grip on something they've held onto for so long.

Leaving my parents alone to themselves at home would probably result in one of two scenarios: they would either relish their new freedom—like I was planning to—or they would die at each other's hands. Either way, I wasn't too concerned at which outcome they chose.

Feverishly, my mom made a final check around the room to be sure I had everything.

Antihistamine and Dramamine.

Student ID card, calling card. For emergencies: credit card.

First aid kit and sewing kit.

Poncho. Flashlight.

I was back at summer camp. I tried to remind myself she meant well.

While those were what she considered necessities, there was one thing—rather a bunch of things—I couldn't live without: My TV, DVD player and movie collection. Besides a laundry basket full of DVDs, I also had three brown paper bags filled with an array of titles ranging from pop culture and cult staples to foreign films, many of which most people have never heard of.

Everyone needs an escape. Mine came in special edition director's cuts with deleted scenes.

Not only was I a student of all genres, I had also studied any and all movies about college. Without an older brother or sister to clue me in on what to expect from college, I chose to frame my idea of college life around *Animal House*, *Van Wilder*, *PCU*, and even *Dead Man on Campus*.

I stood in the middle of my room, stretching both arms out. I easily touched both walls. I now lived in a taupe-colored brick closet with a steel sink and pressboard furniture. My own personal disposable prison cell. All I could think about was how many people had copulated on that mattress in the decades before I was here. Out of everything my mom packed, I was most grateful for the can of disinfectant she had already used to douse every inch of the room.

With everything put away, there was little free space available, and there was still another person to cram in here.

If you ever question if God has a sense of humor, try moving into a two-person dorm room without knowing who your roommate will be. This cruel fate was delivered by a roommate-drawing lottery system where numbers are attached to people and paired at random. Two complete strangers were selected to be pit against each other for alone time and whatever precious mutual space the room provided. Only by luck would your sanity survive living in a brick box in a completely alien society where self-destruction came in numerous forms.

I was mostly concerned about "alone time." In other words, I just wanted time to jack off to the porno I kept stashed away in a few select DVD cases. *Fight Club* was blondes. *Gladiator* was red heads. *Clerks* was brunettes. My categorical spank cinema was stashed in these cases away from the 'rents' prying eyes, all four of which had yet to stop surveying my new quarters.

Mom tried to conceal her preformed tears but the red circles around her eyes gave her away. My dad, standing with his hands on his hips, tightened his lips and gave a fatherly nod.

"This will do," he said, granting his blessing over the room.

There was absolutely nothing else that could be done to the room. Nothing more could be disinfected, organized, shelved or folded. Yet, they still lingered behind. I needed them to leave, but they stayed as long as they could.

Promise you'll call as much as you can, mom said.

You can borrow my car when you come home, dad said.

Mom told me never to carry too much cash.

Study hard, dad said. "Don't party too much."

Mom again: Always tell someone where you'll be.

"Never go out alone."

Dad's last bit of advice: "Make us proud."

With that, they made their way out the front door. Finally.

Don't get me wrong, I can't deny what they'd done for me up to this point in my life, but when you're on the threshold of a society fueled by booze, random public sexual acts, an overabundance of fried food and ditching classes, you don't want your mom standing over your shoulder waiting to give her input on every situation.

Hugs. Mom's brave face wore off as her eyes burst open in big sloppy globs. Dad shook my hand.

Off they went, packed away inside the family minivan with the bookshelf that wouldn't fit inside the room.

The nest they would return to in a matter of hours was now officially empty.

It was two when the 'rents left. My dad had made the rush to get up early and pack the van so he could get me here and drop me off so he'd get home before five in the evening. Why? I don't know. That's just how my dad operated. Decades of working in a nine-to-five environment, he couldn't shake the thought of not having his day end at the same time.

Getting my parents out of the way was, I thought at the time, the one thing holding me back from a party life that would be the envy of everyone. Wrong.

From my view in the middle of the street that dead-ended at campus, to my surprise, there was barely a soul around me. Ready to embark on changing my life and I stood alone. The few people carrying in lava lamps and beanbag chairs into the dorms across the street were unapproachable.

In full disclosure, I'd never really started a conversation with someone, let alone someone I never met. I know it sounds retarded, but it was one hundred percent accurate. Almost anytime I had even fathomed such a thing as initiating a conversation, the fear of being scoffed at and dismissed kept my mouth shut. I had always looked for an in, an excuse or reasonable explanation to talk to someone. This meant, up to that point, I'd had a rather meager social life. Putting it as nicely as I could to shield myself from the apparent truth.

There I was, in the center of a universe where virtually everyone was in the same situation, a place where we were all new to a culture we'd only heard about, and I was too chicken-shit to introduce myself to a fellow incoming freshman. For a while, I was doomed to repeat my anti-social high school life.

Calling myself a social turd would be an understatement.

The worst part about my life was realizing I didn't have one.

With the minivan well out of view, I reached into my pocket for cigarette. After a couple of years of hiding my smoking from my family, I had perfected the art of flattening a pack of smokes and a book of matches into nothing thicker than two credit cards. As my one single recordable act of rebellion so far, I didn't want to explain to my parents the reason for the box-shaped bulge sticking out of my pants in the middle of my thigh.

Smoking whenever I felt like it was the first act of freedom I enjoyed. I could keep a smoke behind my ear at all times and no one would rat to my parents.

The beauty of not knowing anyone also had a perk. No one knew me. They didn't know where I came from, or anything I'd done, or not done, up to this point. I could create a new Chris.

Taking a seat on the three-foot high wall surrounding the dorm, smoking my cigarette, I stared at everything around me. I had a perfect view of what appeared to be lecture halls and another dorm across the street. My new home was concrete, brick and overly tidy landscaping in the school colors of purple and gold.

I was here. I was in college. I was on my own. I was already doing something I wasn't supposed to. Sure smoking would probably kill me, but at this point who would notice if I wasn't here?

The plot in my continued rebellious reformation had been planned since high school. Puffing away, I hashed out my socially scandalous downfall.

Things to do:
- Get drunk for the first time
- Try pot
- For the love of God, lose your virginity

The first cigarette was gone. I walked down to the ashtray, threw it out and lit up another.

Then I noticed this guy. Of the half-dozen people around by then, I noticed him helping some dad-like guy carry a couch from the rear end of an SUV into the dorm across the street. The way he interacted with this girl, who followed behind with a pink comforter in her arms, and her parents, I'd assumed it was a boyfriend from her hometown.

That's one more girl that was off limits. Granted, that's assuming I'd have enough balls to test those limits. The status quo said no.

She was pretty, her body cut the way all freshmen girls seem to be at first. Tight-bodied from years of high school sports and healthy metabolism. He was a bit muscular, his arms looked like he was born that way instead of being manufactured during hours in a gym. He was dressed in just jeans and a T-shirt, but they looked like they were cut just for him.

That little picturesque scene of guy and girl across the street, I wanted it.

Envy. One of the Big Seven that had been ingrained in my head since elementary school.

"These are paths to which the devil will steer you away from the Lord's eternal home," I remembered Sister Mary What's-Her-Face saying in first grade.

I had one. I wanted the rest.

Lust. Greed. Sloth. Gluttony. Wrath. Pride. And a side of fries.

Envisioning upcoming parties, I wanted the chance to replay the scenes from those college movies. The chance to win the girl. The opportunity to become a campus social icon worthy of the front page of the student paper. There would be a way for me to become the king of every party by grasping every opportunity that came my way.

The only things I wanted to do were the ones I'd always been told I'd regret when I got older. Things my whole life I've been told would destroy me. I wanted to rebel from the command-givers at every chance I had. I was planning my spontaneity. Now I know how big of an oxymoron I was.

The guy, the girl and the set of parents had finished unloading the SUV. They were far enough away that I could only see mouths moving without sound. She hugged the adults, they got in the vehicle, and they drove off. The guy said a handful of words to the girl before she went back inside without him.

This guy stayed outside looking around. He saw me, the mope standing by himself on the opposite side of the now-empty street. He strolled over, casually glancing around him the whole time. His mannerisms said he wasn't heading my way but the straight line he was traveling in my direction said otherwise. By the time he got to me, he had pulled a cigarette out from behind his ear and stuck it in his mouth. He slumped up against the wall beside me.

"Got a light?" he said, bumping me with his elbow in a nonchalant way as the cigarette hung from his lips.

As I passed my smashed book of matches to him, I noticed his eyes almost hidden behind his straight dishwater blonde hair. They were the palest color gray I had ever seen. They were almost white, but not enough to give off a creepy albino vibe. In any case, they grabbed my attention and riveted me on the spot.

"Thanks," he said.

He plucked one of the last cardboard strips from the book, struck it, and raised it to his cigarette. He handed them back to me, commenting on how my matches, with their torn edges and lack of a cover, had seen better days.

"I … I … know," I said before diving into the story about how my mom thought I had quit smoking after a teacher had ratted on me after seeing me smoking at school and then my mom made me smoke in front of her and eat the butt before promising me I would never smoke again.

I just started rambling to explain my crappy matches. Hell, I just kept talking in solid, run-on sentences because he started the conversation.

The story continued on to how I perfected smashing half a pack of smokes and a book of matches by pressing the cigarettes between two textbooks. And then… he interrupted with a deep, soft chuckle.

"Alright, alright. I get it. You're good."

Shut up. Just shut the hell up. You're making an ass out of yourself. That's all that was going on inside my head. That's the reason I don't just go up to people and start blathering on. I didn't respond, thinking he'd just bashed me the way I had always feared. Smoking in silence, I wanted to just cower and leave.

This guy remained reclining against the wall, taking long puffs off his cigarette. Holding in the smoke, he loudly forced it out in long exhales. I finished my cigarette, twisting the smoldering cherry off the end of the butt as I tried thinking of something to resurrect myself from my blubbering introduction. Apparently my past conversational triumphs had followed me to my new college life. With nothing, I headed towards the ashtray again.

His outstretched arm stopped me, an open pack of cigs in his hand.

"Here. Have another."

"Na … ah," I declined in a spluttering utterance that was my distinct manner.

"C'mon. I don't want to sit here by myself."

"What about your girlfriend?" I asked. "She doesn't smoke?"

"*What* girlfriend?" he said sounding generally surprised.

"The girl you helped move in across the street."

"Oh, her. She's not my girlfriend."

"Friend? Sister?"

"Never met her before. She was cute and I saw an opportunity to get her name and make a charming appearance in front of her parents."

You just walked up and started carrying her stuff?

"Yup," he said, apparently thinking nothing of it. He inhaled again.

After that blasé explanation, I knew I needed to listen.

This guy saw the girl and his in. He went for it. He had nerve where I had nothing. I hoped that what I wanted to learn, he could teach me. Especially anything more worthwhile than what I'd learn from any of my future professors.

Accepting his offer for another cigarette, I propped myself back against the ledge next to him. I started to mimic his stance even down to how he crossed his outstretched legs and how he surveyed the empty streets around him.

As I lit my third smoke in a row, he stretched out his arm again, this time his hand was open.

"Ethan."

I grabbed his hand in a power grip.

"Chris."

My cigarette was buried in between my fingers down by the knuckles, just like him. He looked around slightly. I looked around slightly.

Enter Ethan Costello into my life.

If only his exit out of my life would have been as simple as his entrance.

Luck has never been that good to me.

FOUR

As time recedes from the passages of life we are all doomed to suffer the incorrigibility of being misguided. We make our preparations to propel ourselves into one life-defining moment, but we'll probably miss it. Most of us, blinded by things unnecessary, will do anything to keep to the safe areas of our lives so we don't have to make the choice to plunge in.

We'd rather sit and watch than take a stand and participate. Apathy is the new black. Commercialism, a good distraction from important things, is the new God. It doesn't matter what is contained inside your character, but what you own that makes you an important person.

Because of our own stupidity, many of us will not notice the passing of the moment when the meaning of life is handed to us in our own unique way. Our safe holds on things that we think matter will never allow for drastic measures to be taken. Because of this we are damned to a life not of normalcy, but rather a life of domestication. We work fifty hours a week, save our money, and buy insurance just in case some turmoil may enter our sad existences. The sad part is that sometimes, the moment never comes.

The idea that property has overcome our personalities is the single reason we'll all miss the best part of our lives. It's people, not possessions that make our lives worth living. The person we'd thought we'd never meet, the people we always ignore. They all have tremendous stories that we need to hear to expand our definitions of who we are.

It's a desire for human contact, a longing to reach out to others, to be held, to be kissed, that we all crave. Instead, we gather materials around us, stupefy ourselves into believing the images on our televisions are the greatest teaching tools of the world around us.

It's the simple act of shaking someone's hand and saying hello that we're all losing by consuming. There is no consolation in shopping that cannot be out-matched by talking to a friend. Still, we collect and horde, hoping he who dies with the most toys doesn't die. We'll overwork and miss our families just to think the lack of our presence will all be for the betterment of those who want nothing more than to see us.

We'll toil all of our lives just to end up where we were when we were born. Scared.

FIVE

Ethan was dead.

Ethan was dead.

I couldn't even force myself to believe it. No matter how many times I repeated it I couldn't convince myself it was real. There was a chance I wasn't completely sure I heard everything correctly, what else could that screaming voice on the other end of my phone mean?

Ethan was dead.

I called his mom back. Busy signal.

In my hangover haze, I couldn't think of who else to call. All of the planning my parents had done for me, all the emergency plans and I couldn't remember the one for when your best friend committed suicide.

I called Ethan's phone. I could hear whatever random punk song that was his ring tone this week. It was just in my head.

Voicemail.

"Ethan. Message. Leave one."

I didn't.

Another phone call to his mother. Nothing.

There's no way in hell this could be real. On the couch, in our apartment, I was starting to panic. I looked around, looking for anything to help me. I wanted some kind of signal I was having a nightmare. Wake up, Chris. I wanted anyone to say it. The lingering nausea reinforced the reality. Wake up. Somebody just please *dear God* say it.

My phone made a muffled noise when it hit the floor. I don't know if I dropped it or threw it. Either way, my slowly awakening arm couldn't hold it anymore.

My cigarettes were the first things I saw on the nearby coffee table, and they were the one thing I needed. My hands shaking, I barely managed to pull one from the pack. My best friend just killed himself and the one thing that could console me would one day, in all likelihood, kill me. In irony, I find peace.

My Zippo opened with a clink. My entire body trembled. It took me seven tries just to get the damned thing lit. I took a long drag and tossed the closed lighter onto the coffee table. It made a thud before it slid off the end and fell on the floor.

Tremors of cold ran through my veins. I felt every rush of blood coursing through my body. My legs ached as I sat hunched over. I gripped my head, rocking back and forth. I was too numb to cry.

Ethan was dead.

No.

Not him.

No way.

It couldn't be.

I was passed out when he killed himself. I was either out getting drunk or working on my hangover when he was preparing to check out.

Another drag.

Still shaking.

The carcinogens were infiltrating my lungs, killing me second by second, marking every last breath like a countdown clock. I wished they'd work faster.

I picked my phone up off the floor.

Another call to Ethan's mom.

Still busy.

She was probably on the line with 911. It wasn't with his dad. Scrolling through my phone, my thumb accidentally fumbled through all of the features, failing to find the one I wanted.

Calendar. Camera. Settings.

"God damn it!"

Finally, I got to the one I needed.

Missed calls.

Home.

That's it. My mom probably called because I hadn't talked to her in a few days.

Ethan never tried to call me.

I sighed with a sense of relief.

Somehow I felt better because I didn't miss a call from him. He never even tried to call me. It made me feel better.

A picture of what might have happened push all other thoughts aside. I imagined the back of Ethan's head splattered all over something. Furniture, the inside of a car, whatever. The self-righteous feeling I had moments ago was instantly gone.

The feeling instead was now coming up the back of my throat.

I threw the blanket off my lap and scrambled for the bathroom.

Not enough time for the toilet. I made it to the bathroom just barely as I took a half-dive in the door. My cigarette was still in my hand.

A burning sensation ran up my esophagus as a mess of black sludge sprayed all over the bottom of the toilet and sink cabinet. Anything I ate or whatever the hell I drank the night before hurled all over the floor. I tasted French fries, Jack Daniels and the familiar flavor of stomach acid.

The bathroom wasn't that clean to begin with anyway.

The sudden rush to spew the contents of my stomach wasn't from the news of Ethan's death. It wasn't from the booze. Not even the image in my head of the gas pressure from the gun barrel blowing his eyes out of his sockets.

It was my own sigh.

As the breath of relief escaped me, so did any bit of respect I had for myself.

Ethan was dead and all I cared about was me.

I was happy for a second that he didn't try to call me. I didn't miss the call that could have saved his life. It didn't even come. For a short instant, that little inane fact made me feel good.

Then it made me sick.

At a point when my best friend was dead, all I cared about was clearing myself of any responsibility. No one could blame me for it. I was sick with myself. Disgusted with temporary happiness.

Lying there, face down on the checkered linoleum floor, a pile of my own puke inches from my face, I was left with everything I deserved. I had washed my hands of culpability.

Ethan's dead.

This is probably how Pontius Pilate would have felt if he'd only known how he would go down in history. Me, there on the floor of the bathroom, I knew my role. Still, I wasn't crying. Not for me. Not for Ethan. I just wish I hadn't woken up for that phone call.

I rolled onto my back, took one last drag off the smoke before extinguishing it in the vomit. It sizzled and stunk, but I couldn't care less.

Call me Chris the Asshole.

SIX

"Well, Chris, what brings you to this utopia of higher education? Here in search of nirvana or to discover the treasures of knowledge the dead left behind to keep us guessing for centuries?"

I'm serious. That's how he talked sometimes.

A monosyllabic grunt of confusion was my response. It came out like it was my native tongue.

"Okay, let's start with your major." Ethan asked.

"I, uh, don't know. Undecided, I … guess."

"Undecided about being undecided, huh," he jabbed and laughed. "Don't think anything of it, I have no clue either."

My lack of a major upset my parents. They couldn't fathom how an eighteen-year-old recent high school grad didn't know exactly what he wanted to do with the rest of his life. They suggested going into business. I said I'd think about it. With three introductory business classes already on my schedule, it seemed to be the route I was taking. Or it was taking me, I couldn't decide, hence, declaring myself undecided.

Ethan tugg
ed on his cigarette and turned to face me, giving me a tap on the chest with the back of his hand. He said he was just messing with me and that it really didn't matter about what we planned to major in. It's just the same get-to-know-you crap everyone exchanges until they can find some inane detail they both like to talk about. Until they find common ground.

"It's amazing. For centuries educated people have populated this earth and still when two people meet for the first time, they just want to size each other up," he said. "We'll compare how much we know about whatever. If it isn't that, it's something stupid like what kind of cars we have or what suburb we grew up in."

Obviously finding a topic he enjoyed, Ethan kept going. His rant was a lot more put together than mine.

"The continuation of humanity has done nothing for us. We're all still apes smacking our puffed-out chests to see who's bigger. And because of that, we're all fucked."

"Yeah," I said like I could actually grasp that. I was still tripped up on "utopia of higher education."

Despite the rough start, I was able to hold my own during the conversation. Despite how most of my views obviously came straight from a textbook or were wrapped in movie quotes, I like to think I did OK.

Or, at least he made me feel like I did.

We stayed outside in that same spot for hours. Minivans and SUVs came and went as parents and kids already dressed in purple and gold unloaded clothes, bedding, mini-fridges, speakers, and whatever stuff people thought they needed to survive. The same scene I had gone through earlier that day replayed itself about every two minutes.

Get the keys from a student volunteer at the front desk. Go to the room. Haul stuff in. Say good-bye to the 'rents. Go back inside. Come back out. Look around. Start talking to people. As far as that went, I guess I fit into that little part of campus life.

Ethan and I talked about where we were from, what we did in high school, and any good-looking girls that walked by. He said hi to every brunette.

We swapped our get-to-know-you crap. Then we dove into more detailed anecdotes from our lives or any other higher world knowledge.

Ethan Costello died at birth.

His umbilical cord — his maternal link — got tangled around his neck and choked him during delivery. As she shoved him out, he was dying. As Ethan saw it, God was done with him right there.

But, some fresh from med school doctor didn't want to be ridiculed by colleagues about how his first delivery ended in death. Dr. Go-get-'em went to work resuscitating the purple lump right there on the delivery room cart, mere inches from the mother's spread open legs. This doctor who was too young to even grow a full beard brought Ethan back from the dead before he even had a name.

"I figure since God didn't want me on this planet, and since I flipped him off right away, I can do what I want," he said.

This is where my straight-from-the-book ideas came in. My whole life until this point was a Catholic schoolroom. This question had been answered before me a million times.

"What if God has a plan for you, and you overcoming that was the first step?" I asked.

"If there is a God, and his idea of getting a plan off the ground is killing a baby, I'm not sure I want to be in his good graces," he shot back.

The response sounded nearly rehearsed, but he had a point.

The rest of Ethan's pre-college life played out in a small town in the middle of nowhere. I'd never heard of it. There, as he explained it, it's commonplace to graduate high school, relive whatever glory you had there for the next ten years while in the meantime working some crappy job and most likely getting married.

The town elders — those who also never left town, or their parents or grandparents — frowned on anyone who dared being unwed and without children by thirty. Most had kids before their twentieth birthday. Theirs was a society of children raising children.

Then it was hunting, snowmobiles and football games. Beer guts and mullets. Big screen TVs and pickup trucks. In a rare case in the dumpy little hometown, a few kids went to college. Sadly, Ethan said, they usually returned to work in the accounting offices of the few remaining factories their parents worked at to pay for their kid's school. These new college grads would live in a world where dressing up is a polo shirt and khakis.

"My hometown is occupied by the white trash that clogs the natural flow of human evolution," Ethan said. "It's a psoriasis scab on the clean complexion of the earth."

Ethan wasn't going to be one of them. He vowed with a particular vengeance to never go back. He was determined. That was the source of his drive, to never have to go back home.

I was jealous. At least he had a reason other than just doing what you're told.

For the majority of my life, I did what I was supposed to. I played the part of the seemingly normal Catholic high school student. Good grades. My idea of fun was watching movies. One after another. Six a day on the weekends. Me and my TV.

FBLA. Golf team. Retreat team. Dated a little, if you can call it that. Debate team. Didn't drink. Worked part-time. Ethan thought it must have been tough to balance all of it at the same time.

It was easy if you didn't have a social life. Going through life, step-in-step with what your told, is the easiest thing ever.

Do this. Done. Go there. Gone.

After a while, after years of instruction, you learn how to float so accomplishing the bare minimum appears to be excellence. The fun part is when you trick yourself into thinking that the things you're doing aren't only the right choices, but they are the only options. Before long, you start liking what you first hated. I imagine that's how the Nazi soldiers operated. Constant instruction and mind games meant they didn't know what they were doing was wrong. It was all they knew.

Even with all of my high school accolades, smoking was my only rebellion. It's probably no coincidence that's how I met Ethan.

We kept talking about everything and nothing. Religion was a prime topic.

"You can't put too much stock in faith alone," he said. "If Adam and Eve didn't fuck up in the Garden of Eden, none of us would be here."

I asked, "What about original sin? Their acts marked all of us for eternity."

"Yeah, but we've found a way around it. Voilá, baptism. Original sin is just a myth created to get people to join organized religion. Baptism is just something we think will set us free when all it does is bind us to more rules."

Rules. Ethan didn't seem to like those.

He continued, "If the Bible is one-hundred percent accurate, we're all children of incest. Adam and Eve made Cain and Abel. Cain killed Abel. Two guys, one girl. Cain had to sleep with his mom so we could survive. The same thing with Noah, his wife and their kids. All incest. I doubt all of those motherfuckers—and I mean that literally—looked as pretty as the great artists characterized them."

I never thought of it that way. Somehow, our religion teachers failed to make that point about our long lines of incest-ridden heritage. All those years of Catholic school and Ethan was the one who put it all into perspective. Some of what he said made sense.

Still, I had a comeback to that one. "Maybe that was part of Adam and Eve's punishment for their fall from the grace of God, the fact they didn't give birth to another female immediately."

Ethan looked a little puzzled and pulled off his cigarette. "Maybe," he said. "Could be. I don't know. I don't have all the answers. I'm here looking for them too."

We kept talking. More religion. Girls. School.

Then our conversation came to a grinding halt. Death hit our interaction when we ran out of cigarettes. Without an excuse to keep us out there, we had no reason to stay. Besides, Ethan wanted to go check out campus. He invited me, but I lied and said I had to finish unpacking. As if my mom left anything unfinished.

I declined mostly because my comfort level with him wasn't as high as I would have liked. Sure, I was fine with just talking to him, but throw another person in the mix and I was back where I started. Sitting in my room seemed like a better option.

"I'll stop by later and pick you up," Ethan said. "We'll go hit some parties."

That is the one thing we both knew we wanted to do, and at this stage,

I wasn't going alone.

He went left. I headed inside.

I sat at my desk, staring at the neat row of shrink-wrapped textbooks lined up with the brand new notebooks and binders. Despite my anticipated rebellion, I was overly organized. Everything was neat and orderly.

I did nothing but try to absorb the guy I had just been talking to for hours. One part of him seemed to be an arrogant prick. He seemed too cynical about too many things. In parts, his simplistic views were annoying. I feared he was just some quasi-anarchist nut-job whose explanation for everything wrong with everything was somehow God's fault. Or maybe it was a mix of some hippy view that the betterment of others is more important than taking care of yourself.

I'm sorry, but altruism is for idiots.

Still, there was something about Ethan. His views couldn't be traced to political lines. No religious dogma seemed to blind him. He hated everything equally. At least that was refreshing.

Immediately I knew I wanted to co-opt his views, his articulation, everything.

I wanted to be him. Ethan was everything I wasn't.

Then there was my roommate.

The thick wood door slammed against the metal bunk bed behind it.

Stan The Man came into my life.

Out of breath like he'd run full-on to the doorway from wherever the hell he came from, he looked around the room.

This bleach blonde spiky-haired, eyebrow-pierced figure inspected the room from top to bottom. His pink and blue-stripe T-shirt and cargo shorts were wrinkled just the way fashion ads dictated. His tan was so perfect that even his exposed ankles showed no sign of sock lines. Under one slightly muscular arm he held a duffle bag under the other, a tie-dyed blanket. A piece of paper was in one hand.

After hulking in the door for a few seconds, he looked at me, saying nothing. He looked at the piece of paper. Then the number on the door.

103.

"This is Prentiss Hall, isn't it?"

He looked confused.

"Eeey … yeah," I said slowly.

As soon as I said it, he flopped down his stuff and turned around outside the door. No hello. No, "My name is…" No swapping of biographical bullshit.

Like that, he had turned and was gone. He returned the same way less than a minute later, carrying two purple plastic totes stacked on each other.

He nearly tripped over his other crap on the floor before slamming down more next to it. Every trip outside and back in was more hurried than the last. One time he overshot our room by about four doors. He kept that spacey look on his face. He kept huffing.

He'd come in, drop in the middle of the floor and look. He'd look at me at first. Me, in my gray high school T-shirt and jeans. Me with my skinny self. Me, with my scuffed up shoes. Me, in my neat little organized corner desk by the window. It was the first day of college and I was sitting at my desk, by myself.

This chiseled-faced model wannabe wasn't impressed with me.

More stuff. I thought it'd never end. Television, DVD player, stereo. We now lived at the electronics department at Big Box. A land of duplicates. Two of everything. Our own little post-modern ark.

After a few more trips, I'd thought he'd be done. And then nothing.

His pyramid of boxes, totes and clothes lay dormant before I realized he wasn't coming back for a while, or not at all. Maybe his marathon moving style gave him a heart attack. I looked out the window to make sure he wasn't dead on the sidewalk.

He never said anything to me other than the one sentence.

"This is Prentiss Hall, right?" Then nothing.

His ambivalence was apparent.

I stayed at my desk. My stomach rumbled with hunger.

SEVEN

Lying on the bathroom floor quickly lost any appeal.

I pulled myself up without a drop of puke on my clothes. After a year of chugging down booze and then later throwing it up, I had mastered the art of chucking without adding any of it to my attire. At least I had that going for me.

Ethan had gone home for the weekend. Nothing was different in his goodbye. He just got up and left. Maybe he felt he needed a break from everything at school. Yeah, that's got to be it.

By the time I had gotten ahold of his mom, when she could talk coherently, Ethan should have been back in the apartment. He should be watching movies or playing video games with me on the couch or rehashing the weekend's partying. Instead, I'd be dreading my first trip to his hometown.

I didn't know what I could do at this point. Answers were all I wanted. I wanted to know what everyone else did.

With every suicide, there's the big question: Why?

As I slowly pushed open the door to Ethan's room, I fully expected him to be in there. It should have been a joke. Ethan would be inside the room, with the curtains pulled, fully ready to laugh his ass off at my expression. It would have been the ultimate sick and elaborate joke. I would have jacked him in the mouth right then and there.

Still, I would have felt better to see him alive and well. But he was neither.

Walking through his room, I took in everything, attempting to play detective. I wanted to find some clue. I imagined a romanticized suicide note. I wanted to hear why it wasn't my fault.

His mom had already done the same at her house, completely pissing off the responding cops by rifling through his bag, jacket, dirty laundry, everything. She found nothing. All she found was her son backed up to the concrete wall, slumped over in a pool of blood. It trickled over the floor and weaved into the drain. Pieces of him were everywhere. The wall, the ceiling, the floor. His father's handgun rested at his side.

His mother later said she never heard a thing. She and his dad had gone out the night before. It was one of those second first dates. To try and see if they could rekindle a relationship that had spawned a son, an overworked father and too much space between them.

Apparently, it was like trying to light a fire underwater. Too many things plaguing them to fabricate a clean slate. They went home, and she went to bed alone. Ethan's father left to catch a last-minute plane after a familiar voice on his cell phone told him to do so.

She ignored her natural motherly instinct to check on her son before she went to bed. He should have been sound asleep in his.

Judging by the tone in her voice on the phone, Ethan was five years old again. He was her boy, the child who leapt from her womb twenty years ago. He was her dead baby. Again.

She had gone down to the basement to do a load of laundry Sunday morning when she found Ethan. Her involuntary self-preservation instincts blocked the realization, but she smelled him first. Nothing clogs your nostrils quite like the contents of someone's head and bowels spread all over a damp basement for twelve hours.

That's when she called me. Me, the guy passed out on the couch. Me, out getting drunk as Ethan took a gun, loaded it and unloaded on himself.

He should have been back by now. He should be in his room reading. We should be watching a movie. He should be at the library. He should be at work. He should be anywhere but in a black vinyl bag with a tag on his toe.

Tiptoeing around the room, my prying eyes took in everything in plain sight.

I invaded everything of Ethan's.

The glow of his fish tank illuminated the bottom half of the room. It was just enough so I didn't have to turn on the light. Shadows created by the water and fake coral statues created pockets of darkness. Coupled with the hum of the water pump motor, the room felt alive and dead at the same time. Wanting to view the room as he left it, I fumbled through, in whatever light was there.

A part of me itched as I thought about how long Ethan had planned this.

His mass media book was open to a chapter on the birth of television. His sweatshirt hung on the back of his chair. It was his favorite. Dark gray, tattered with an extra large hood.

The twin bed with its flannel sheets and blue comforter looked like someone had just slept there. The white shoes tainted with black sludge from basement parties looked like someone had just taken them off. The empty carton of cigarettes looked like someone had just left to get more.

I didn't touch a thing. I didn't want the cops here questioning why everything of his had my fingerprints on them. They'd probably ask what I stole or what I was hiding. I didn't want to answer any of those questions.

Black and white photos taped to the wall showed last semester's photojournalism final. There's the shot of a girl down by the lake as seagulls flew overhead. The professor praised that one. There's the photo of his desk, a cigarette burning in an ashtray. A Jim Beam bottle was in the background. Notebooks were spread everywhere. It was his self-portrait. He failed that one.

Next to the photos, a poster immortalized a frail old man dressed in rags clutching his guitar. Picasso nailed it. The perfect poster boy for depression.

Fully in Monday morning quarterback mode, there were clues that Ethan was depressed. Yeah, he had to be. That's the answer. It's an easy conclusion to come to following a suicide. After-the-fact.

But how? The guy who everyone knew. The guy who always knew the right thing to say and had an uncanny ability to unite people in any situation. The guy who I wanted to be, wouldn't have done this.

I didn't know what I could have done beforehand. That's assuming he was depressed. That's assuming it was a suicide. By even thinking that, I felt better for split second. Self-preservation. Again, I tried to play it off like I had no responsibility.

In all so-called tragedies, everyone looks for clues as to why it happened. Examination of every little detail takes place. Everyone wants answers. They want someone to blame, just so long as it isn't themselves. It's finger-pointing at its finest.

I was no different.

Greed.

In my sanctimonious attempt at self-defense, the finger was pointed at me. By seeing I didn't miss a call, I tried pointing it right back. It was the worst thing I could have done. It's immediate abandonment.

I closed the door to Ethan's room behind me. It was about time I cleaned up the bathroom floor. The little chore of scrubbing my own vomit cleared my head. The rancid smell and the simple task took my mind away from everything.

Scoop, wipe, flush.

Since I couldn't get any emotion out of myself, I might as well get something done. Mission accomplished. There, I had one less thing to worry about.

Again on the couch, I was alone. There was nothing else to do.

It was time to deal with reality. No more attempts to keep busy.

Deal with it.

Don't hide.

Cope.

Ethan taught me that.

EIGHT

Take a header off a building.

Dive in front of a train.

Hang.

There's plenty of ways to kill yourself.

The Cobain cocktail. The Buddhist self-immolation technique. Seppuku. Jonestown Juice.

Creativity can turn your personal demise into art. But beware, some methods are less a guarantee of immediate death. Others are sure things.

A Beretta in the mouth.

Throughout the course of human history, untold numbers of people have committed suicide, many repeating the successes of others. More than thirty thousand a year alone in the United States.

Those who fail at suicide are doomed with the indignity to live afterwards, forever shamed by not even being able to off themselves correctly. You're at the lowest part of your life. You think you're ready to die. Ready. Aim. Fire. You miss the important part of your brain.

The cut isn't deep enough.

The rope breaks.

Before your declaration of intent for death, you've failed at life. Relationships, work, everything. The world's out to get you. It's now worse: you can't even kill yourself properly. You just can't do anything right. You are the now the world's pissing pot.

A German factory worker was discovered after swallowing sixty sleeping pills. He survived. It was his tenth suicide attempt. Before the pill incident, the gun jammed, he threw up the rat poison he ate, and the time before that, the hair dryer in the bathtub didn't work.

Some people just aren't meant to die at their own hands. Cancer, liver disease or AIDS are just in the cards for some. Like it or not, God's got a way out for us.

Learn from others' mistakes. Plan.

But don't be an idiot about it.

Forget about dressing up, dropping a handful of pills in hopes you'll be discovered all pretty like you died in your sleep. Girls are often found in their beds, gussied up in their prom dresses, their hair done perfect. They think they'll look beautiful after their death. They want to be immortal.

Instead, these flesh Barbies are found covered in vomit as their bodies, doing their jobs to halt the self-destruction, try to expel the poison. Then they shit themselves.

You spend all your life puckering your rear, constantly preventing from crapping yourself. Instilled at potty training, we keep all the shit inside. Finally, after your death, you can relax. That's the best part, assuming your corpse is discovered quickly.

Lying there in your own feces, your stink will invade the neighborhood. After a few days you'll be so bloated and rank that no one will want to come in and see you. Mommy and daddy will have to throw out everything in your room because it will reek of death.

That's a nice way to leave a lasting impression, princess.

Wear a diaper if you're set on it though. If that's just the way that you have to do it. If that's the suicide technique that sums you up as person.

Don't church up when you're doing it either. That's just annoying. It's not "transitioning." It's not "retiring." Or "going into the hands of the Lord."

It's suicide.

Death.

Killing yourself.

Say it.

If you can't even call it by it's name, if you have to use some romanticized name — whatever those Emo kids call it, you don't want to die. You might feel like it, but there's a difference.

If you plan to leave a note, you don't really want to die. You're being selfish, giving in to the pain in life, so why would you care if anyone knows why? People in your life have made it hell, so why give them the comfort and peace of mind knowing what really happened?

If you plan your funeral, death isn't ready for you yet. If you're serious, you won't give a rat's ass what the bastards who did you wrong do with your stinking vehicle of life.

If you haven't planned your suicide, you don't really want to do it. You're just panicking. You'll surely die painfully. Call someone. Call the cops. Commit yourself. Call a suicide hotline. They'll listen.

But, if you can hold the knife, toaster or gun without shaking, well, see you later.

A Taiwanese soldier and his transvestite boyfriend wanted to die because their parents objected to their relationship. It was a modern Shakespearian drama. Plastic bags over their heads didn't work. Neither did driving a car off a bridge. So, taking the logical next step, they rented a hotel room and planned to kill themselves. Unfortunately — or fortunately, depending on how you look at it — they weren't smart enough to make it work.

Their makeshift nooses, crafted from electrical wire, caved in the ceiling, preventing a successful hanging. They couldn't asphyxiate themselves because the meter on the gas fireplace ran out. At last, their twelve story hand-in-hand jump out the window was softened by the tin roof of the restaurant below. They ruined a lobster tank and landed on a buffet table. Each had a few fractures but lived to tell the tale.

Don't be one of these people. Do it right the first time, or don't do it.

Monday is the most common day for suicide. Maybe the weekends are so good for these people that they can't face going back to work.

If you're serious about wanting to die, put some thought and preparation into it.

Jump your way to freedom. You'll need a building at least ten stories high for certain instantaneous death. Anything less and you're just gambling on being a paraplegic for the rest of your life. Good luck at a second attempt after that.

Getting to the right height is frightening as hell, even if you aren't afraid of heights. Make sure to bring bolt cutters to get through any pesky locks to the roof. Once you find the right spot, don't neglect your form. A swan dive, the one where you'll split open your head and shoot your spine out your butthole, works the best. Scream the whole way down if you want others to watch.

Slitting your wrist is popular for the "cry for help" suicide attempts. Kids do it all of the time to get mom and dad's attention. They're usually superficial cuts that heal up with a bandage and some ointment.

But, if you're going for the gold, you'll need a razor-sharp knife. Razor blades just by themselves get pretty damn slippery when saturated in your own blood and you've already cut tendons on your other arm. You'd be surprised at how handy box cutters without protectors around the blade can be. And, they can be found at any hardware store.

Remember kids, when slitting your wrists: Down the road, not across the street.

Don't mess around, either. Know the cuts have to be deep. You're not emotionally strong enough to live, so you probably don't possess enough physical strength to get through your skin. Trying working out if you're set on this as your exit strategy.

If you want to make a point, really piss everyone off in a smug fashion, the best way to die is to follow the lead of the Hindus by dying by Santhara. Talk about a ballsy exit—starving yourself to death. That'll show 'em, you'll say. Look at the control I have. I can kill myself by not eating.

Some cultures consider starvation the only legitimate form of suicide because it cannot be done on impulse alone. Find that spot away from everyone and meditate for a long time. A really, really long time. We're talking weeks here. It's rarely done in Western cultures because it takes so much self-restraint. Most of us here in the West are just too weak.

But don't be discouraged. If Gandhi could do it, surely you can.

NINE

Hours later, and still no sign of my panting, spiky-haired roommate.

In the meantime, I ventured to the cafeteria. I say ventured because my first meal of mass-produced college food was an adventure. I never knew the simple act of eating could be a gamble with your health and well-being.

It was one of my first college lessons: Nothing is safe unless I've seen it made in front of me.

Say no to the tray of baked meat calling itself meatloaf. Yes to the cheeseburgers. Anything deep-fried is safe. Cereal is always a good choice.

The meats and cheese concoctions passed off as real food are the reason why Ramen noodles and microwaveable mac and cheese are college student staples. Never mind how cheap and easy they are. The guarantee of life after meal makes them so appealing.

Afterwards, the meatloaf was less than agreeable with me, but I had to go out. I wasn't going to miss the chance to attack my debauchery list, inevitably crossing off the first thing and possibly the rest within hours of hitting campus. Ethan was my Golden Ticket.

Rarely paying much attention to my appearance, I was meticulous in preparation for my first college party.

Shit, shower, shave. Shit again. Damned meatloaf.

This was the beginning of my change. Tonight, I swore, I would begin the transformation to become the person I've always wanted to be. I had already avoided all other people at the caf, sitting by myself. If you noticed me, I was the nerd in the corner table who looked around sheepishly before plunking down his tray and scarfing down his food. No more.

There would be no more talk of action. This would be it. There were no situations I would shy away from. This wasn't like avoiding school dances because I was a putz on the dance floor or I was too scared to ask a girl out. This was grabbing life and shaking it like a British nanny.

I changed clothes. Plaid shirt, tucked in of course. Clean, ironed slacks. New white athletic shoes. Even in college, I got back-to-school clothes. There was no way I was going out in the same ones people saw me wear all day. I didn't want to look like a slob. As if anyone was looking at me.

The next fifteen minutes were spent combing my hair.

Ethan said he was coming over, so I waited.

Other people started to congregate outside. The yellow glow of the streetlights illuminated the amassing hordes of coeds. Even on Day One, they were eager, like me, to do something other than sit around watching movies or playing pool in the dorm basement. Groups of people hummed in conversation, bumping into each other as everyone talked of house parties. Unfamiliar street names and random numbers popped up, as discussions of whether the cops had become privy to the centers of mass underage consumption.

Sanborn. Sixty-six. King. Three-eleven. Broadway.

With every passing minute, more bodies filled the street.

Twitching with anticipation, I still waited by myself. The roommate's pile remained untouched. I was all talk. Ethan came knocking on my door around eight, freeing me from my boredom.

My savior.

He hadn't changed clothes.

"You … uh … late for a Young Republicans meeting?" he asked, smirking a bit.

My clothes. Crap. I thought they looked good. Movies were my fashion consultants. All the high-end frat boys, granted, the ones who categorically lose in the end, are always dressed well, keeping a neat appearance. I thought that was the way to go. Better be overdressed than under. Not in college.

"I'm just kidding," Ethan continued on about my clothes. "If you're comfortable, let's do this."

Too late. I threw my shirt on my bed. I dug through my closet for jeans. I was back in grub gear before we were out my door.

Ethan already found a place to party that night, which did not surprise me in the least.

As I was locking the door, he asked me if I remembered my wallet.

"Leave it," he said. "If you get busted drinking underage in a house full of a hundred people, you think the cops are going to worry about running some ID-less kid through their system? Hell no."

I was surprised. "There's going to be a hundred people there?"

"Maybe," he said, "or it could suck. You want to hang around here instead?"

"Hell no," I said, throwing my wallet in a drawer. I was anonymous in the eyes of the law. My next first act of rebellion, or so I told myself.

He maneuvered through the crowds of people outside, me right on his tail. He'd stop at a few groups, casually asking where everyone was headed. He told people where we were going. I was glad this house was close enough so we wouldn't get lost on the return home. The new home for this little pack of eighteen-year-olds that wanted nothing more than to get "saggy-faced drunk."

As Ethan explained it, saggy-faced drunk was getting so inebriated your mouth hangs open, your eyelids droop like oversized pillowcases and snot slippage is uncontrollable.

More alien names, more strange number combinations.

Three seventy-six. Freedom House. Pink Taco. Five-eighteen.

Ethan finished giving his sly howyadoin's to girls and macho whaddup's to guys. Off we went to begin our deviation from expectation.

The two-story white house on King Street was only a few blocks off campus. The hum of students near the dorms blended with the sounds emanating from our destination. Loud rap music, bottles clanking and the muffled sounds of footsteps sounded somehow exotic to me. It would be the soundtrack of my life from now on.

"Are we invited?" I asked.

That was my one concern.

Ethan stopped just short of the front door, turning his head to look over his shoulder.

"This is college. No one's invited to anything, but they always show up," he said with bravado, as he pulled open the door.

About a dozen people hung around the kitchen table down the tight hallway from the door. Smoke, coupled with the smell of spilled beer, slapped me in the face. The cigarette smoke I was familiar with, but the other smell, although I wasn't certain, had to be pot. That wasn't my crowd in high school.

Guys a few years older than us seemed to run the place. Sitting at the table, complete with nicks, burns and stains, they had a drinking game going. I had never seen one before.

Yes, I was that sheltered.

Socially, I was inept. I'll admit it. In high school a good time consisted of video games, surfing the Internet or watching movies, mostly by myself. Outside of studying for school, I wasted the majority of my teen years staring at a glowing box, thinking it was a window into the world around me. I didn't even notice that I had little contact with real people. My life was planned around prime time and in ninety-minute blocks. I was the standard idiotic American teenager.

Entertainment at the cost of humanity. I loved it.

The worst part about my life was realizing I didn't have one.

Five bucks could get me one at school.

Everything in college revolved around five bucks. It's the deciding factor between sitting at home and getting laid. If you didn't have it, you'd scour until you found it. Freedom, true freedom to throw caution to the wind and get completely blind-ass drunk, came at a cheap price. Despite this new-found knowledge that would become my creed, Ethan bought my way in. While leaving my wallet behind as instructed, I forgot to grab the cash out of it.

I held my red plastic cup, rotating it to see every angle and ridge. I beamed pride just to have one. I planned to keep this one forever. The chalice of my new life.

In the basement, bodies were packed wall to wall. The mass moved in unison. The voices were like the moans and wails from a Southern Baptist church wrapped in a wet blanket. Music was blaring, so people just yelled louder to compete with it. Then I noticed something.

If a fire broke out we'd all be dead.

With only one exit up a steep, narrow set of stairs with a low clearance, a funnel of panicking bodies would pile up at the first sign of fire. Some would die in the stampede, others from the smoke. The flames would roast some alive. At every college party, you take a chance with your life.

Following Ethan's example, I squeezed, shoved, squirmed and shimmied through the crowd to where I thought the keg would be. The pool of beer on the floor deepened with every step.

I thought I saw my roommate in the mess of unfamiliar faces. Either that, or everyone looked like him or everyone looked the same. I was glad I ditched my preppie look at the dorms.

Almost everyone bore evidence of spillage from trying to hold a beer in the wall-to-wall crowd of people in the room. When a tasty blonde whose chest toppled out of her tube top was shoved from behind, I joined the swill-stained masses. Half a beer landed on my crotch.

She didn't even notice that her beer went from half-full to empty right on my pants. Her attention remained on the four guys hitting on her, not the guy wearing her beer. Before I lost my alcoholic virginity, I was baptized. The warm beer spread across the fly of my jeans. I already wanted to go home considering I looked like I'd pissed myself.

Finally, we reached the keg. More lessons to be learned.

There's a hierarchy to serving beer in a college basement. The key was to get your man on the hose. Then, you were surely granted first serving, if you could get into the pile of outstretched hands with empty cups. You'd get served after the house cups, the pitchers and whatever girls were pressing their boobs up against your buddy.

I believe the term "bros before hos" was invented to deter such behavior. It never did. Boobs always won. Five bucks or not, it didn't matter, if you had a big enough pair of sweater kittens.

Ethan weaseled his way in, grabbing my cup and yanking me closer to the keg. Somehow, God knows how, the Hose Man hit our cups immediately.

"Slam it!" Ethan yelled, handing me a full beer.

"What?" I yelled back, "I've never had a drink before."

This is the part in the movie where the record playing would screech to a halt and everyone would look at the freak. There was no record, but everyone found the freak. The eyes that were fixed on the keg were now fixed on me. The crowd stared at me like I was a nun walking out of an abortion clinic.

"Then you've *got* to slam it," Ethan yelled.

All eyes on me. The mouths screamed in Gregorian chants.

"Drink! Drink! Drink!"

They had a taste for blood. I thought they wanted me dead. Instead, they wanted me drunk.

God bless them all.

Ethan and I smashed cups together in cheers as I sent the cold foamy drink down my throat. I choked, spitting up on the first gulp. My body wanted nothing to do with something that tasted like wet, moldy bread.

The yelling changed. "Alcohol abuse!" and "party foul!"

Before the drink returned to my lips, Ethan's was finished. He'd obviously done that before. I managed to throw my first beer down in long, accentuated pushes of my throat.

My rebellion was officially begun. I couldn't help but show a stupid, goofy grin, slopped with beer and foam.

Go Team Me.

Ethan smiled back and shook his head with a smile. He pointed at my T-shirt. Half of my first beer was on my chest and stomach. The first and newest stains joined at my belt.

"Let's get another one for the virgin," Ethan said to the Hose Man.

What? Virgin? Please dear God tell me he didn't just use the V-word to the whole friggin' party.

Deer look this way right before they get creamed by eighteen-wheeled trucks. No toilet in the history of indoor plumbing has ever flushed as quickly as my face.

How did Ethan know that I managed to keep all of my body parts out of the inside of a girl? It's not like I didn't want to. And why the hell was he airing that to these people, who obviously were susceptible to a highly unstable mob mentality?

Telling every female within earshot of this little fact—okay, this HUGE fact — only further limited my chances of being de-flowered.

Screw Ethan.

Screw rebellion. I should have stayed home. It's safe there. No public mocking, no reeking of beer. No false piss stains.

Surprisingly, the unruly horde of booze mongers did nothing but return their attention to the keg. All of my terror was unfounded. Passing me a beer, Ethan summoned me to head back to the stairs.

"Congratulations," he said. "You popped your cherry quite nicely."

Oh, *beer* virgin. I just kept my mouth shut.

Safe for another day.

Jesus, did I panic quickly.

Haunted by my fear of social situations.

We spent the rest of the night at the kitchen table, Ethan talking his way into numerous drinking games, each one more outlandish than the other.

President and Asshole. King's Cup. Flippy Cup. Beer Pong. Ride the Bus. Fuck the Dealer. Spades.

The best ones have the most cursing in their names.

The more tanked I got, the more Ethan had to remind me not to stare at the protruding boobs of the girl across the table from me. I'm sorry, but if the neckline goes down nearly to her bellybutton, she wants people to look at them. You don't dress that way to go unnoticed. As if she just wanted to air them out. Well, they were big enough to have their own set of lungs.

Other than the games and the tits, the rest of the party was an alcoholic stupor. We kept pounding beers, and with each sip, the rotten yeast taste went away. With every one gone, there was a craving for another. More. More. More. That's how parties go.

Gluttony.

Sadly, the most concrete memory I have of the evening was tossing my cookies on the campus lawn just short of the dorms. Mom would have loved that image. Dad's advice was already ignored.

Ethan couldn't help but throw out a deep laugh as he stood next to me pounding a can of beer, laughing in the face of the dry campus rules.

It wasn't even the first week of school, and my pile of puke wasn't the only one. They dotted the prim and proper landscaping all over campus. Bodily fluids blanketed the perfect flower gardens, wilting and withering the sensitive greenery. Purple and gold turned into purple, gold, green, tan, red and, if memory serves, some shade of blue.

I was part of the tarnishing of the perfect iconic representation the school gave itself.

This should have been on my list.

The next morning, I awoke — barely—still blitzkrieged. It was my first hangover. Still groggy from the alcohol, I rolled over in my bed, unsure of how I got there. The taste of fermenting vomit lingered in my mouth. The light coming in from the window only made it worse. Everything in the room was cast in an overexposed white, blurring edges of the furniture, drowning out the colors.

This was how coma patients must feel when they wake up.

Again, I was nauseous and barely made it to my sink. I heaved anything left in my stomach. The pain of not being able to expel anything was new to me. Pulling up a chair to the sink, I passed back out under the running faucet.

I missed my first orientation class, regaining consciousness for the mid-afternoon one. All day, I dry heaved at the thought of food, a cigarette or more booze. Still, I went out that night at Ethan's encouragement.

Another party. Another puke-fest. Another hangover.

Each one got progressively less excruciating. My body was welcoming its new punishment. It had better—there was more to come.

TEN

Why am I always doomed to live my life in a cycle?
Turmoil.
Acceptance.
Comfort.
Agitation.
Pain.
Repeat.
It is certain this is the way life is for everyone, but others seem to live in comfort longer than I can. My insecurities will overcome that stage in sufficient time. If I could live without fear, I wouldn't have to remain in my bubble and avoid new things. It is the only option.

This aching pain inside myself, the voices reminding me of the critics and failures, are overwhelming.

Daily life is mundane. Wake up, class, work, play, sleep. What possible culmination would release me from these eternal cycles? A meaning must be found to justify why. What drives me? Fear. Fear of failure is most common. Continuation for something. Maybe Frost has the right idea: Find simplicity in complex things.

The less we have, the happier we should be.

Instead, we take the exact opposite approach.

Many of us will be too inebriated or stupid to know that our most important moment in our lives is the one before us. As children, we dream of becoming President, super heroes or some other important figure. Nothing seems too far from the grasp of the imagination. Then, every day we are alive, we find peace in keeping the status quo. We refuse to take chances in fear of failure.

We do not make things happen, but rather wait for them to pan out. We wait with open palms for a handout or offering that we think that we desperately deserve. We think the terms "gimme a break" or "that isn't fair" applies to every sanctioned instant of our days. When we think we earn something, it is because we have done an adequate job for a certain length of time.

We are children of the machine that fosters mediocrity.

Those who stand out, those we call "lucky," are the ones who really rule us. They act on every impulse and inclination that comes past them. Those are the select breeds that do what they want, say what they want, and act the way they want without fear of reprisal. Many people have deemed those people assholes, crazy, stupid, and even insane. Those are the people who we should respect, foster, and even fear, for they are stronger than all of us.

They are the ones in the history books.

They are our gods.

ELEVEN

I grabbed for her chest and, without hesitation, my grope was met with an equally firm grab. Hers was at my crotch. That's when I blew it. Literally. Right there in my pants without a second of flesh-to-flesh contact.

That was my sole experience making out with a girl that I had, up until this point, innocently dated a couple of times. We were in her car at our high school graduation party. Needless to say that was the end of that budding romance. Still to this day, I have no doubt that my lack of sexual prowess was the reason we never went out again, despite her feeble protests to the contrary. Why she had to tell everyone, opening me up to ridicule the last few months before I left for college, I don't know.

That was my first sexual experience, if you could call it that, and it was far from being as impressive as the porn I owned. Though to my classmates, as it was told over and over, it was as comical as most of the plot lines in them.

Ethan was intent that wasn't going to happen again.

By the end of orientation week — five days of persistent inebriation, I had conveyed that sacred, hallowed bit of information to him. He could have just laughed. Other people had.

"I wish my grandfather was still a virgin," he said, shrugging off the seriousness of the situation.

Besides, we were plastered.

Ethan explained one night when he was fourteen, he got high, drunk and laid all for the first time. She was sixteen. After doing everything like that for the first time all in the same night, it's been hard trying to top a party like that, he said.

He had completed my college debauchery checklist one night in junior high. He was conquering older women when I was discovering jacking off.

"It's not like it's the greatest accomplishment of mankind," Ethan said. "If that girl would have gotten pregnant, my life would have been over. No, let me clarify that—if *I* had gotten that girl pregnant. Let's just face it, I would be the responsible party. Fourteen? Are you kidding me? Young, dumb and full of cum is no way to go through life."

Ethan inhaled, passing me the joint.

Another thing quickly marked off my checklist.

"Besides, you can officially guarantee every girl at this school that you're clean. Just make sure she can do the same."

In college, drugs are easier to get than alcohol. Every floor of every dorm at every university in every state has its own drug dealer. Some even have their own wannabe Pablo Escobar. Here in Prentiss Hall on the first floor, we had our version, too. I'm sure he had a name, but we just called him The Dealer.

Quickly, through resources unknown to us, he was hooking up the dorm with anything. He was getting coke for the kids on the fourth floor. They would take it and churn out crack for private use. Those amateur street chemists in their tie-dyed T-shirts and hemp necklaces smoked out front, laughing their asses off and constantly jerking their heads around searching for security guards.

They called me Narc. Ethan told me that wasn't a good thing.

The guys in room 205 were riding MDMA. They were the guys with all the black lights and huge subwoofers who always dressed in Adidas track suits. They tried making the room into a rave, but it always ended up with them dancing by themselves to horrible music with a thumping, repetitive baseline.

Room 409 stockpiled Ritalin in preparation for crushing it and snorting their way through finals. They were the preppy kids who worked their asses off just to impress their parents. In the interest of full disclosure, I belonged with them more than with Ethan.

There were rumors of heroin from 312, but those were never confirmed. Three-sixteen was mescaline. One-twenty was 'shrooms. Two-o-one was meth. Virtually everyone, except for the uptight goodie two-shoes who hung out in the lobby day and night, smoked weed. At least at parties.

Class wasn't the only place to expand your mind.

So there I sat, as paranoid as the crack heads, taking a hit off my first joint. A wet towel had been stuffed underneath the door, right by the yet-to-be touched pile of my roommate's crap. Five days since he amassed his belongings and he'd yet to return.

For me, it had been a week of disparaging hangovers, remedied by deep fried cafeteria food and more drinking. As I sat through all of the get-to-know the school classes, small groups and general college survival seminars, I prayed I didn't crap my pants. I hadn't pooped solid all week and I couldn't have been happier.

Puff, puff, give. That's the only etiquette I needed to know about smoking pot. Ethan had fashioned a filter out of a toilet paper roll stuffed with dryer sheets to exhale through. He'd obviously done this before.

The sheets, Ethan told me, were powerful enough to pull dried farts out of underwear, so they should work on pot smoke. To me, it was the same smell.

"Here goes nothing," I said pinching the joint as Ethan had shown me. Puff, hold.

In my lungs, the smoke felt coarse even after smoking half a pack of cigarettes in yet another basement party that night. Ethan looked back at me, as my face clenched and my eyes watered. It felt like a half-hour had gone by since I inhaled. Still, I held it in. Man up.

"Chris ... you can exhale now," he said.

My hold over my lungs let go, as I began coughing and choking as an uncontrollable lurch took hold of me.

Ack. Arg. Ogfh. Repeat.

Someone was putting out cigars on the back of my tongue.

A thin string of drool began escaping my lips.

Fire ants were feasting on my trachea.

The joint dropped from my fingers as Ethan grabbed it off the floor away from my kicking legs. He grabbed a bottle of water from the fridge and passed it to me.

With hand spasms, I pulled back on the water. The urge to hack up a lung went away with every slurp. My lips detached their firm, suctioned grip from the bottle as I grabbed for more air. Out of breath was an understatement.

Ethan complimented me on my puffing power, shaking his head and scoffing.

Again, I had failed. I was trying to be someone I wasn't. I had no business attempting to be some kind of rebel when I still was little short of a pathetic loser.

"You know Iron Lung, you'd be a lost cause if you weren't so willing to try," he said. "'A' for effort."

Never mind, I said, it's not worth it. I can't do anything right. I know who I am, I tell him.

"What's the point in changing that?" I rhetorically asked.

That's when Ethan changed. He wasn't smiling. He glared at me, and threw the joint down, and with his foot, smothered the weed into the carpet.

"Hey, my floor," I said. "That's going to be coming out of my security deposit."

"Fuck your floor," Ethan quipped back.

"Listen," he said, leaning forward in my desk chair.

"Self-determination is realizing your weaknesses and not letting them define who you are," he said. "You can either toe the line or make something of yourself. Standing out means being open to absolute scrutiny, but blending in, following the herd, doing what you're told, that's admitting the defeat of mediocrity."

"But everybody smokes weed," I said. "Is this just because I can't smoke a joint?"

Inching closer to me, those gray eyes darting at me, Ethan said it had nothing at all to do with pot, sex, drinking, school or anything else. He explained the only reason he asked for a light from me the first day was because he saw me standing there nearly convulsing in awkwardness.

Me and my inability to move. Powerless to go forward on my own.

I was so uncomfortable, Ethan couldn't stand it. He didn't need a light. His Zippo was in his pocket the whole time, he said.

Drink only if you want, he said. Smoke only if you want. Do what you want.

"Fuck everyone else. Don't do it because everyone else is, but don't be swayed away from it because you're not the first to do something," he said.

"We're all born different. Look at it this way, our birthmarks distinguish us from everyone else, but they don't define who we are."

"After millennia of human occupation of this planet, we're still finding ways to stand out. It's only after years of teaching, breeding and grooming that we learn to be like everyone else."

Dumbfounded, I just stared at him.

Maybe this is what I needed to hear.

Or, maybe it was because I was high. On my first time smoking though? Ethan told me I probably wouldn't feel anything on my first time. Then I realized the contact highs in the cloudy basements prepped me for this. They were so choked with second-hand that I missed my first high, technically, because of the energy of the room and the newness of it all.

While this was circulating through my head, Ethan continued. The passion behind what he was saying was undeniable. He believed every word he said.

"There is no alternative," he said.

Go out and choke the world until it spits blood. Give it a near-death experience to force its change.

Destroy stereotypes.

Set fire to complacency. Burn Rome with your ideas.

To be swayed by the threat of public embarrassment is to give up. It's becoming part of the system.

"Everyone will do their best to destroy you, pick apart everything you ever do. Don't give them enough power to do that. To change your life all you have to do is change your mind."

I listed to the Word of Ethan.

Maybe he was right. Since I came to school craving change and decided to chase it, maybe I was already a different person. I've always wanted to get drunk, high and laid, but I never made the effort. In one week I was already different from when I stepped out of the minivan.

Everything Ethan said made sense.

Yup, I was high.

TWELVE

Confusion.

There it is.

There's the emotion I needed. It's not the one I want, but it'll do—for now. At least it's better than nothing.

Here's the most stable person in the world, the epitome of cool, and then he goes and does something stupid like kill himself. It made no sense, not based on the little information I had. I didn't even know what questions to ask. No one had anything.

Still, it was up to me to start making the calls. I knew Ethan's nearest and dearest at school and it was my job to let them know. Before I even went through the numbers in my phone, the nausea returned. It would be the same questions over and over followed with the same response.

I don't know.

I don't know.

The more I knew I had to say it, the less I wanted to.

The guys from First Prentiss. People from work. People from just around.

It suddenly became apparent how many people he knew. The list was around fifty or so. Those are just the ones I could think of off the top of my head and whose numbers I had. That's not including the dozens of people that were inevitably going to question me when I run into them on campus.

Damn, that guy was a social bastard. Van Wilder didn't have shit on him.

The phone calls began and I gave answers that seemed distant. I tried telling myself that it had to be done. Do the job. It's not you. It's your duty. That only works in certain situations.

I had some idea what people were going to ask, so I planned what to say.

Suicide is by far nothing new. For as long as people have been living, they've been taking themselves out. Methods have changed, but the end result has always been the same. So have the emotions, questions and answers that have followed.

Yes, I'm shocked too.

People always want to know the same things.

No, he didn't leave a note that we know of.

Yes, I thought he was fine too.

No, I didn't notice anything.

I became the official spokesman of Ethan's suicide. It was my first chance to put recently chosen my public relations major to use. Finally. If you can't decide on a major, you either go with psychology or somewhere in the communications field. I chose the one with more money.

"I'm sorry, but I can't answer to any reason why he would do this," was my favorite answer.

Talking my way around most things, I answered what I knew and dodged what I didn't.

His mom found him.

The basement.

I switched from a confused, surprised and grieving friend to a PR agent of death, or, as I liked to call it, the voice of Ethan's self-induced sudden mortality.

It was a softer, yet long-winded way of saying "suicide." It seemed a gentler term than telling the truth, a nice way of staying away from a recognized simple word with a bad stigma to it. It was something people could understand. And it put less on me, the roommate. The best friend.

Self-induced sudden mortality.

Yes, I'm going to the funeral.

No, I don't know when it is.

It was being in a car accident, watching all of the faces in passing cars with eyes glued to the carnage. People say they detest violence, but if it's slapped right in front of them, they can't look away. They want to know every little detail.

I doubt it will be open casket.

Yes, a gun will do that.

I'm sure it was gruesome.

No, I haven't seen any photos.

No, I don't want to see any photos.

Some people asked more questions than others.

Unfortunately, as the virus that is suicide infects the healthy veins of humanity, no one is asking anything new. It's always the same. The answers are always the same. Nothing's new. With suicide, everyone talks in clichés. I was no different.

With the little bit of info I had, I was able to talk around most questions. I was better than I thought I'd be. By the end, I was even convincing myself. Everyone wants to sort out events that could have led to someone's self-destruction.

I could have sold a school board on installing cigarette machines in schools.

"They're going to smoke anyway, so we might as well bring in some revenue off it," I imagined saying.

Ethan would have been proud.

"Sure I'll call (insert name here)."

Collin, Nick, Aaron, the Bens, Eric, Gage, Zach, Dan. Katie, Jean, Meredith, Lisa, Christi, Kristi, Kristen, Kirsten. Ox, Roofie, Bubba, Mickey, Mikey, Nova.

"I've already told them."

Two dozen phone calls later and I was getting sick of it. My cell phone battery already died once and the sun was going down.

No, I don't know what they're going to do with his stuff.

I don't know if we should have a memorial service here.

I don't know.

I don't know.

No matter how hard I tried, the faked slickness wore off. Calling people, knowing in a few seconds they'll burst into tears. It's the worst thing I've ever had to do.

This was what police chaplains must go through every day. You wake up, get dressed and go to work knowing you're breaking the news to loved ones of the recent stabbed, shot, beaten, crushed and decapitated. They attempt to console mothers and fathers of dead sons, husbands and children of deceased businesswomen who were crushed on the Interstate on the way to work.

With those little white collars, at least God has those guys' backs. I wondered where He stood in my situation. I was trying to smooth over the death of my best friend.

No.

My best friend's suicide. Again, I could spin circles around my drinking buddies, but I still couldn't completely convince myself.

The little face I put up to make myself feel better was breaking down.

This time, however, it was for survival, not self-gratification.

Calling Heather was another thing I had to do.

Heather. I didn't even have her number.

Heather was the last on my list.

She should have been my first.

THIRTEEN

Sunday.

The worst day in college.

It's sitting around with a hangover and nothing to do. Getting through a week of drunken trances, and crippling headaches that followed, was easy because there was always some job to be done.

Eat. Class. Laundry. Study. Video games. Movies. Crap kicking.

Find more parties. Get laid again. Prank your neighbors.

The week long orientation seminars were over. The chances of getting up and meeting people in a structured environment, those sardine cans of people packed into the same situation, had completely escaped me. I still kept to myself. I was the quiet kid, keeping still in the front of the room.

Still, with the week of parties, my checklist was nearly complete.

Things to do:
- Get drunk for the first time.
CHECK, CHECK, CHECK, CHECK, CHECK, CHECK.
- Try pot.
CHECK.
-For God's sake, lose my virginity
NOT SO-CHECK.

Don't get me wrong. There were opportunities to take care of the entire list. Getting a college girl in bed is easy. It just depends on whether you'll be proud of it the next day.

At this school, there was an eleven-to-one girl-to-guy ratio. Nursing and education, the school's biggest sellers, kept the school freshly packed with wannabe servants of the idiotic and invalid.

Every guy had fantasies of all these post-high school tight bodies slithering out of skimpy white nurse's uniforms waiting to hand out sponge baths. Or, it was having long hair knotted tightly on the back of their heads, a pair of thick-rimmed librarian-style glasses perched on their noses as the buttons on their blouses were unfastened auspiciously in a seductive manner. Discipline for the bad boys.

Guys saw eroticism in the mothering figures of their childhood. Freud was onto something.

It was hot for teacher, praying for an educator-on-student sex scene made popular by our over-watched porno.

For further examples, see my copy of *Gladiator*.

But, judging by our parties, Ethan had the student population broken down already.

Eleven to one.

Half of the girls were fat or ugly.

Five-point-five to one.

Two of them had mental issues, baggage or both and therefore not worth any long-term effort.

Three-point-five to one.

At least one or two of these girls disdained partying or went home every weekend. Others had already picked up a new boyfriend at the first party. They were the needy types who only felt their lives were validated if they were in a relationship.

Attachment as a security blanket.

Then there are the complete bitches. They won't so much as acknowledge your existence unless you have a crotch rocket, wear Armani jeans or own the party house. They'd sleep with you if you had all three. It's just another form of prostitution. You don't pay for the sex, but the stuff you buy gets you laid.

Status as sex currency.

According to Ethan's calculations, there was about half a decent girl to every guy at every party. For those of you who are less inclined at math, you'd be competing against at least one other guy for every girl. That's even assuming the party wasn't a complete sausage fest.

The key to getting a girl in the sack with minimal effort, Ethan said, is to not jump on the same girl as everyone does. Then you're left with a room full of girls with all the attention focused on one. No girl wants to sleep with you after the eye candy at the party shut you down. No girl wants to know she's second choice.

In every chick-clique, there's the one that stands out. It's common for college-age women to group together. The best looking one recruits others that are sub-par compared to her. The theory is when seen by a group of potential mates, she'll appear to be more attractive than she really is. Her ugly friends will make her stand out.

Beauty by comparison.

Avoid all contact with her. Be a dick if need be. Talk to her friends instead. Somewhere in that group, there will be one decent-looking friend. Shoot for the late bloomer who had to rely on her personality to get through life instead of just dropping the neckline of her shirt and shoving her mostly-exposed tits in the faces of hump-hungry idiots.

As the night progresses, the friends will come to like your sense of humor, the nice way you offer to get them beer and mainly—and this is important — you pretend to not give a shit about their friend. The one who always gets the spotlight.

Secretly, every college girl, or high schooler for that matter, hates any friend that is hotter than she is. Sure, they say they all love each other in the sorority kind of way, but it's all bullshit. They'd just as soon drop her body into the Mississippi River with a dry cleaning bag over her head than admit more guys want to get into her pants.

Loyalty in college is in short supply.

But, that hottest-of-the-hot friend always knows where the party is. Her flavor-of-the-week boyfriend always has friends. It's friendship out of convenience, just to meet new people without any work.

That, unfortunately, is where I fit into my relationship with Ethan. I'm getting sage life advice from him and he's getting a project. I was his pet freshman.

His lesson continued, explaining the bigger the asshole you are to a girl, the more she notices you. The fact you didn't pine over her all night will really piss her off.

"Then, in the back of her naïve little brain, she's wondering what makes *you* so special. This only works if you're remotely good looking and free from any flesh-eating virus that has taken over your face. You," he told me, "You're fine."

"By the end of the night, she'll want to know why *you* haven't tried to get *her* into bed when *everyone* has tried."

It's social Rohypnol.

By the time you even talk to the Princess of the Party, she'll be undoing her pants. She'll screw you just to spite you. She'll think she's the player, not the played. Like all other men, you're putty in her hands, she thinks. It will repair her temporarily-frayed ego.

Drunken hook-ups as therapy.

To me, preying on the holes in every girl's psyche just to get your rocks off was low. It's just short of date rape. I didn't like the idea. Whatever happened to common introductions, talking and seeing what happens?

Not that I've ever done it. Not by then, at least.

The downgrading of every woman while pretending to build her up is done every day in every college town, in every classroom, in every study group, in every non-college town, in every bar, in every office.

Everywhere men or boys have ever stepped a foot.

Don't hate the player, hate the game, Ethan said. He added, which I abruptly ignored, was that this technique was only to be used in extreme circumstances.

"Don't become some sex-crazed idiot," Ethan said.

But that's parties.

It was Sunday.

There had been no sign of my roommate since his first few grunts at me. His crap remained in a pile, pushed farther back every time the door was opened. He could have been dead for all I knew.

My skin felt like leather from the smoky basements and lack of non-carbonated, hops-free liquids. My eyes could barely open, swollen from constant irritation. They leaked white goop.

It was noon and I was still in bed. According to my usual, proper, get up and do something routine, I was a failure. I have should been pre-studying, cracking open my shrink-wrapped three hundred dollar textbooks and get a start at future assigned readings.

I should have been getting prepared. I wasn't.

I will do nothing today, I told myself. I will not be productive.

Sloth.

My smile as I laid in bed was undeniable.

FOURTEEN

Don't exist.

Live.

Get out, explore.

Thrive.

Challenge authority. Challenge yourself.

Evolve.

Change forever.

Become who you say you always will. Keep moving. Don't stop. Start the revolution. Become a freedom fighter. Become a superhero. Just because everyone doesn't know your name doesn't mean you don't matter.

Are you happy? Have you ever been happy? What have you done today to matter? Did you exist or did you live? How did you thrive?

Become a chameleon—fit in anywhere. Be a rock star—stand out everywhere. Do nothing, do everything. Forget everything, remember everyone. Care, don't just pretend to. Listen to everyone. Love everyone and nothing at the same time. It's impossible to be everything, but you can't stop trying to do it all.

All I know is that I have no idea where I am right now. I feel like I am in training for something, making progress with every step I take. I fear standing still. It is my greatest weakness.

I talk big, but often don't follow through. That's my biggest problem. I don't even know what to think right now. It's about time I start to take a jump. Fuck starting to take. Just jump—over everything. Leap.

It's time to be aggressive. You've started to speak your mind, now keep going with it, but not just with the intention of sparking controversy or picking a germane fight. Get your gloves on, it's time for rebirth. There IS no room for the nice guys in the history books.

THIS IS THE START OF A REVOLUTION. THE REVOLUTION IS YOUR LIFE. THE GOAL IS IMMORTALITY. LET'S LIVE, BABY. LET'S FEEL ALIVE AT ALL TIMES. TAKE NO PRISONERS. HOLD NO SOUL UNACCOUNTABLE, ESPECIALLY NOT YOUR OWN. IF SOMETHING DOESN'T HAPPEN, IT'S YOUR FAULT.

Make this moment your reckoning. Your head has been held under water for too long and now it is time to rise up and take your first true breath.

Do everything with exact calculation, nothing without meaning. Do not make careful your words, but make no excuses for what you say. Fuck 'em all. Set a goal for every day and never be tired.

FIFTEEN

Fear.

There's another emotion.

I was scared to go running to Ethan's hometown to face everything there. Okay, terrified. At least I wasn't too arrogant to admit that.

I had called my parents. One part of me wanted to call them first. As my independence grew away from them, they were still the first people I ran to when things got truly messed up beyond my own repair.

They were stunned. Mom cried. That surprised me, yet it didn't. She barely knew him. The only time they ever talked him were during the few times they came to visit me.

Their visit coincided with Parents' Day. The campus was scrubbed extra clean for that day. Students in school polo shirts walking all over greeting people with their perfect teeth and all-American appearances, giving the same tours for pre-application high schoolers. These picture-perfect representations of no one I knew were walking brochures. These campus models would always end up topless at parties, but still managed to act like they were better than you.

Their fakeness made me sick.

But the only time my parents actually talked to Ethan was when they took him out to eat with us early sophomore year. They felt it necessary to meet the new roommate. This was only a few months ago.

Hung-over and shower-less, Ethan still managed to charm the crap out of them. He faked interest in school sports, politics or whatever topic my dad brought up to keep silence from the table. Ethan hated all of that stuff, but he kept perfect poise under pressure like he did it on a daily basis. Conversation kept going as Ethan played the part of the rough-edged college student with goals, aspirations, and dreams.

By the time my dad got his steak sandwich, he would have donated Ethan a spare kidney if needed. Mom would have given him a hummer under the table before she stuck her fork in her Asian salad.

All my parents knew of Ethan came from what I told them over the phone. Keeping the truth from them, all the while making it believable, was a full-time job.

Yeah, we partied a little. Only when all homework was done. Always in moderation. No, we don't mess with the wrong, trouble-making crowd. Always stayed out of fights. Drugs? They never asked.

Their immediate willingness to console me was no surprise. They must have asked a dozen times if I was all right. I was, I said.

Liar.

What they don't know doesn't hurt me. Their ignorance is my bliss.

After hours of phone calls selling people on the new, dead Ethan, I was tapped. I had no ambition to stick around in the apartment anymore. It was just all a reminder of what could have been done differently.

Walk. That's all my brain was telling me to do.

From Ethan's room I grabbed his sweatshirt. Something wanted me to believe he was still there. His room was no longer his. It was the museum of who he was. I thought being inside that sweatshirt, something he rarely took off, would help me get inside his head. I wanted desperately to know why.

Thoughts I didn't want to have circulated inside my head as I walked, unsure where I was heading. With my iPod blasting angry white boy music, I wandered to clear my head.

Past the corner barber shop, past the football players' house. Slowly my destination was inevitably becoming campus. With my head wrapped in the gray hood, I tried to keep my concentration on the music. Past the front of Prentiss Hall. Where I had met him. Every spot on campus had a memory.

Ethan.

Wasted out of his skull.

Freshmen year.

After the school had bought an antique clock he decided to christen the 150-year-old timepiece his own way. Hunched over on all fours, he shoved his fingers knuckle-deep into his throat. In the middle of the campus, Ethan made his statement on the waste of school money with stomach acid, beer and pizza. Even after an attempt at pressure washing, that puddle of mouth excrement tarnished the metal permanently.

I stood near the spot as emergency poles cast a blue light on the metal, highlighting the faded patched where Ethan had puked.

"Push the button if you're being sexually assaulted," our orientation guide had told us.

Sure thing.

Excuse me, Mr. Rapist, stop for a bit while I send for help.

Thanks.

The biggest emergency those poles would get were frat boys cruising through campus thinking they were funny, or worse, original.

Around the corner was the former fishpond. It's where I killed all of the bug-eyed oversized goldfish last year. That was not my intention, mind you. It was Ethan's dare.

I had no idea I would kill them when I took a flying leap into the pond just off the side of the Performing Arts Center.

But by morning, two grand worth of fish were floating on top.

Maybe it was the fluid in my Zippo, or the detergent residue on my clothes. Hell, maybe it was my Odor-Eaters.

Whatever it was it was poison to those koi.

Of course, I couldn't be lucky enough to have a janitor come and scoop them out with no one noticing. Oh no. Some terrified animal rights nut was the first to find the two-dozen koi floating ass-end up. From what I read, she was "traumatized."

An editorial in the student newspaper called the incident one of the worst acts of animal cruelty in school history.

Ethan called it the worst cannonball he'd ever witnessed.

Campus terrorism as a time killer.

Yeah, I felt bad, but it was Ethan's dare and the lighter was his present for my nineteenth birthday. It was that night we got schlitzed on Schlitz and some Jamaican green from The Dealer. That was the other part of my present.

"Be impulsive," Ethan said after chunking on the clock.

Okay, so it wasn't a real dare, but he put the idea in my head. I just started running and jumped. The fountainhead jabbed me in the ass cheek when I hit bottom.

By my calculations, the dead fish were his fault.

My walk was only clouding my brain more.

There were few things on campus that didn't remind me of him. If it weren't for him, I would have spent all of my time in my room. By myself.

Studying. Over-preparing for a boring future.

And I kept walking. Through the cafeteria, through the student union. Everything was as it should be. Sloppy dressed college students picking up late-night food. Plastic silverware, straws, salt and pepper shakers. Styrofoam everything. Paper napkins. Ketchup packets. Nothing had value. Everything disposable. Go in. Get out. No one will know you were there except for the trash you left behind.

Keeping my head down inside the hood, I pretended to hide as to avoid anyone I knew. All I wanted was someone to stop me and say something worthwhile.

I wanted to hear it wasn't my fault.

When the inspirer of your transformation puts a gun in his mouth, you should really reevaluate your relationship. My savior offed himself in the laundry room. I then questioned if I had put too much stock into our friendship.

I'll bet this was how the Romans felt after killing Christ and he did his magical reappearing act from the grave three days later.

SIXTEEN

Then there's Stan. The roommate from freshman year.

The fashion magazine cutout that plunked his stuff down and left. The one that didn't return for a week.

It was Monday.

I had my newfound declaration of intent to slack off, but that was for Sunday. It was the new week and the old me wouldn't let my college career slouch before it even stood up.

I woke up early, ironed my clothes and read the first two chapters of the textbook. Classes hadn't even started and I was already doing homework. Old habits die hard.

That's when the door flung open the same way it did a week ago. It smashed into his pile of crap, toppling over a few purple totes. The guy in the door was wearing the same clothes he left in.

Figuring to impress my professors, I dressed in an Oxford shirt, tie and khakis.

Up and down, he eyed me. Then he huffed.

"Oh my God, you're not a Mormon are you?" he said. "You selling Jesus door-to-door?"

"N … n … no," I said back.

He didn't wait for my answer before he began digging through the totes.

He fished through one, pulling out bottles of all different sizes. Shampoo, moisturizer. Frantically pulling through his things, he was unaware I was trying to sneak by him.

"Excuse me," I said sliding flat against his closet door.

He snapped upright, his head whipping back and his highlighted porcupine blonde hair nearly stabbed me in the face.

"Stan," he said. "Everyone calls me Stan The Man."

Chris, I said. I asked where he had been the whole week.

He plopped down conditioner and something that exfoliates on the sink.

"Here and there. Partying. Up all night, crashing wherever. College is unreal man. I haven't slept in days."

He panted out short quick sentences.

"I met this girl. Sophomore. She's a crazy bitch. A biter. Stay away from freshman girls. Freshman fifteen, right? You start dating a girl now and by the end of the year she's a walrus. Sophomores and up, okay?"

Cologne, facial toner, bronzer.

He kept talking, never waiting for a response. At this rate, as sweat beaded on his forehead, he was burning a hundred calories a minute. Coke head, I'd say, based on my vast experience watching Pacino in *Scarface*.

From another tote he pulled out a polo shirt and khaki cargo shorts similar to what he was wearing. He threw them on my bed.

"Hey, I'm going to move stuff around later. This place looks just like everyone else's. I had trouble finding this one."

"Fine, whatever," I said. "I just don't want to be late for class."

He still clogged the doorway. I slid by him, clutching my overstuffed bag against my body. He smelled like a porn film set — body odor, secreted juices and cheap liquor. At least that's what I guessed they smelled like.

With Stan's funk lingering around my head, I was off to my first class. My first class of college. The place where, if I didn't like a class, I could drop it so long as it didn't have anything to do with my major. Right now, I didn't have one, so any class was fair game to toss off my schedule.

Now that campus was populated with people heading for classrooms and not searching for basements, the median age upped significantly. Non-traditional students were everywhere. Either that or there were three professors for every student or a lot of super-duper seniors.

I know now the non-trads were the ones that would make a class suck more than the homework. At their ripe old ages, they had an opinion on everything. The degree was just a piece of paper, because they already knew everything about anything. The worst part was they always had something to contribute to class. Even if they weren't asked.

They would talk about conflicts and wars that ended long before anyone else in the classroom was born. They mentioned them like they were current events. They regurgitated Freud, Hemingway and Einstein like they were classmates in elementary school.

But I wouldn't learn this until much later.

My first class was in a packed auditorium. It was the same one where half of my orientation classes were. "Getting to know your school" involved formal lectures on where the fire exits were in every building and where to find the Diversity in Action office. No wonder why everyone stopped going to those things by the end of the week.

The seats were the same as when the hall was built, which was around the early nineteenth century when no human was taller than five-foot-six. That meant my long legs that made up most of my six-foot frame were jammed in between the non-reclining seats. My knobby knees barely fit, even when I sat spread eagle. The best seats were at the end of the row, but that meant standing up every twenty seconds when someone wanted in or out of the aisle. Still, I took the gamble.

"Excuse me, sir," one girl said, as she wanted into the row.

Sir? Either she thought I was a non-trad or the professor.

The hall began filling as the beginning of class approached. As soon as I sat down after letting someone by me, I'd have to stand up again. Showing up early for class was pointless.

Then the professor came in.

I eyed my classmates in between scribbling down every word he said—even the clearing of his throat—as he went through the syllabus.

"Your first test will be in two weeks," I scribbled verbatim.

Some people I already recognized from parties. Most were dressed like they were going to one. Girls had done their hair, put on jewelry, and doused themselves in the most expensive perfume they could find. The guys were the same. Many dressed more aptly for rap videos than higher education. Skin was definitely in. With plunging necklines traced by miles of cleavage, it was obvious some girls were going to try to T&A their way to a BA. Not that I'm complaining.

I was sitting in the middle of a Gap ad.

This class is brought to you by Burberry.

Intro to Sociology. It's a class everyone takes, no one goes to and not a soul fails. They're gimme credits taught by only the oldest and most boring professors. This one was no different.

My parents chose this school for me because of the small class sizes. The university advertised the average class size was fifteen. Plenty of personal contact with professors, a brochure said.

The asterisk always means something.

From the thirty-second row in the double-tiered former performance hall, the sounds over the loudspeaker seemed to emanate from someone standing behind the podium. I was so far back I couldn't make up any other distinguishing characteristics. He never looked up from his notes so we could see what his face looked like.

He was just a talking gray mop wearing a green blazer.

"Oh cool, our professor won the Masters," a voice from behind me said. I didn't know if he was joking. But if he was, I got it. If he wasn't, God help the future of this country.

One group of girls was auditioning for American Idol.

The final will account for fifty-percent of your grade, the mop said. It will be open book and open note, he said. You can elect to take it home, he said.

That's why no one showed up. On the first day, he gave you a paper that screamed, "Here's when to show up!" That's why everyone took the class. With an open-book testing system with exams drafted word-for-word from the book, why the hell would anyone take notes? Still, I wrote everything down. This could be a test.

No one else wore a tie. Only me. Not even the professor. I slowly undid the knot.

Twin guys looked like Abercrombie models.

The voice from behind the podium was waning under the growing hum of incessant chatter from others. It got louder and louder as the students soon learned the professor either didn't notice or didn't care how loud they were talking. Half the class left in the first half hour.

I stood up, let another person pass and crammed my legs back in. My knees were getting raw from the constant friction inside my khakis and the seat in front of me.

The class size was then down to about two hundred. Maybe the school got their magical class size number by doing a head count at the end of each hour.

A girl was prepping for a Banana Republic two-page spread in *Maxim*. This wasn't class. This was a fashion statement.

Everyone was pretty. No one was ugly. But me.

My tie was now undone.

My office hours are from noon to one, Monday through Friday and seven to eight in the morning on Tuesdays.

This is when I began to realize what college was. I wasn't writing anymore. I stuffed my tie in my bag. I should have kept listening.

"I will be taking a mid-semester break for two weeks. During that time, we won't be meeting for class," the professor said.

I should have written that down.

Nike. Structure. Ecko. Corporate Punk. Dolce & Gabbana. American Eagle.

Some people look like they were sponsored.

Dockers. Stafford. That was me.

Levis. Hanes. That was Ethan. He must have been the only freshman not in this class.

Two of my shirt buttons were undone by the time the professor walked off stage. That was his way of saying class was over.

The line of my classmates anxious to leave gathered next to me. I was holding up the show. I hurriedly tried to stuff my notebook into my bag. Instead the contents tipped out the front onto the floor. Pens rolled underneath the seats down the slope to the front of the room.

My first impression to the class was classic college movie stuff. I was officially the token nerd. Never mind the tie. The exit spoke for itself.

Pages in hundreds of dollars worth of textbooks were crushed and torn by passing feet as people flowed into the main aisle where my books were. I fumbled my way through scooping everything up as quickly as possible as the line of people impatiently huffed behind me. Help only came by them kicking things closer to me.

That's when I saw her.

Hazelnut brown hair. Big chocolate cake eyes. Cinnamon freckles on her nose. No visible brand names.

I stared. She noticed. She smiled.

No clue what to make of it. It could have been the start of a laugh. It could have been out of pity. It could have been nothing more than a smile.

I should have followed right behind her, scrapping my stuff and chasing after this girl who showed visible interest. Especially because I was at my geekiest. Especially because the third thing on my list hadn't been crossed off.

I say I should have. That means I didn't.

With my books back in my bag and my dignity still on the floor, I headed out of class with my head down.

Nice start, ace.

SEVENTEEN

Outside the commons I saw the last thing I expected. A group of people gathered closely around one another, each one clutching a lit candle surrounded by a paper cup.

A vigil.

One part of me wanted to think it was for someone else. The other part of me wanted to know, if this was for Ethan, why I wasn't told. I had, after all, told everyone he committed suicide. I had been the bearer of bad news. It was I who was Ethan's PR agent of death.

Slowly I approached the circle of about thirty people.

From the light glow of the overhead lights and the flickering of the candles in the cold breeze, I couldn't make out faces. Slowly walking over, I only recognized a few people from around campus, but no one Ethan and I hung out with.

There were a few of the Goth kids that were always in front of the liberal arts building. Some were the zealous drama students who smoke hundred-length cigarettes on the picnic tables near the theater building.

It must have been for someone else. I wanted to know who else's death timed so well with Ethan's.

There were all of these students on a Sunday night, hovering around each other wearing as much black as they could pull out of their closets. They stood in silence.

Circling around the outside, I didn't see anything but more unfamiliar faces dripping tears. Some of these strangers hugged each other in comfort. I eyed the crowd for a face who could answer why they were outside, obviously mourning something. Still I lingered, unable to find someone I knew. There was no way I was going to intrude into a stranger's grief when I couldn't deal with mine.

Ethan taught me how to spot the people who would talk. Usually on the outside, looking around. Not too involved in what's going on, but still aware. I tapped a black trench coat near its shoulder.

The coat turned as a lanky guy with blue-dyed hair looked at me. He was covered in so many piercings it looked like he fell face-first into a tackle box. Obviously a liberal arts major. Philosophy, I guessed.

What's this for, I asked.

"Schome kid killed himschelf," the face said through a mouth of metal.

"Who," I asked.

"I'm not schure," Tackle Box Face said. "I think he wasch a junior."

"W … wait," I said. "You're here and you don't even know who it's for?"

"I've scheen him around campusch. He alwaysch wore a schweatschhirt like yoursch. Maybe I'm thinking of the wrong guy. Maybe it wasch you I'm thinking of."

Since Tackle Box Face knew as much as I did, I asked the person next to him. And the next. The next. Everyone was giving the same answers.

Some student. A guy. Sophomore. I had a class with him last semester.

My roommate knew him.

It wasn't until the fifth person I asked that I got a name.

"Nathan."

"You mean Ethan?"

"Could be," a brooding Emo told me through the locks of black hair covering her face.

It was for Ethan. A vigil for Ethan and no one bothered to tell me. You can't fathom that sense of rejection. The effect of that kid's suicide was nothing I could have comprehended. At the same time, I was jealous of his fan base.

Envy.

But Ethan was affiliated with none of these people, as far as I knew.

There was this puddle of people who wore black head-to-toe on a daily basis, part of an open expression to mourn someone's death, and most of them didn't even know who lived the life that preceded it.

Then I just started getting pissed off when I realized what was really happening.

If there was a tragedy to be had, these people couldn't pass up the opportunity to become part of it. To them, it was a fun excuse to cry and show everyone how in touch with their emotions they were. The angel of death paid someone a visit two hundred miles away and these assholes wanted to grab at his wingtips for fun.

Crying for someone they didn't know.

How empathetic.

How pathetic.

"What in the *fuck* is wrong with you people!"

Wrath.

In my disbelief that these death aficionados would celebrate a suicide, somehow I had lingered my way into the center of the circle. I was glaring at these suicide groupies in front of me. Less than twelve hours after Ethan's mom found the body, and the all-new dead Ethan was the latest fashion statement on campus.

Rigor mortis as a social event.

Let's just say these mortality fans were digging up emotions inside of me I didn't know I had. I was yelling the way you yell at the taxi driver who just cut you off during rush hour. It was the way parents yell at a four-year-old for spilling grape juice on the new white couch.

"You don't even know who the *hell* he was and you want to fake how much you're going to miss him!"

These fatality followers. They could summon emotions like fashion models in front of a camera. Like televangelists exorcising demons.

I was still yelling at them. It was less anger than it was frustration. I just couldn't understand any of this. Their faces were telling me the same about me.

"Why don't all of you go kill yourselves and give someone else something to mourn?" I yelled at them. "That's if anyone would even care." This was the way your boss yells at you when his wife leaves him. The way you suffer for his failures.

It's okay. Let it out. Let it all out. Don't hold back.

"Jesus H. Christ! Fuck *all* of you!"

Fuck, fuck, fuck. That's about all I had to say. Substantively, my little tirade wasn't much. Who cares, it made me feel better.

Appalled, the crowd leered back. Coughs of disgust and more weeping. At least this time they were actually upset. One voice in the throng spoke up from behind me.

"What's your problem? Why don't you leave us alone and let us mourn our friend," a pigmy chick with a green streak in her hair shot back at me. "Who are you to tell us what we can and can't do?"

Your friend? I had hung out with him all through college and these fakers didn't even know who I was.

"Fuck you Emo. You don't even know his name," I yelled, pointing sharply at the short girl. "I was his damn roommate and I've never seen any of you before. This is just damn sick."

"Get the hell out of my way," I commanded as I pushed my way through the rabble.

Rage. Disgust. Confusion.

It's all coming out now.

I had found everything I didn't want. I had wanted noise, anything to drown out all the Ethan. I had wanted a distraction and all I got were reminders.

Now all I had was the commune of death fans in my head. Everything was obscured. These suicide sycophants. Ethan's dead and these people are his phony friends. I started trucking across campus away from the crowd. They started singing some sad song, something I've never heard before.

Everyone just shut up.

Ringing phones. Questions. Music blaring in my ears. More questions. No answers. Ethan. Repeat. These toadies were singing some depressive bullshit to calm themselves.

At first I wanted noise. Anything but silence.

Once you get what you think you want, you'll sacrifice it all for what you had.

Everyone just shut the hell up.

Ethan. Ethan. Ethan.

I kept hearing it.

Who else has to die for me to get some silence?

"Ethan."

A hand grabbed me, spinning me around and stopping me in my power walk across the yard.

It was Heather.

Heather and her Cappuccino skin. Her fudge brownie shoulder-length hair was tangled up in her scarf, perched just above the collar on her red Old Navy pea coat. Her overloaded backpack forced her to hunch forward a bit to compensate for the weight.

She put her gloved hand to her mouth in embarrassment when she realized I wasn't Ethan.

It was something she found out long ago.

"Oh Chris, hey, I thought you were Ethan."

The sweatshirt.

"Where is he? I haven't been able to get hold of him for two days."

No one had told her. Ethan didn't tell her he went home. I hadn't called her. She didn't know.

I stood there, huffing from my walking sprint.

Saying nothing, her expression changed.

"Chris, what's wrong?"

She had gone from surprised to confused. Scared wasn't too far off. I just stood there as the charlatan mourners kept singing about a block away.

"What is it?" she asked. "Chris, say something. You're scaring me."

Ethan's gone. Ethan went home. That's how I started to tell her.

"Oh, I wonder why he didn't tell me," she said.

I could think of a few reasons. But I didn't say that.

She asked when he was coming back.

"Never."

"What? I don't understand," she said.

Of course you don't, I thought. You never got it. And there was no way to keep her from understanding it anymore. I looked at the ground.

"Heather," I started and paused. "Ethan committed suicide last night."

There I said it. There were plenty of other ways I could have put it.

Self-induced sudden mortality.

Ethan blew his face off. He wanted nothing more to do with any of us. He figured a gun blast to the face was better than everything he had. It was better than us.

There's a thousand different ways she could have reacted to hearing that someone she's been humping for about a year just swallowed a live round.

There would be no more soft moaning from her seeping through the doorways of our apartment. No more shrieks of orgasmic delight from the other side of Ethan's door.

You can deny it, try and trick yourself that the totality of the circumstances was impossible. You can just pass out. If your mind can't handle it, your body will respond accordingly by sending your stunned ass to the pavement.

You can throw up. That's another of the body's responses.

You could just start screaming. Drawing attention to yourself could make you feel better. Make the suicide about you, not the dead one.

Heather chose none of these.

She just stood there, mimicking my dumbfounded and numb stance. Her eyes pooled up with tears, her lips quivered as her head tilted slightly to the right.

The poor girl couldn't come up with anything. She was trying to say something. Something that needed to be said. Something that needed to be asked. We stared at each other until the reflection of a tear came down her cheek. It started in the inside corner of her eye by her long eyelashes and trickled down to the crease in her nose. As soon as the droplet passed over her upper lip and into her agape mouth, I was staring at the ground again.

No one was singing anymore. My headphones stopped blaring as they hung from my neck. There was finally silence.

Silence. Sweet fucking silence.

After hours of making phone calls to Ethan's drinking buddies, delaying telling his girlfriend, I was not in the mood to make another person cry. The faked smoothness I had been using to deliver the news to our shared idiotic friends was wearing thin. I couldn't bullshit Heather. I just couldn't bring myself to do it to someone who obviously loved this guy so much.

I pulled off Ethan's sweatshirt.

"I'm sorry," I said, handing it to her. I shouldn't have been wearing in the first place.

I left her standing there, silent. Like me, she craved answers but I couldn't give her any. I could only speculate.

Walking home, I realized my handling of the situation only worsened things. Out of anyone, Heather should have got the answers. She should have been told the truth from the beginning. She deserved better than just being left standing alone clutching that sweatshirt. It's me that should have been left dumbfounded.

The wind made me shiver as I pulled my arms into my T-shirt. There I was, cold, isolated and desperate for something I knew I couldn't have.

A solution. A remedy. Anything.

The silence continued except for my own footsteps. I hated it. Alone and confused was the last place I wanted to be.

Somehow I knew I deserved this.

EIGHTEEN

My first college class went down as a beautiful failure.

I just wanted to sit in my room. I wanted to pout. I completely forgot Stan had wanted to play Martha Stewart. He said he wanted to rearrange things, but I was barely paying attention. I just wanted to get past his porno stink and get to class.

From outside our room I heard the blasting of whatever trendy hip-hop song had been played three times an hour on the radio. I couldn't tell you who it was by or what the name was, but I had heard it so much during orientation week that I had all the words memorized. Different basements, same thing.

On the marker board etched in disgusting penmanship was a slogan like the labels on all our laptops, "Virginity robber inside."

Welcome to my world with Stan The Man.

Stan was type who scoured for the easiest girls to get on—the drunkest or skankiest—and bring them back to the room. He'd leave them. I'd clean up. He'd be off doing something else when I made sure these girls got home. Without pressing charges. By the end of our tenure together, I'd have to wake up four girls left passed out and naked from the waist down.

How many venereal diseases he was carrying, I don't know, but he was the reason disinfectant and shower shoes were invented.

Grudgingly, I reached for the door handle, fearing for my life what was inside. It was locked. This early on, I had learned the only people to lock their doors were scared to have all of their stuff stolen. Or getting high or laid. Or they were chronic masturbators. Stan was the latter.

My key still in the lock, I opened the door and stood in the doorway interrupting Stan's very private moment with himself. There he was, stark naked sitting on my bed in its new location, his neck arced up at the television, spanking off to *Gladiator*, at least what was in its case. My presence didn't even phase him. He kept on churning away like a milkmaid on deadline.

"What are *you* doing on *my* bed?" I yelled, my voice cracking like a second bout of puberty was on its way.

On the screen a pale red head was bent over the edge of a couch, a pair of hips pumping her from behind.

"Just … close … the … door," he wheezed as he worked his kung-fu grip. "I'm … almost … there."

He threw a towel over his lap. At least it was his towel.

Without enough time for me to leave the room, his faced filled with creases and all the blood in his upper torso rushed upwards. He growled the way two dogs fight over a bone. Then he whinnied like a horse after a race. His orgasm was the soundtrack from *Animal Planet*. It pains me to admit that I know that.

With a wipe of his hand on the towel, Stan stood up, his erection still at full bore and pointed at me. I spun around, knocking my head on the back of the door.

"What in the *hell* dude," I sneered, peering over my shoulder to make sure the beast had been re-sheathed.

Stan wrapped himself up in the towel and grabbed his shower basket from his desk. I jumped out of his way. He said nothing as he let the door close behind him.

I was afraid this was his idea of roommate bonding. He hadn't lived there for more than two hours and already he had found a way to violate where I slept.

Before he had copulated with himself, Stan had turned our room into proper housing for a psychotropic harem. Tie-dyed fabric fastened by strips of duct tape hung from the ceiling. Posters of Playboy models in lingerie covered every inch of the closet doors. By the way this guy obviously only thought with his dick, he wasn't masturbating. That was his idea of studying.

His idea of enlightenment was rubbing one out.

Another poster, "In case you need to celebrate," a sort-of calendar giving historical importance to every day of the year, was on the wall opposite the desks. On my birthday, the toaster was invented. That's the most exciting thing that happened that day, historically. I'm less exciting than toast.

All of the movable furniture, which was only loft bunk beds and my mini fridge, had been shuffled around to create more space behind and around Stan's desk. My bed was pressed up against the wall by the widow. My things were now in a pile as all of his took up the space mine once did.

The girl on the screen was moaning in pleasure.

The feeling was not mutual.

Since my bed had just been the arena for a one-person tug-of-war, I carefully removed its sheets and put them in my clothes basket. The rest of my morning, before my next class, would be dedicated to the campus laundry machines in the basement. At least I got to put those four rolls of quarters my mom gave me to good use.

Our laundry services consisted of six washers and six dryers, only half of which worked. A thirteen-inch TV was chained to the wall. A load of laundry, from beginning to end, cost five bucks. It seemed steep, but it was another example of how the university profited from the laziness of its population.

Five bucks ruled my world.

I dropped my coins in, started the load and went upstairs.

Stan had come back from the shower down the hall. At least now he had his boxers on.

"Hey, we're going to have to work something out with this kind of stuff," he said. "I don't mind if you do it when I'm here, I just hope you're the same way."

He explained he wasn't gay, he just knew it was going to be difficult to find jack-off time with two people in the same room. It was one of my concerns when I first got here, but Stan changed all of that.

He went into a story about how he and three friends were on a road trip over the summer. They took turns spanking off into a Subway bag and passing it on to the next guy. He didn't remember what he did with the bag. I was sure it was somewhere in our room right then.

Masturbating with three other guys in a car. Sure, that's not gay. Whatever you have to tell yourself.

Still, he proceeded with talking about plans for "personal time." I would have just rather tried to put his personal exercise regimen out of my head.

"Just stay off *my* bed," I said as I hosed my mattress down in Lysol.

The shirt he put on for the first day of class summed him up perfectly. One arrow pointed up with the words "The man." Another arrow pointed down. That was for "The legend."

I'd seen it in some movie before. Or a couple. It was anything but original, but Stan thought it was.

And I like to think that would be only the time I encountered Stan pleasuring The Legend. I say I'd like to.

Nope.

I'd wake up at night and hear him going at it. If it wasn't him by himself, he was with his nightly scrapings from the bottom of the party barrel. It's not like he was a bad looking dude, it's just that he didn't like putting any work into it. If there was the least bit of resistance, that wasn't the path Stan wanted to take. Stan was my first inspiration of who not to become as I went after my checklist of debauchery.

Thanks, Stan.

To make things worse, when I returned to put my sheets in the dryer, they were gone. Someone took *my* damn sheets. In less than a half hour, someone snagged used bed sheets from the community machines.

If I didn't watch what was mine, someone would steal it.

Lesson learned.

NINETEEN

The all-important, self-sustaining Your Friend Has Killed Himself List — things to do before dealing.

Shower.

Pack. That list had a list within itself.

Black pants. Black shoes. Black shirt. Black tie.

None of these things I had, so it was a shopping list. Screw it. Why not buy a suit? Designer. Use the credit card. This constitutes an emergency. Another sub-list.

Order is the false return to safety. We can't prevent terrorist attacks, but stashing gas masks and canned food in our bunker-like basements, that we can do. Preparation is the illusion of security.

Simple tasks give us a certain sense of control.

Suicide is no different.

Confirm train ticket.

Feed Ethan's fish.

These little missions seemed easy, but by writing them down ensured I wouldn't forget anything. It was categorizing things so everything was in its place. Organization. This comes first. This comes last.

When things are most tumultuous, the order of a list, a compilation of easy things to do, is comforting. I couldn't help Ethan, but I remembered to pack a toothbrush. An explanation for what happened was far from my grasp, but letting my professors know I would be gone gave me a feeling I was doing something worthwhile.

Lock the door.

Crossing off each line gave me a point of accomplishment. I was closer to completion.

Error. Correction. Redemption.

There was only one thing left to do.

Leave.

Stay busy and it will all go away.

It was time to go to Ethan's house. His mom said I could stay there.

The police had finished their work.

While all homicide investigators are told a suicide should be investigated with the tenacity of a homicide, it rarely happens. One person. The gun at the scene. It's near the body. It's possible the person could have done it himself or herself. Close to calling it a suicide.

Suicide: The intentional taking of one's life.

But if they rule the death a suicide, there's all the second-guessing for everyone. There's the social stigma on a family after their son checked himself out of Hotel Life.

Suicide: Considered a grave public wrong in most cultures.

Friends and family feel guilty because they couldn't stop it. Often family members will hide notes or weapons to deny the inevitable. They'll call a suicide a police cover-up. They'll call state and federal authorities to review the investigation. The family doesn't want to believe it was a suicide. That, and they might not get their insurance claim filled.

It's not a dead body. It's a payday.

The person in the black bag is nothing more than a non-breathing dollar sign. It's not your fault Uncle Louis killed himself, but why can't you benefit? Your insurance agent will give you a million reasons. He's got his own lists.

If there's a note, some cops would consider the investigation over. If someone leaves a note and goes out in the middle of nowhere, the cops call it a "clean" suicide. The note makes the person's intention known and the family aren't the ones who find the body.

Ethan's was far from clean.

Cops have lists too.

Weapon at the scene?
Check.
Injuries self-inflicted?
Check.
Motive to take his own life?
Not-so check.

If there's a history of mental illness, done. Drugs and alcohol? Yup, it was a suicide. When it's ruled a suicide, the cops can go home.

Suicide: Not a crime.

The coroner takes the body away and the family is left with a room filled with bits of bone and brain matter spattered all over the wall. The half-melted face spread all over everything. The insides of eyeballs on the dryer. Clumps of skull stuck to the washer.

Ethan's mom had called a crime scene cleanup crew the police recommended. Their job is to take something out of the pages of a homicide investigator's handbook and make it fit for *Better Homes and Gardens.*

They had lists too.

A guy in a biohazard suit came and pulled out buckets of blood and any bits of Ethan's head stuck to the concrete.

It's not suicide. It's Art Deco.

The crew restored the room to the way it was, just a little cleaner. Dead Ethan gone. The smell of coagulated blood and death was replaced by the scent of a warm dryer in the damp basement. The concrete was scrubbed clean with cleansing agents you have to be licensed to carry.

Everything was back to normal. Nothing happened. The property value would barely flinch once all the flashing lights outside stopped drawing unwanted attention to the house.

It was a visual way of allowing everyone to continue on as usual. There'd be no mess to haunt the minds of the ones who claimed to love him. Ethan was dead and already partially forgotten. He couldn't even stick around as a stain in the basement.

A two-hour train ride later and I arrived in a small southern Wisconsin town. A sign at the station said Lancaster. I told the cab driver the address Ethan's mom gave me.

TWENTY

It was rush season.

Die-hard pledges of one frat were forced to wear barnyard animal costumes. Yeah, they said they weren't forced because hazing had been outlawed. But, if they wanted in, they had to wear them.

Ethan and I were in the cafeteria. A cow, a pig and a chicken were sitting behind him. A form of one of them was on my tray. Which one, I wasn't sure.

And out of nowhere, Ethan started talking with the pledges. He explained his view of the Greek system. Groupings of friends based on superficial guidelines. One frat wouldn't let in anyone with an American car. One sorority didn't allow black or fat girls. Most frats could give a rat's ass about GPA.

All these rich kids show up on campus without friends, but they've all got money. Then they realize they can pay some dues, get into all of the parties, and have their lives mapped out for them. The Greek system was nothing but a grouping of people more insecure and afraid than those who followed them. The freshmen without friends.

"They were all scared once and would do anything to fit in like just like you," Ethan told the cow, pig and chicken. "Don't buy your friends."

And they didn't. None of them joined. They all swore not to prove their worth with stupid gimmicks. They scrapped rushing. Ten minutes earlier, they all were prepared to fuck a goat to get into a party. Instead they partied with us.

Ethan Costello was an enigma. As much as I tried to parrot his every mannerism, I couldn't figure him out.

He could drop a six-beer bong and then go right into arguing a point until he had everyone convinced that his opinion wasn't subjective, but pure fact.

People found him captivating. Maybe it was the way he stayed in control in almost every situation. Maybe it was the way he could talk to any girl. Maybe it was the way everyone wanted him at every party. Like me, many strived to be like him.

If we only knew.

The clunking noise of a gun dropping from a dead hand, the tree falling in the woods no one heard, was a knife to the heart of our view of Ethan Costello.

We all went looking for answers.

Suicide is always followed with one thing: blame. Everyone wants to cleanse themselves of any wrongdoing on their part. Like everyone else, I too wanted absolution.

I can't tell you anything more than what I saw or learned afterwards. It's a matter of replaying clues and anecdotes in my head to try and sort things out. You won't know everything, because I don't know everything.

Like everyone else, I replayed events that could have led to Ethan's demise. One thing immediately comes to mind.

Around five-thirty in the morning is when he knocked on my door. It was early October.

"Are you up?" was the first thing I heard. Ethan stood in my doorway.

"Hey, is it cool if I come in?" he whispered.

Already he knew he was always welcome in my room. This time he asked.

"Can I talk to you?"

So I sat up.

"Yeah." I rubbed my eyes, looking at my alarm clock.

"Come with me," he said with an uncharacteristic strain in his voice.

Something was obviously wrong. I hadn't seen him in four days.

"Dude, can it wait for two hours until I have to be up?"

"If I ever ask for anything from you, this is it," he said.

Unwillingly, I got out of bed. Oh, that comfy twin-sized mattress five feet off the ground supported by nothing more that a few screws and some bent tubing. The bed with a me-sized warm spot under the covers.

In my groggy state, I unintentionally put on my roommate's Nikes after jumping into some jeans. They probably cost two hundred bucks. Label whore.

Ethan ushered me out of the door as I grabbed my jacket. At that time of the year, it was questionable if it would be forty or seventy degrees outside.

Something was bothering him. Normally, if he had something to say, he'd just say it without holding back. Not this time. At five-thirty in the morning on a Tuesday, it had to be something monumental for him to take me outside.

I followed him to the front of the dorms. Except for the rain, all was quiet. There was this unreal trembling feeling in my stomach I couldn't shake. It was working its way into my mouth. With the little I knew of him, besides how much he could drink and basic biographical information, I didn't know what to expect.

There was one section of the concrete wall in front of Prentiss Hall that became our spot. It was where business was conducted, where party information was shared, where people met up after class. If anything was ever going around campus, the word of it spread from right in front of the wall near my dorm room.

As soon as we affixed ourselves to our usual spots — Jay and Silent Bob-style — Ethan lit a cigarette. His first drag seemed to come out in slow motion. The look on his face meant he had something to say. The lack of him speaking meant it was something important. It was painful to watch as his expression showed he was searching for words.

Something was going on behind those gray eyes. Something was brewing behind his lips. The rain broke through the tree limbs, plopping heavy droplets onto his hair and shoulders. He was wearing that gray sweatshirt.

Watching Ethan smoke, realizing I was staring, I fumbled through my coat pockets for a smoke myself. It would help me wake up and give me something to do. Keep busy. That was my defense mechanism.

What the hell was I worried about? Nothing, but I was.

No cigarettes. They were still on my desk.

Ethan extended his hand. Once again, that hand held an open pack. This time he pulled back.

He flicked his smoke out into the street. He reached into the front pouch of his sweatshirt. He pulled out two cigars.

"These are appropriate," he said, not looking up at me.

"What's the occasion?"

He lit mine before I was able to ask anything else. I wouldn't have anyway. I knew better. Staying quiet, I wouldn't let my input, filled with my usual tripping over my own tongue, seep into the conversation.

Screw the parties. Forget the sharing of mutual boredom easily remedied by campus terrorism. Never mind idle time in the cafeteria. This was when our friendship was founded.

I was the only one who might listen, he said.

He said I would understand.

He was wrong.

He sat puffing away at his cigar for what seemed like an eternity. His uneasy demeanor was excruciating to watch. I soon forgot my worries and finally reopened my mouth.

"What's up?"

Those words broke the silence that only that time in the morning could offer. There was no one else around. Ethan didn't say anything.

God I am stupid. Keep your mouth shut. You're here to listen.

Puff.

The smoke grew thicker from our cigars, engulfing our faces.

Puff.

I was starting to get anxious again. It was the first time I saw him at a loss for words.

Puff.

He kept looking at his feet.

"I was supposed to be a father today," he said.

Dad, Daddy, Dada, Pops, Pa. Each term for the same paternal figure carries different meaning. Father has it's own. He used that word, father, and no other. He knew what that meant. It almost seemed as if someone had told me it before.

My mouth was stuck open.

"What?" That was the best I could do.

It was a simple story, he said.

He and this girl he dated through high school had split up senior year. It happened after the abortion. After a Valentine's Day dinner and date, they went to her parent's empty bedroom and got to it. Days later, she was throwing up. She stole a pregnancy test and used it right there in the bathroom of a gas station. It turned blue.

My Valentine's Day ended with a hug.

Ethan adamantly opposed the abortion, but she didn't want to mess up her college scholarship with a baby. She was going to a different school. He wanted to raise it. He had no say in the matter. In terms of parental rights,

Ethan was nothing more than a sperm donor.

"Once you squirt, you no longer matter," he told me.

She had the abortion a month later. Her parents never found out. Ethan never said a word to her after finding out his future son was sucked through a tube. He assumed it was a boy.

Ethan was too calm as he told me what he was still pissed about. He told the story as if it didn't happen to him. It was like a joke, but the punch line never came.

That's just the way he was.

Still smoking his now soggy cigar, Ethan told me it all. The rain beat down harder and harder as the minutes ticked away.

I kept staring at him. Either the nausea came from hearing the news or from inhaling off the cigar. In case you haven't noticed, I have a weak stomach.

As the saying goes, in life there are no certainties. That's bullshit. There is one.

Chris will puke.

"Something needed to be done to remember this day," Ethan said. "Thanks for having my celebratory cigar with me."

It was exactly nine months to the day after the conception. Nine thirty-day months. He skipped the extra from the odd months, he said.

He envisioned a boy. A nine-pound, six-ounce healthy baby boy. He would have coached T-ball. Given him his first car. Ethan would have been a good father.

"Don't be dumb and make mistakes like me. There's more to life than getting drunk or getting your rocks off. I did all that. All it left me was empty and mourning the death of my unborn son," Ethan began.

I was half-listening. I was more concerned with how if that kid had been born Ethan would have gone to school closer to home, if at all. He would have devoted his life to that child. I would have never met him. College up to this point would have sucked.

"Go out have fun, but do something else besides getting wasted all of the time. Make friends, not just drinking buddies. Take something from this place more than just a collection of bottle caps," he continued.

In lieu of raising his own child, Ethan took me up as his pseudo-child. His pet freshman.

"There are unlimited possibilities inside the walls of these buildings. The hardest thing is finding out which one was meant for us. Until then, I'm going to try and take in as much as I can. I'm going to do all of the things my son never got the chance to do."

That's when I realized it.

That abortion was the best thing that ever happened to me.

So what if I think that way? Every time someone dies, someone profits. I'm no different. Baby Ethan's loss. My gain.

After our conversation, Ethan told me not to tell anyone. The surprising thing was that he thought I actually had someone else to tell. I had met the guys from the rest of the floor by that point, but I was in no way up to gossiping level with any of them.

That morning changed nothing. The next day, he acted like nothing happened. He acted as if it was just another normal Wednesday. Tuesday morning didn't happen.

Sure, now I can say this could be a reason for Ethan's suicide. Of course, he couldn't handle the loss of his unborn kid and used a Beretta to turn his face into a crater. That would have been the simple answer.

If he would have done it right away that night. Not more than a year later.

It seemed like too simple of an explanation. My absolution wasn't coming that easy. I owed Ethan that much.

The abortion does, however, add more irony to the campus work-study job he took soon after.

The campus health clinic.

If you needed a pregnancy test, condoms or cream for your outbreaks, you talked to Ethan. He was the monotone voice on the phone and stoic face behind the counter. He said he took the job for unfettered access to whatever medications were available only with a prescription. Antidepressants and drugs for ADD were fun to party with.

If you crush up two Ritalin's and snort them while getting blitzed, it'll keep you up all night. It's a steady high, not the peaks and valleys like coke or meth. All without the random nose bleeds.

Ethan knew he'd never get caught clipping pills, even if they ever checked the inventory. He knew this because of the sheer number of drugs they haphazardly handed out to students on a daily basis. It wasn't that our campus was filled with a mass of apprehensive, panicking students riddled with chronic depressing pain or obsessive-compulsive disorder. Well, not more than any other campus.

"It's just the nurses answer to everyone's problems," Ethan would say.

Have a bad day? Here's some Zoloft.

Finals got you down? Have some Paxil.

Molestation memories coming back? Try Xanax.

Saviors come in pill form, too.

These people handing out the pills like M&Ms took up shop at school because they failed at *real* nursing. The university could have saved a ton of cash by firing the "nurse practitioners" and setting up medication vending machines.

The nurses never checked to see what prescriptions you were already on. They never screened for mental illness. They never checked to see if the round pills turned you into a homicidal sociopath.

The campus nurses thought they were curing the mental anguish of the student body. They thought depression was rampant in college and 50 mg yellow pills of sertraline HCl could protect you from yourself.

Instead they were free-sampling their way to a sniper in the bell tower.

Ethan snatched boxes of antidepressants, antibiotics and whatever other multicolored pills fell on the floor. One time he accidentally ended up getting loaded on estrogen supplement pills. For a few days, he was *too* in touch with his feelings.

I saw his job as ironic not because of the drugs. That was the perk. The sheer irony came from his favorite part of the job—poking holes in every one of the ten condoms you got for a dollar.

Little did the most of campus know—except for the few friends Ethan warned—that the thin layer of latex that ruined sex did nothing to protect them. They should have just stuck their hands into the used needle containers in the bathrooms. With the STD rate on campus, and people like Stan perpetuating them, it would have been a better idea.

Barely any of the rampant coed sex was safe, if people bought their wares from Ethan.

Thanks to his work with a safety pin, Ethan was steadily jotting down more appointments for VD treatments and unwanted pregnancies. He created seventy-two abortions the first year.

They bought the condoms, and then needed to return for the Penicillin to get rid of the clap.

Some might be appalled. Some might call it perverse.

Was it wrong? Sure. Was it funny? Yeah, if you knew about the joke beforehand.

Ethan never got how weird it was that his child was killed and he created more dead babies. Hurt others because someone hurt you. It's a survival technique.

"It's job security," he said.

Very few people go around hurting other people for the fun of it. People only hurt strangers after being the target of pain. And harming those you don't know only lasts for so long. Then you start hurting the ones you love.

I know this.

Heather knows this.

Ethan knew this.

TWENTY-ONE

The secret to making a leak-free beer bong is to apply a silicone sealant on the funnel stem before jamming on the hose.

A dash of salt will take away the taste from even the most vicious of beers.

Two aspirin before crashing will prevent most hangovers. If not, drink the super strong electrolyte stuff they give to babies for diarrhea. Slurp down a bottle of that the next day and you'll be ready to start guzzling brews by noon.

I knew these things before I took my first midterm.

Mine was the prototypical college experience. You could have scripted it.

It was somewhat like a rehashed college movie where dick and fart jokes are wrapped around a time-tested plot. Partier has a life-defining moment and reevaluates his existence. Then, he gets serious, wins and celebrates by more partying.

There wasn't much else to jot down except going out and getting blasted on whatever was within reach. We lived for the weekends. And Thursday night. And Wednesday night.

Sure, we got smashed and fell down quite a bit. But, in a four-year college setting, that's not only acceptable, it's encouraged. There's no other explanation for why the library would close at five on Friday and not open until eleven the next morning. The administration wanted us to go out and fulfill our God-given right to chase tail while in an alcoholic stupor.

They benefitted from it more than we did.

You get busted drinking on campus. They get free labor. It was work hours in the form of whatever they chose. When Ethan set his record for alcoholic counts in the dorms—the one where I took part of the rap—we were sentenced to twenty hours each. The majority of those came from vacuuming the hallways of The Thirteen Floors of Whores, the all girls dorm on the edge of campus.

Nice punishment really.

When a girl hears a vacuum cleaner outside her door at eight o'clock on a Saturday morning, she just expects it to be the regularly-scheduled cleaning lady. Not cleaning guys. Let's just say those towels on the way to the shower weren't always pulled up as high as they should be. The cabaret of cleavage was worth the ten hours we bilked out of the job two weekends in a row.

You get busted drinking off campus. They still found a way to give you work hours. You could get busted at a house party in Alaska during summer break, and if the school found out, they'd punish you. More work hours. We'd have challenged that rule, but the school's got better lawyers. Besides, in college, you have no rights.

Except for the right to remain intoxicated. Anything you do and say while in the state of inebriation can only be held against you for comical reasons.

Why else would there be twenty-seven liquor stores in a town of twenty-five thousand townies and eight thousand college students? Why? You fool. Because of underage alcohol sales.

You have the right to a Forty. If you cannot afford one, a Forty will be provided for you. Hopefully. If your friends don't suck.

Going out and getting drunk at noon on a Tuesday fueled the economy. We were balancing budgets with every shot, every beer bong, every keg stand.

Going to underage parties in cramped basements, drinking crappy flat beer followed by questionable hook-ups is an American tradition. George Washington would have done it. Jack Kennedy was the king of it. Dubya, anyone?

Ethan Costello promptly went from some random name to a secret password into a release from all inhibitions for those who wanted freedom. True freedom for five bucks.

Every party he went to he made more friends. The guys who rented the house. The girls who knew guys at more houses. Girls who didn't have boyfriends. The girls who rented the houses. Those foreign names of party houses from the first night of college became our regular stomping grounds.

Three-eleven. The Pink Taco. Freedom House. Sixty-six.

Each place was a temporary cure for our Saturday night wanderlust.

He had united us all. He made sure no one was left behind party-less on a Friday night.

Envy.

Friday and Saturday nights we went out in herd. En masse, we'd take control of a party, keeping it running at our break-neck speed.

First Prentiss wasn't just the name of a dorm floor. It was a mindset. A hazy one filled with drunken antics, but a mindset nonetheless.

Collin was the one who tried to pick fights with total strangers just to watch their expression. It would have gotten annoying if it wasn't just so funny.

Aaron would be the one to fall down the stairs on his ass. Not all the time, but if someone did, nine out of ten times it was him. And everyone noticed his butt slides into the basement.

Zach would start screaming at people about the weirdest shit. Give him half an ounce of grief and he'd make a huge deal out of all of it. Drama

Queen, extraordinaire.

Eric was the man-whore. If anyone out of all of us was going to get laid, it was most likely him. He wasn't the best looking dude on the planet, but he made his shit work.

And it wouldn't officially be a night out without Gage taking his pants off in public. Parties, after-hours eats, bars. It didn't matter. He would drop trou and claim to have a reason for it.

Occasionally, we'd bump into my roommate and his polished friends. Stan the Man and his pretty, pretty man-princesses. Looking for their nightly scrapings. Flashing the shocker hand and laughing like it was brand new.

They'd stand together using crappy pick up lines and trying to find the drunkest girl in the room. The one with the glazed cow-like stare and dripping makeup. The one who lost all control over the volume of her voice. The one with hair flattened in the back proving she's already been on her back tonight. Either passed out or spread open.

When Stan wasn't on *my* bed, watching *my* porno, punching *his* munchkin, he and his parasitic friends wanted the sure thing. They were the scum left on the floor when the party cleared out. That's how he went from his self-designated "Stan the Man" to become known as "STD Stan."

You know those fish that cling to huge whales, cleaning them while still feeding off them and getting a free ride, that was me to Ethan. I got into the parties. He got a social project. I wondered if he could get credits for it.

He'd do the talking—I'd do the watching.

Usually, I was the quiet one, sipping my beer in tiny intervals. When there was nothing to say, I'd take a drink. New people, I didn't do well. Since that's all the first few months of freshman year was, I was drinking a lot. Nervous, take a sip. Anything to keep me busy. Show me a picture from early freshman year and I'd show you me standing in the background.

Me, the breathing wallpaper. You'd have to look hard to notice I was there. But, slowly I got better, more confident as everything lost its shiny coat of newness.

There were plenty of parties to work on the list of wickedness.

In the breaks that were sobriety, there was that pesky education that needed attention. Surprisingly, the majority of us were still doing well in school. It didn't matter what your major was. The beginning of a four-year school—so chock full of classes about world history, philosophy, biology and computer science—was just a weeding ground to see who would fall into the caverns that were academic suspension.

If you can't make it through classes freshman year, if you can't seem to grasp the basics of higher education, you should just drop out. Seriously, if doing a four-page paper on some war or a seven-minute, how-to speech on *anything*, is just too much for your little mind to handle, then prepare for the embarrassment of being a dropout.

Stop wasting mommy and daddy's money. Just get out now so other kids can get your spot in class. Go back to your high school job of pushing carts at a Big Box, hoping someday to work your way up to a department manager and marry the cute girl from Housewares.

Barring any life-altering event, like your own suicide, getting though college isn't that hard. Go through the motions, get the degree and get out. Sometimes it's okay to follow directions.

"You have to learn to work inside the system to change it" was Ethan's advice to me. "Just remember to keep your mouth closed so you don't swallow any of their crap."

The parts of college that didn't reflect my inebriation I saved to report to my parents. It's what they wanted to hear. It's not lying just because it isn't the whole truth.

What they don't know doesn't hurt me.

Still, I needed explanations for why I didn't return their phone calls for a few days. Saying I was in the library was just saying it. They needed proof. Bullshit only spreads so thin.

So, with a schedule filled with Gen Ed classes rehashing what I learned in fourth grade and a sampling of business classes, I made dean's list first semester. Ethan did too.

Go Team Us.

While The Dealer and the rest of the dorm had figured out their roles in the illicit drug trade, Ethan found the much more lucrative product. He became the official Beer Baron for Prentiss Hall.

Within weeks of stepping foot on campus he had set up an army of people willing to buy him stockpiles of booze to fuel the supposedly-dry dorms. After a while, his suppliers stopped charging him their handling fee. No one could figure out why some people were so willing to buy a freshman truckloads of alcohol. I suppose it was out of sympathy as upperclassmen remembered their own freshman situations. They just assumed the function others had played for them. We all were characters in the banned booze circle of life.

Or maybe Ethan was just that convincing.

He got so many different customers that he could no longer sneak it into the dorms in a backpack alone. The administration said no alcohol in the dorms. Security guards were posted at the door to look specifically for that. Our lives were guarded by overweight snitch students, most of them future cops, who threw a yellow polo shirt on and considered themselves the

Elliot Ness of campus prohibition.

Always looking forward to a challenge, Ethan joined the intramural hockey team just to have an excuse to haul a bulging bag, supposedly filled with pads and whatever else, into the dorms after ten at night without security ever being the wiser.

With his new extracurricular venture and our conflicting schedules, sometimes I'd go a week without seeing Ethan. He'd be off somewhere doing something while I spent my time doing homework, playing video games or avoiding STD Stan's attack on the war in his pants.

I'd like to think the quick immersion into all things surely had me cured of any inhibitions I had previously had. That was not the case. It was Ethan. It was all Ethan. Slowly I was getting my drinking legs firm enough to hold me up, but Ethan was still my crutch. I drew my party poise from him.

Any kind of self-esteem I had built up was all from his approval. If he was proud of me, I was proud of me. I looked at him as an example of how to live my social life.

Go. Go. Just keep going.

Don't ever stop.

Carpe diem and whatever.

Without jobs and cushy class schedules, we were free to do anything. And we did.

Lust. Gluttony. Greed. Sloth. Keep 'em coming.

Hangover to blacking out and back again.

It seemed like a fucking circus sometimes, but I kept buying tickets hoping to make center ring. If I said I was staying in, Ethan would ask if that's what I really wanted. I never said yes. It was four-day binges followed by a week of sobriety to catch up on missed homework. Ethan made sure that was still priority numero uno.

He tried teaching me about exceeding expectations by abandoning them.

"Set your own goals," he would say. "Don't live to appease to the standards others have set up for you."

Live like a cancer patient with one day left and, yet, still like someone who knew they would live to be a hundred.

Party for today. Study for tomorrow.

When not terrorizing campus hopped up on pharmaceuticals and forties, Ethan was logging a record number of hours at the library. Not the local bar, The Library, but the actual place with the books and the desks and the computers. Some people somehow graduated never having seen the inside. But not Ethan.

Let me clarify something here. It wasn't that Ethan liked school. He figured since he was going to college he might as well do something else besides get smashed all the time, although that had it's perks.

His dad's advice was, "Learn something besides what the bottom of a bottle looks like."

Our dads weren't too much different that way.

More clarification.

Ethan hated asinine jokers that used the library like a dry campus bar. You know the type. The ones who yell at their friends across the room, blare music from their laptops or try to pick up women there. It's the ones who couldn't stand people's attention not being fully directed at them. It's the ones who craved to be stared at, even if it was in pure disgust.

STD Stan comes to mind.

Ethan went there, studied and left. I think he liked it because you could be left alone there. There in a mass of books, tables and pseudo-cubicles were hundreds of students at any given time, all doing the same thing and barely interacting. Ten students would be waiting at the same printer for what seemed like an eternity and no one would interact. They'd rather stand in absolute silence than say something to someone they've never met, but yet they shared the same study time for months. It's the ones who had phobias of unarranged personal contact.

I come to mind.

Ethan liked the library despite all of its faults. The socially-dependant and the socially-challenged.

It's that a library has no memory. In another four years, the majority of those inside would all be different, studying the same things, reading the same subjects. Books checked out by people who have long since died would still be read by those who are just beginning to live.

A library doesn't judge you. It lets you in. You use it for whatever. You can leave when you want, possibly borrowing a piece of it. It puts the campus whores to shame.

But, the main reason Ethan liked the library was because every second he spent nose-deep in a book kept him miles away from his hometown. It prevented him from being the white trash that clogged the flow of human evolution. Someone gave him an opportunity and far be it from him to waste it.

Education, he believed, would set him free.

Knowledge—not inebriation—was the best escape.

Further clarification needed.

No matter how hard he tried, Ethan couldn't sit silent as he ingested what he was supposed to be learning.

Anytime I'd go with him to the library, I would watch his irritation with any subject. He'd be reading, lean back in his chair and mutter at the book.

"Bullshit," he told a theology book.

To my sociology book, "This is crap."

It didn't matter what subject, whether philosophy or biochemistry. Half of the time they weren't even books for his classes, just whatever he pulled off the shelves.

Current Applications of Religion.

Politics and the Middle East.

Issues in Criminal Justice.

Still an undeclared major, he took the mixed-bag bouquet of classes.

Dirt Science. That's what everyone called it.

Bowling. Hell, they gave him credit for it.

By the third week of class, we all knew getting a degree was just going through the motions to please professors, at least the ones who failed in the field they were attempting to teach. The easiest professors only wanted a rub to their bruised egos. If you're lucky enough to find the ones who actually enjoyed teaching, you might learn something worthwhile.

Study. Test. Study. Test. Study. Paper. Study. Final. Repeat.

That's college.

That's what Ethan said.

Still, present or future, he wasted none of it.

Even with struggling to grasp something that wouldn't bore him into a coma, there was one area where he undeniably excelled. He was the social butterfly with big, bright wings. Trust me, even if you didn't think you did, if you went to our school, you knew Ethan Costello.

The guy in the T-shirt and jeans but somehow stuck out in the crowd of guys in T-shirts and jeans. You know, the guy with the tag-along. That was me. I was learning under the wing of my personal guardian angel.

But Ethan sometimes played the part of the devil, too.

TWENTY-TWO

Homecoming is the last pure American holiday.

Hallmark hasn't touched it.

There's no fat guy dressed in a red suit that breaks into your house and gives you stuff. The pilgrims had nothing to do with it. Jesus didn't die at homecoming. There's no St. Whatever of Homecoming. No flowers are sent. You don't buy anyone gifts. The only thing you buy is a commemorative T-shirt with a clever slogan and enough booze to harden your liver into a football.

Sure, homecoming was supposed to be the day for alumni to come back and re-taste the good life. Supposed to. In reality, it an excuse for every college student to wake up early — earlier than they would fathom for class — and get stinky drunk by noon. Or, if they're good, nine.

Kegs and eggs.

Beer & Bagels.

Mimosas. Screwdrivers. Irish coffee. Bloody Marys. Beer bongs from the roof to the road.

There are plenty of recipes out there if you want to drink your breakfast.

They should just call it Drink Day.

We'll get to that later.

And it's always been a tradition for all college students to make sure they were tossed even before the parade at ten in the morning. That is, all college students who lived like we did.

The only problem was that the school cracked down hard on drinking during homecoming after some dumb-ass rugby player fell off the team's float and split his head open. The crackdown came the year before we started school.

The school blamed drinking. I, like many other students, blamed the low tolerance of student-athletes. Sure they could kick most of our increasingly-flabby asses, but we could toss down a case of beer before they could run a mile. Sure their skills got them scholarships, but at least ours didn't create the new prohibition. Us smart. Athletes not.

So the cops and rent-a-cops the university employed were on heavy lookout for open containers every year after that. A girl could get raped in the middle of the street, but if neither of them had alcohol in their hands, it wasn't the concern of Johnny Law. Selective attention comes in many forms.

"All containers banned at parade," the headline of the student newspaper read.

Ethan became obsessed. The Beer Baron's ingenuity came into full force. Someone tried telling him he couldn't do something. It only focused him more.

It wasn't good enough to drink beforehand and then hang out. Oh, no. Not good enough. It wasn't good enough to stash it in bathrooms in restaurants along the parade route.

No, Ethan had a plan.

Afterwards, it sounded simple, but me and the rest of the First Prentiss boys had to give Ethan credit because he's the one who thought of it first. Ten turtleneck sweaters, ten boxes of wine and twenty feet of clear tubing later, we were in business.

The instructions were simple.

1.   Remove bladder from box of wine.
2.   Cut hole big enough to insert end of hose.
3.   Insert hose.
4.   Tape wine bladder to stomach.
5.   Put on sweater.
6.   Pull up tube.
7.   Put on jacket.
8.   Insert tube into mouth.
9.   Drink, stupid.

Knowing how cold it always was by homecoming, we had plenty of reasons to repeatedly tilt our heads down to the collar of our sweaters. Breathe hot air onto your hands. Heat up your face, whatever. The newly-added protruding guts went unnoticed. This was college. And all of the alumni had them too.

"Wine's a different kind of buzz altogether. I promise you'll love it," Ethan said as I duct-taped my bladder to myself. My nipples poked through the sweater from the cold bag of Riesling.

But it worked.

Six blocks of the city's main drag — and I use that term loosely—was closed down for an hour. That created even more animosity between the townies and the school. These townies with their complaints of how dirty, drunk and dyslexic we all were. These people who lived in a college town all their lives and still managed to complain at every instance of late night noise and a few plastic cups in their yards.

Yes, Gertrude Miller of 308 Sandborn. It was I who stole your precious garden gnomes! I repainted them and put them back. I thought you'd like the *Reservoir Dogs* in your front lawn. The letter to the editor, the one where you called me a "ruffian," wasn't the fond show of gratitude I was hoping for. That, and saying you "knew" it was a college kid was a bit assumptive. It could have been the high schoolers.

Terrorism as a time killer.

Besides, the college was built in 1885. I doubt even crotchety old Ms. Miller was born before then. The school was here first. College kids party. Deal with it or move.

Anyway, homecoming. Parade. Bladder of wine making me nip out.

Huff Street was lined with lawn chairs and couches occupied by red-eyed students and glaze-eyed adults. It was as if the school had pissed its colors over all of them. Walking down the route, our wine guts protruding out under the turtlenecks, Ethan, the rest of the boys and I searched for girls. Cops eyed us like pedophiles at a preteen beauty pageant.

The Man was pouncing on anyone who failed to realize the new parade route policy. The open container fines, and subsequent work hours, racked up as poor saps were getting pinched before the first float went by.

That didn't stop the Beer Baron. He put his hands over his mouth, rubbing them and blowing out his nose, the whole time sucking down merlot. It felt like it was fifty-degrees out, but he feigned cold hands. All the time next to a fat cop, who obviously had skipped his agility test for a few decades.

Ethan winked at me. The balls on that guy.

Coast is clear, that flashing eye told me.

I stuck my chin into the turtleneck, using my tongue and chin to dig around and find the stray hose. I only imagined how I looked. After my spastic jaw adventure, I just started sucking. The sugar-water wine didn't feel as cold in my mouth as it did against my body, but I was happy nonetheless.

Aaron, Collin, Gage, Zach, Eric, Nick and the Bens all followed suit.

School: zero. First Prentiss: one.

These are the future doctors, lawyers, accountants, salesmen, public relations representatives and teachers of America.

Go Team Us.

The search for prospective women was rejoined. Me, I was too occupied in amazement on how no one noticed me tripping off a bladder of wine.

After a half a dozen sips, I realized none of the cops were none the wiser. I just unrolled my turtleneck up over my mouth and kept the hose in there permanently. Sure I couldn't scream at the passing floats like everyone else, but I wasn't up on day without classes to hoot and holler at Student Senate or at cheerleaders wrapped up in leggings and sweaters.

Floats passed and I kept drinking.

And, yes, Ethan was right. Wine is a completely different buzz altogether. The lack of carbonation means you don't get as full as you usually get with beer. It's not as debilitating as drinking straight liquor. The middle ground is amazing. It's like being stupidly drunk and ridiculously high at the same time.

More floats, more drinking. The guys were socializing. I was slurping.

Then I started getting hungry.

"Eden," I said, wiping the back of my hand over my eyes. "Weave gosh two heat the calve fur sum each."

That's what I said. In my mind, it was crystal clear.

And Ethan looked at me in amazement. He tapped my stomach and felt nothing but an empty bag against my skin.

His response was simple.

"*Oh shit!*"

The last float had passed and my bladder was tapped. That's five liters of

Riesling that had become as warm as my piss in the two hours since I'd started it. Not a wise idea if you need longevity for a full day of drinking. Pacing myself was something I hadn't mastered yet.

Blowing into my hose, my stomach re-inflated. And I giggled. That's right, giggled. High pitched. Like a girl.

"Buddy, we've got to get you to the caf for some eats," Ethan said, one hand on my shoulder to steady my swaying.

"Hats watt eye sex."

Ethan had to keep me from stumbling into the street as I barely made it off the parade route on my own. Ethan and the boys were dragging me to the cafeteria. Then plans changed.

I threw up all over the lawn. And Collin's shoes.

Chris will puke.

It's called CVS, or Cyclic Vomiting Syndrome. It's a condition where you have repeated, stereotypical bouts of intense vomiting during times when you're normally healthy. It can also be triggered by emotional stress. I looked it up.

Unfortunately, getting wasted doesn't help either.

Throwing up, I don't remember. Getting to the dorms, I don't remember. The only reason I knew this was because the guys told me later. Besides a good buzz, wine will also erase any memories created during the stupor. Sometimes many memories long before it, too.

Winos have no childhoods.

Because no one I knew had any intention of going to the football game, and everyone else was, First Prentiss partied in the dorms. They forced me to take a nap against my will.

My big bee-stung swollen tongue couldn't detach from the roof of my mouth far enough to form a coherent word.

"Wash tea fork, ewe bass turds?"

"Call the exorcist!" Nick yelled. "This one's possessed!"

"Nah, he's speaking in tongues," one of the Bens followed.

Shoved into my bed, I passed out in minutes.

In all the ruckus that is homecoming, little did I realize that while I was lying in bed, my comatose ass was fair game.

I noticed nothing.

Hours later, I awoke naked except for my underwear. My skin felt slimy. It was covered in something I couldn't quite make out just then.

Sitting up, the wine reclaimed its ground in my brain. The gravity of the situation took a while to get in there too. Was it still homecoming? Had it been homecoming already?

This is when my memory fades back in.

My legs caught my hop down from my bunk and wobbled me over to the mirror.

Head bald as a cancer patient's. Black magic marker cocks went into my mouth. "I (heart) dick" was bannered over my forehead. They misspelled "transvestite" on my neck. My skinny, shaven legs looked like they belonged on a girl. I had no body hair except where my boxers were. No one was brave enough to venture down there.

The mirror told me I had been conspired against.

You could say I was pissed off. You could also say I freaked out. If you really wanted to, you could say Ethan deserved to get punched in the face. I say he did.

There was clamor in the hallway. I stuck my head out there.

Hyenas don't cackle that loud.

These are the future quacks, ambulance-chasers, money-pinchers, door-to-door salesmen, PR flacks and substitute teachers of America.

And I ran down after them, but they didn't budge. They were laughing too hard.

Ethan took my right cross to the cheek and stumbled back from the surprise. But he just kept laughing.

"Chris," he mustered out as he doubled over. "You … look … like … that …"

He paused as some of the guys were pushing me back.

"You look like that kid from 'Powder.'"

No matter how hard I charged at them flailing my arms, a bald and eyebrow-less kid in his underwear doesn't seem that threatening. They had trouble holding me down because my hairless body with its shaving cream coating made me too slick for their drunken reflexes. Gage got hit in the balls. Aaron got smacked in the head a few times.

Finally, they were able to pin me and get me settled.

Another party. Another college lesson learned.

It's not really homecoming unless someone's body is temporarily changed beyond just the brain cell count. Cuts, floor burns, head wounds, random acts of shaving. They're all part of campus life.

If you graduate without a new scar, then you didn't live. You just stole good oxygen.

A shower took the marker off. Some clothes and a beer in my hand, a few Ritalin up my nose, and I was good as new. Not good like completely settled, more like new like a newborn baby. Hairless as one, anyway. Getting my eyebrows to grow back, however, would take weeks.

People tend to look at you a little differently when they think you're a Skinhead. It's not a fun experience.

I'll just leave it at that.

TWENTY-THREE

My taxi pulled up to the two-story suburban home around five o'clock.

An American flag waved in the front yard, the same as in the rest of the neighborhood. This yard was the only one with ceramic shamrocks in the flower beds and trendy rock garden landscaping. Kids rode their bikes in the streets and cul-de-sacs common in the spurring development project on the outskirts of the small town.

It was far from the "asshole of the world" as Ethan had described it.

It was a slice of Americana.

Kathy Costello and I had never met before. In the three years of school, she never came and visited her son. Ethan's dad hadn't either. Our first encounter wouldn't be an exciting one, like a graduation or to celebrate a birthday. The circumstances surrounding how we would meet couldn't be any worse.

If nothing else, we would serve as momentary distractions for each other.

Forget what you're here for and it will all go away.

The woman who opened the door was attractive with brown hair pulled back tightly into a ponytail. Cat-eye glasses hung on the tip of her nose. I guessed her age somewhere around forty, but the last few days probably aged her significantly. Through her tight black pants and matching shirt I could tell her body had been well taken care of. I could see her bra lines arching around her C-cup breasts. She'd been nipped and tucked to look too young to have a college-age son.

Let's just say it. Ethan had a hot mom.

She invited me into her home without detaching the cell phone from her ear. I tried being as polite as possible, asking if I should take off my shoes and where I should set my bag. She answered by pointing me upstairs towards Ethan's room. In our many phone calls since her first screaming fit into my ear, we'd already discussed that's where I would be sleeping.

"I haven't been able to bring myself to go in there," she'd said before over the phone. "We'll close it off or sell everything to get it out of here."

As I stood there in the entryway, she yelled into her phone, "No, I don't want mushroom caps. I placed the order for portabella and, damn it, that's what I'm getting. I don't care *how* you get them."

There was still final funeral planning to do. She had to work out the kinks for the hors d'oeuvre caterer before the wake tomorrow. There were still phone calls to be made.

Sure, Ethan was dead. The real tragedy would have been if his mourners were served steamed broccoli instead of buttered asparagus.

Prepare to prevent unwanted surprises.

She left me in the entryway and continued to yell into her phone. On the hallway table was a copy of his obituary. A Celtic cross icon was next to a photo of a much younger Ethan.

> **Ethan J. Costello, 20**, of Lancaster, passed away unexpectedly at home March 15.
>
> He was born Aug. 28, 1986, in Lancaster to Steve and Kathy Costello. He was attending college out of state.
>
> He enjoyed reading and writing. He often celebrated the Irish heritage of his mother's side of the family.
>
> He is survived by his parents, grandparents, numerous aunts, uncles, cousins and friends. He was preceded in death by his great-grandparents.
>
> Visitation will be held at 2 p.m. Thursday at Waters Funeral Home, Lancaster. Funeral will follow at St. Patrick's Catholic Church. Burial in church cemetery.

Ethan's life was summed up in ninety-seven words. "Passed away unexpectedly." That's a nice way of saying he blew his face off. "… celebrated the Irish heritage …" That's a nice way of saying he got drunk a lot.

Obituaries never say how someone died unless its from a "long courageous battle with cancer" or in a car accident. Families want to tell everyone their loved one is dead, but they never want to say how. Especially with suicide. There's too much for everyone to talk about there. Then begins the speculation over chemical imbalances, homosexuality, drug use, alcoholism or whatever reasons might fuel the gossip.

Passed away unexpectedly.

Self-induced sudden mortality.

They were a lot prettier terms than that ugly word. The word no one wanted to say, let alone tag to the death of a college kid.

Suicide.

Say it.

The blame almost always falls on the parents. Their son's death was their failure. They were horrible parents. They're bad people. People will say anything to make others look bad. By comparison, those constant critics are better than all of us. They should feel good about that.

With Kathy still on the phone, I started peeking around the immaculately clean house. The carpet was still embedded with lines from the vacuum cleaner. The wood floor in the hallway glistened. The couch was undisturbed with fluffed matching pillows and throws. The big plasma television didn't have a spot of dust on it. It looked like no one had lived here since the house was decorated, but someone was always cleaning it. The dining room table, with a crystal chandelier overhead, was set for three people.

"Chris," Kathy called from inside the kitchen. "Honey, can I get you anything to drink?"

She was already calling me Honey.

I eyed pictures of Ethan in the living room. Studio photos of Ethan and the family, all dressed in blue sweaters. By the look of Ethan, the picture was only a few years old. Everyone bore a greased smile, dad and him with hands on mom's shoulders. Everything looked normal.

I heard Kathy in the kitchen. A rattling pill bottle followed by the closing of a cupboard door.

That picture was a reminder to all that everything was perfect. Mom. Dad. Son. Nothing's wrong.

An open door off the living room was an office. A large dark wooden desk sat in the middle. A glass gun cabinet to the right. Shotguns and handguns were displayed on hooks. One hook was empty.

Kathy called again from the kitchen. I walked in as she was going over a list on a yellow note pad on the counter. She was off her cell phone. I told her I was thinking about getting a hotel room so I wouldn't be a burden on her and her husband.

"Nonsense. Don't waste your money," she said, not looking up. "You'll stay here. Don't worry about bothering Steve. He's out of town on business until later this evening. You can sleep in Ethan's room. Besides, it will be nice to have a young man around the house again."

Again?

Like the one that was here a few days ago?

Like the one who died in the basement?

She wanted me in his bed, something I told her I would feel uncomfortable doing. Actually, I was terrified she even thought of such an idea. For the couple of nights I would be in town, she would have a replacement son. She could pretend I was Ethan. She could convince herself her son was still alive. She would tell herself the sounds upstairs were actually her son's footsteps. The shoes left at the front door and the jacket on the coat rack could be his.

In her head.

Ethan wouldn't have to die in her mind for a couple more days.

There are times in our friendship that I pretended to be Ethan. I pretended to have his confidence. I acted like he would in situations.

What would Ethan do?

I didn't have enough training to mimic him so his mother could lie to herself for a few days.

Kathy told me where a hotel was near the funeral home. She insisted that I at least stay at the house until dinner. The smell of rack of lamb wafted from the oven.

Still standing in the kitchen, leaning up against the marble counter with her perfectly round butt sticking out, she scribbled on her list. A sense of order. The illusion of control. She couldn't bring Ethan back, but she could make sure everyone had a nice meal.

I twitched for answers. Somewhere in this house, I was sure to find a reason why we were burying Ethan tomorrow.

"Do you mind if I give myself a tour?" I asked.

"No, not at all," she said. "Ethan's room is up the stairs and to the right."

I left Kathy to her list as I tiptoed up the stairs at the front of the house.

The room was nothing I expected, especially comparing it with how we lived at our apartment. A dark green and red plaid duvet covered the bed. The kind of plaid a mom picked out. When her son was twelve.

A shelf was covered in trophies—hockey, golf, and baseball. Ribbons from science fairs, debate team and mock trial were thumb-tacked to corkboard. A stash of comic books lined the shelf above his overly-organized desk. One wall had poster with a hovering space ship headlined by the words "I believe." A bookshelf against the opposite wall held science-fiction novels with titles of *Time, Space and Invasions*, *The Science of the Unknown* and *Files from Roswell*.

This wasn't the room of the Ethan Costello I knew. This wasn't the breeding ground of the Beer Baron. This was the room of a nerd who spent his time cooped up, poring over books about alien life forms and other topics that would prevent him from ever, ever getting laid. This was more like my room.

"He was a geek," I whispered to myself.

Ethan never gave any hint he was ever interested in any of this. His only talk of high school was how much it sucked. And the weekend parties. Never once did he say anything about being involved in anything resembling the things I did. Judging by this, we probably would have hung out together if we grew up in the same town and went to the same schools.

Maybe that's why he picked me for his project. His pet freshman.

I had no idea who the person was that once lived in this room. The person I called my best friend. It added another layer to this already complex person, this difficult situation. Instead of answers, I was handed more questions.

Was he ashamed of who he was? When was the Ethan we all knew formed? When did this transformation occur? When did the person in this room and the Ethan I knew separate?

How did he fool us all? Did he convince himself he was this new person?

I rifled through his room. Socks bunched together, folded underwear, T-shirts in the dresser. Dress shirts and ugly outdated ties in the closet. *Playboy* under the bed. Everything you'd expect to find of a high school kid away at college.

Nothing you'd expect from Ethan Costello. The father of Drink Day. My savior. Even after two thousand years we don't have Christ completely figured out.

Nothing in here giving me my answers.

There were parties. There was a life back at campus I needed to get back to. All I wanted was to have this mess cleaned up and tied up with a neat little bow. I hoped this would be done by Saturday night.

It's not like Ethan was going anywhere.

TWENTY-FOUR

Halloween. Everyone plays make-believe, giving your inner child the recharging it desperately needs. And there are always great parties.

Freshman year, the party of choice was the Attic House. It was a two-story five blocks off campus. If underage consumption was a religion, this was the Vatican.

Even as early as we arrived, the yard was filled with pink piles of puke.

The smell of rancid rotting fruit stuck in my nostrils, almost evoking my inevitable reaction to throw up.

"Oh, must be jungle juice night," Ethan observed. "Well, we know you're going to toss up tonight."

"I look forward to the opportunity," I said.

Chris will puke.

The basement had a keg. Drinking games took up most of the living room. A narrow set of stairs just off from the kitchen led up to the attic where the jungle juice and shot bar stood.

Five bucks for freedom.

Sixteen-ounce Holy Grails in primary red and blue plastic.

The wooden floor creaked and moaned under the weight of the hundred people already up there, the costumed drinkers following us in making it worse. If this thing gave way, we'd all surely die. Circling footprints of cigarette ash and stale beer made swirls around the floor.

Ethan and I had been at this house before, but this time it was nuts. The cramped mass of about four hundred drunkards clogged the air with their alcoholic breath and various flavors of smoke.

Ethan went as Bluto from *Animal House*. With a pillow shoved under his sweatshirt that read "College," a four-day stubble and a curly black wig, he played the part perfectly. He even kept a bottle of Jack on him.

My last-minute costume was a pair of plastic red horns, a tail and pitchfork. With a red T-shirt and black pants, I looked the same as about ten other devils there.

For the first part of the night, things were the same as every other night in every other house. I kept pressed against the walls of the attic tending to my drink while Ethan and the boys toured the revelers.

Two 32-gallon garbage cans filled with jungle juice kept us fueled. A mix of fruit juices, Kool-Aid and a ton of booze. It was mostly Everclear, but the juice masked the harshness of the grain alcohol. The Attic House boys made stuff noteworthy in all partier's minds.

Irreversible blindness was always a possibility.

You spill a glass on your shirt, touch a burning cigarette, and you're a human torch.

Other than the usual miscreant antics, nothing was out of place. Drinking games, shots and random movie quotes. Without anything else, this story would be pointless.

Until I noticed her. The girl from my Sociology class. The girl who smiled.

It was around midnight.

Dressed as an angel, I could see the sparkle from the glitter around her eyes even across the room. Her wings were perched just above her shoulders and a halo hung over her head. She was glowing in my blurred vision. My already intoxicated infatuation.

Cut to the slow motion sequence. Cue the soft pop song.

She caught me staring.

She smiled again.

At least I think she did. It was hard to tell because she was with a group of friends. She could just be looking away and laughing about something someone said. Or she could just be laughing at me. The loser who dropped his crap everywhere. The dork against the wall.

But she kept looking right at me. Smiling.

"What are you doing?" Ethan yelled over the loud music and clamor of the room.

He, too, had noticed that smile.

"Nothing," I said.

"I can see that. That's the exact opposite of what you should be doing right now." He had to shove his way past four people to move the six feet to stand next to me.

"That girl's into you. There's no way she's not loving you right now after you've been gawking at her. She wouldn't be beaming if she didn't. She would have gotten a restraining order instead."

He shoved me forward.

"Get over there."

No. No way.

"She's the girl I told you about from my Sociology class," I said.

She's out of my league. She's too pretty. I mean I'm not the ugliest guy here, but there's better prospective cock suppliers for her to choose from. Approaching a girl like that, despite how she seemed to be looking at me, I knew I would be an unmistakable failure.

By this time, Ethan had turned my inaction into a public discourse. The guys sided with him.

"Go, bitch," Collin said.

Use the fact I had a class with her to start the conversation, he said. It's that simple. One thing in common is all it takes. If not, offer her a shot at the bar.

She's the angel, you're the devil, Aaron said.

Just do something, they said.

Still, it wasn't enough for me. I stood there, gripping my cup, sipping faster and faster in a nervous tick. Jungle juice wasn't something you want to do that with.

"Your roommate's over there now," Ethan said, pointing towards her.

In my hesitation, STD Stan, dressed as a pimp, was going after her while his flanking date rape-posse was homing in on her friends.

Stan put his arm around her.

She looked uneasy, laughing a little bit.

"Her face screams, 'Save me!' Virginity doesn't lose itself. Go!" Ethan said, shoving me in her direction.

I was slammed into a quarter-ton Care Bear with a beard. And I apologized.

"You know all of that advice I gave you?" Ethan said.

Go for the friends to get the best one. Stroke the ego. Girls hate each other.

"Yeah, I remember it," I said.

"Forget it," he said. "It's not going to work here. Besides, if you don't do something soon, I'm going to beat your ass, right here in front of her."

Ethan looked me square in the face, his eyes and mouth tight. Those gray eyes glowed in anger. He was dead serious.

"Fuck it!" I said, slamming the rest of my cup and tossing it at Ethan. "I'm going in."

The boys were happy with this. "Get 'er buddy," one of them said. The rest was muffled by the music and shouting.

I was on my way over there. I was making the move.

Thank you, Ethan. Thank you.

"Stan, what the hell's going on, man?"

It sounded like I was actually happy to see him.

STD Stan. The virus in a purple and leopard print velvet hat and matching jacket. He could go fuck himself. If he hadn't already tonight.

Wrath.

I stuck my right hand out and left it out there. To shake it, he'd have to pull his arm off the girl. It's something I figured Ethan would have done. How I knew that, I don't know. And he shook my hand, his slimy arm slithering off the angel.

Then the angel was smiling at me. Victory number one.

"Not a whole lot, just talking to these honeys," he said, apparently thinking his dress finally matched his persona. Stan the Man. STD Stan. The social disease. This girl was a much higher caliber than anything he's left in our room to clean up. She wasn't passed out and not even close to it.

And then she spoke.

"You're in my Sociology class, aren't you?" she asked me.

For the audience at home, I want to make this abundantly clear: She talked to me. First.

It's something simple, but I can't express how mighty those few words were. They were normally just the start to the major-year-hometown repartee, but she started it with me.

This was how David felt after Goliath was on his back like a bitch.

Still, I looked back at Ethan. He was scowling at me, jerking his head up and down to get me to not look at him right now. That ass-kicking was on its way.

"Uh, yeah, I think so," I said. "Monday-Wednesday-Friday, nine in the morning, right?"

"You're the cute one who sits in the back," she said, stepping closer to me and away from Stan.

I had no response.

Cute. She said *cute.*

Cue *We Are The Champions.*

So I just started with the B.S. banter. She thought the class was a joke. I did too. She was a nursing major. I was undecided. Blah, blah, blah. The standard freshmen exchange of basic information.

She never said anything about where my eyebrows went. They were there, just barely growing back from my Homecoming shaving.

By then, STD Stan and the boys got the hint.

Her name was Heather.

And there in the middle of our conversation, as I was slowly building up some confidence, the one thing that could ruin a party happened. With one utterance, my night would draw to a close.

"Caaahhppps," a voice bellowed through the floor.

This house had been busted before, and never a minor has been ticketed. The guys at the house knew the boys in blue.

Party legend has it that they helped the cops chase and arrest the neighborhood's resident wife beater, forever earning them a free pass. From then on, all they had to do was clear the house to appease the neighbors when things got out of hand. No tickets. That was the unwritten rule.

Ethan came over, saying we needed to slam as much of the jungle juice as we could before heading out. I said I was busy talking. Frantically, I thought of something. Anything to prevent leaving this girl. The girl who owned the back of the head I'd been staring at since the book-dropping incident.

But Heather said it was time to go.

"But I don't want to go home just yet," she said.

One of her friends agreed. The rest were cutting their losses and going back to the dorms.

Think, you bastard. Think. There must be something. Ethan, dear God, help me. He was too busy at one of the garbage cans, dunking his cup in and sloshing back the contents repeatedly.

"I paid my five bucks, I'm not leaving sober!" he yelled.

My eyes back on Heather, I said, "Uh … we … uh … should be able to … umm … find something."

Ethan had *finally* got his fill and said us four should pair up together. Ethan, Heather, the yet-to-be-introduced friend and me.

We left the attic together in rank-and-file with the rest of the party. Down the stairs, we tried to assemble a plan. We all agreed that some form of deep-fried food was the best course of action. Heather knew of a place neither Ethan nor I had heard of. It was a townie hangout, she said.

The friend's name was Kristi, Heather told us.

She was pretty, but nothing worth writing home about.

Outside the front door two cops were counting people leaving. I was around number two hundred and eighty-something and there were still plenty of people behind me.

Partygoers shuffled their numb feet in a feeble attempt to not seem drunk as they herded past the youthful officers.

"Nice costumes, boys," Ethan said to the cops.

"Move it, wiseass," one said.

"That's not very nice, sir," Ethan rebutted as I grabbed him by the sweatshirt and pulled him out.

"Wait," he said.

He stopped on the front lawn. Hordes of drunken, stupefied faces passed.

There was one more thing before we left.

"Either of you ladies have a camera?" Ethan asked.

You'd have to know him to notice he was slurring his words.

Heather pulled a silver digital camera from her white sequin purse. Ethan pulled the bottle of Jack from his pocket.

Telling me how to pose, I threw my fist in the air making devil horns with my fingers as Ethan took a pull off the bottle. He was a perfect match to the infamous image blazoned across campus dorm walls nationwide. The best part the cops were right in the background.

As soon as the flash went off, so were we.

Or so we thought.

"Hey, wiseass!"

The cop had noted our flaunting of the situation. Sure, everyone got a free pass. Only if they didn't do something stupid like chug from a bottle in front of the cops.

This time, cue the *Cops* theme song.

Bad Boys. Bad Boys.

Damn you, Ethan.

The cops walked over to us, the way cops walk over to dumbass college kids. Their hands were on their belts by their guns, their chest stuck out to accentuate the badges. Big gun, little dick syndrome.

"Good evening, officers," Ethan said, using his sleeve to wipe the spilled whiskey from his lower lip.

The cops were almost standing on our toes as Wiseass Cop grabbed for the bottle.

"You twenty-one, there fella?" the other cop said.

"Nope," Ethan responded without missing a beat. "You?"

Chiming in, I said, "Shut up, dude."

"You know I could bust you for underage consumption, public intoxication, underage possession, loitering and open container right now?" Wiseass Cops said. "You *and* your friends."

With that, Ethan's face switched gears. He got serious.

He knew my parents would freak. It'd be part of the permanent-record crap they always spewed at me. The girls, the ones we just met, would undoubtedly be screwed too. All because Ethan wanted his picture taken.

"Gentlemen, there's no need for that," Ethan began. "It's my fault. You're right. I am the wiseass. There's no need to get them involved. They just wanted to go home."

"It's too late for that," Wiseass Cop said.

By this time, the lawn was empty and the front house lights had been turned off.

"I'll make you a deal. You ticket me for all of it and I'll pay it. Fine me and a check's in the mail. I'm guilty," he said. "All you have to do is let my friends walk away."

He'd obviously done this before.

Tell a cop he can write four tickets and he won't have to show for court. No young cop wants to sit in a courthouse during the cattle-call of misdemeanor court when he could be defending the world against evil. The defendant might not even show. Tell a cop you'll plead guilty and you might slide. Well, Ethan would be stuck, but he was throwing himself on the fire to save us from getting burned.

St. Ethan of Costello. Patron Saint of Drunken Idiot College Kids.

The girls' nervous looks turned to thankfulness.

"That's not the way it works pal," Wiseass Cop said.

The other cop looked at his partner, "C'mon, that's not so bad."

But there was no arrangement. Wiseass Cop's ego had been bruised. Ethan was just a punk to him and this was a chance to use his handcuffs. Letting his friends go meant Ethan still got his way.

Pride.

"Too bad, kid," Wiseass Cop said, grabbing Ethan by the shoulder to turn him around. His hand went for the back of his belt where he kept his handcuffs shoved down his pants.

That's when Ethan took off running.

There was no struggle. In a quick twist, the officer's grip came loose. So was Ethan. On foot. Without hesitation.

Wiseass Cop's actions were just as quick. His partner was only a few steps behind.

Off into the distance they went, the sounds of three pairs of feet and the jingling keys trucked off into the dimly lit streets. The other cop yelled about a ten-something-or-other over the radio as he ran behind to catch up.

He described Ethan.

"White male. Six-feet. *Animal House.*"

The chase was on.

"West on Fourth."

For a guy who spent his time camped out at the library or working on a beer gut, Ethan sure could haul ass. Especially when two cops who looked like they spent all day in the gym were chasing him. He had a lead on them by at least twenty feet or more at all times.

He'd obviously done *that* before.

Heather, Kristi and I couldn't help but stare. It's all we could do. The cat-and-mouse headed down the sidewalk, across a lawn. With three hoisted bodies over a wooden fence, the chase was out of view.

We stood by in the lawn for only a few more seconds before we seized the golden opportunity to get the hell out of there before backup arrived. The cops hadn't asked for our IDs. Like I carried one anyway. They had no idea who we were. Or who they were chasing.

"I hope he's okay," Heather said.

I said, "Don't worry about him. Ethan knows what he's doing."

That was far from the truth. I had no idea what Ethan was thinking.

One minute we were leaving a party, and the next he's high-tailing it from two All Star officers. For all I knew, as the foot pursuit was far from my sight, Ethan could have been getting corn-holed at the jail right then.

Again, all I wanted was Ethan right there next to me to tell me what to do next. I needed guidance. I needed direction. My whole life, I've never been far away from someone to tell me what to do or how to act. Ethan had been that for me. Now, he was gone.

What would Ethan do?

We stuck to the alleyways in the opposite direction Ethan went and headed back towards campus. Food was an unaffordable luxury right now.

No restaurant. Ethan's dead sprint put us ahead of the cops. That's where we wanted to stay.

"Does he always do that?" Heather asked about a block away from the party.

"It's the first time he ever did it in front of me," I responded.

"Well, we owe him a lot. If it wasn't for him, we'd probably be in the back of a squad car right now," Kristi said.

They caught that too.

St. Ethan of Costello. The Patron Saint of Self-Sacrifice.

Maybe altruism isn't just for assholes.

Sirens wailed. The game was on. Ethan ran and the entire police force took that as a jab at their manhood. Or, it was just an excuse to speed through town. With a hard crime rate near zero, these young cops wanted anything to get their rocks off.

The girls felt awkward walking back. I could tell by their silence. I shuffled my feet, kicking at the gravel alley. Anything to keep from staring at the angel next to me. Anything to keep me occupied. Anything to prevent me from having to speak and fuck this all up.

Sloth.

In my head, Ethan was still running. He jumped a fence, and another. And another. He tried hiding in some bushes or behind a house, but kept running. It wasn't hard to imagine.

More lights and sirens lit up the night around us.

It was a matter of minutes before the dorms were in sight. The noisy crowd in front of mine told me ours wasn't the only party that was raided that night.

"It looks like ours wasn't the only party that was raided tonight," I said.

Thank you Captain Obvious.

Whatever. At least I said something.

Closer and closer to campus and I was blowing it. This was my opportunity to finally lose my virginity.

Lust.

And it wasn't to some random girl. This was one I liked. She offered me into her world and I couldn't even get through the door.

She did say I was cute.

Pride.

Nope. I said nothing. It was Kristi that broke the silence.

"Isn't that him?"

There was Ethan, talking it up with the tweakers from the fourth floor. He was just leaning up against the wall, his costume had been scrapped somewhere along the way. The sweat hadn't even dried off his forehead and he was nonchalantly hanging out in front of the dorms like the increased police presence in the surrounding neighborhoods wasn't all about him.

That sneaky son of a bitch.

"Ethan, what the hell?" I yelled from down the block.

"Chris, girls. You made it back," he said, standing up straight. "I was worried they snagged you."

He was huffing. The chase hadn't ended long before we spotted him. Where did you go? How did you lose them? What are you going to do? They were questions we all asked at about the same time.

"Outrunning the cops isn't that hard," he said, the slur from his speech was gone. He'd run himself sober. "They're packing an extra forty pounds around their waists with their batons, handcuffs, pepper spray and the like."

"And their guns," Heather finished.

"Yeah, that too," he said puffing off his cigarette. "The cops aren't designed for foot races. Their fat asses are designed to ride in cars."

"My dad's a cop," Kristi said.

Whoops.

Heather laughed. She was looking at Ethan the way she looked at me earlier. That smile was for him now.

"On that note, I'm going in," he said. "There's no reason to stand out here and jeopardize everyone else."

He explained how he would turn himself in the morning. "Without a bottle or a blood-alcohol content, all they can get me for is obstruction of justice," he said. "I'll get a fine and some community service hours."

Okay, now there was absolutely no fucking doubt in my mind he'd done that before.

"Chris, make sure these ladies get home safely," he finished.

Ethan headed for the door, but before he got there, Heather said one thing.

"Thanks."

"Chris would have done the same for me," Ethan said, pulling open the door and standing in front of the security guard. With a wave of his hand, he went through the next set of the doors and on his way into his room.

And then there's the walk to the Thirteen Floors of Whores.

In the five hundred feet from door to door, I filled out the verbal questionnaire that was Ethan's life.

I'm pretty sure he's serious about turning himself in.

Yes, Kristi, he's single.

Yeah, it was cool he took the bullet for us.

The girls both pulled out their keys for the front door. Heather was in first, opening it for Kristi.

"You guys want to do something again some time?" Kristi asked.

"Sure as shit," I said. "That is if Ethan's not in jail."

They didn't like the joke. Never make fun of St. Ethan of Costello in front of his followers.

"Well, have a good night," Heather said, forcing a grin through her teeth. She just pulled back her lips.

It wasn't the same smile.

She turned. She and Kristi walked toward the elevator.

I wasn't invited in. They were going to bed. Ethan was probably in his already. This was not the way I wanted to end my night.

The door clicked shut.

TWENTY-FIVE

Let my life begin now. It wasn't meant to be done twice. Only one shot. If I cherish what I have and never stop learning from my mistakes, then my life will be what I make it. Never let it be what someone else wants. Still, that simplistic a declaration won't suffice. I can't afford to settle. I must never be ashamed or afraid to admit when I am wrong. Admitting my fears, confronting them head on, is the only way to overcome them. Fear is the thief of dreams.

Those were his words.

A journal.

Inside his desk, buried under old high school papers. Every one said "Good Work!" in large red lettering. I pulled it out like I was recovering a lost relic, careful as not to disturb anything or make any noise.

My search was over.

The brown leather was soft and moist, showing constant care. It was important to him. Half of the pages contained some kind of writing. Some I might have witnessed their creation and not noticed.

If the cops gave two shits about Ethan's corpse in the basement, they would have looked for this. If Kathy, downstairs yelling into her cell phone again, gave half a shit about her son, she would have found it.

Slowly I unrolled the wrap-around cover. I opened to the first page.

Ethan was speaking. His voice was clear. They were words echoing ones he'd told me.

Lead feet drag hastily behind an imagination faster than the sunset. A day passes with no forward motion, a stagnant, dreary dream. Dare I dream of bigger things? It only makes reality seem trivial. For the part of me that has died a thousand times, rest well my friend. You'll never be forgotten. Please, tell me, was it worth it? I'm sure I'll regret it all someday. There's going to be a time when I'll wish to escape to my former self. I shouldn't regret how I've lived my life, but how I have never lived it enough. I'm always searching for something to remedy my problems, something to make me who I desperately feel I need to be.

I read at his desk.

I wanted clarity. My craving for absolution worsened.

How this journal still remained in the top drawer of a desk, waiting for anyone who cared to find it, showed how quickly everyone wanted to clean up the mess Ethan left behind.

No sense in worrying about the past.

No use crying over spilled milk. Or spilled blood.

It was already too late.

All I wanted to do was flip to the end of the book.

This could make everything clean.

I wanted to cheat by fast-forwarding.

I wanted to scene-select my way to the final chapter.

Roll credits.

I just wanted to hear it wasn't my fault.

From birth, we strive to know more about anything in the world we are now guests of. Our grubby little fingers latch on to whatever we can grasp, constantly examining things and making assessments on them. We're born as a purple fragile lump of nothing, and everyday we have to kick and scream to stay alive. Once we learn to express ourselves through writing, music and other forms, the footprint of knowledge is so ingrained in our minds that we cannot deny it. From daily gossip to the meaning of life, we strive to forever know more each preceding day. It is both a gift and curse. All of us are both blessed and burdened. It is in our own strife to reach divinity. The knowledge we possess about our own world makes us immortal. Our lack of it makes us fallible.

The lost art of journal writing.

There were no dates. About two hundred pages.

That's a guess because there were no numbers.

It was just a big jumbled mess of random thoughts.

The instructions to life according to Ethan.

Some assembly required.

Be the good guy, love the sweet woman, and don't forget the little guy. There's always someone out there who will be lost that you might be able to help. Don't ever underestimate anyone. It's time to start living that way and stop writing about it. It's time to start living the life you are losing with every second. Too often I find myself wrapped-up in the monotonous day-to-day events. There has to be more. Maybe that's what my life is meant to be, a constant search. This perpetual scavenger hunt for something I'm not sure exists, all the while I bumble through every day trying to find an end when all I really did was the dishes and laundry. The easy way will never be the good way.

No "Dear diary."
The pulpit of his life.

Failure still means attempt.
I would rather fail than just watch.
My passion and energy cannot be wasted.

Sermons to someone.
No daily events. No idea when he wrote.
The entries started in clean print.

When the moon rises, I don't have to be the same person as when the sea extinguished the sun. Why can't I be two people? Just because Superman struggles with it doesn't mean it can't be done. All it means is that it won't come without difficulty.

Then scribbling.
The act of contrition to himself.
His Sermon on the Mount.
Some he wrote to himself.
Others he wrote for himself.

You have never felt love because you were afraid of the pain. You never felt joy because you trembled at the thought of it leaving. You must move forward without fear. It's not about having all of the answers, but knowing which questions to ask. If there is one way to judge someone's redeeming qualities, it is his or her willingness, eagerness and ability to learn about the world around him or her.

With every page the writing was less legible.
The confession to the person he called I.
Bless you, Ethan, for you have sinned.

I imagined him pouring himself into these pages.

But for how long?

And why?

I see three people in the mirror.

The boy I was, the person I am and the man I will become.

Like God, I am three in one.

They all fight, toil and doubt.

Unless all three are willing to move forward, all will be stagnant and with regret.

The boy is still alive. The man will soon come.

Who will I be when the day is done?

One doesn't like two, two has learned from one.

The man isn't sure where he is.

Time wants to separate them all.

Pride interrupts, hate spoils, love lingers.

The mirror lies.

There is not three.

There is only one.

I call him me.

"Honey?"

Then I closed the book. The voice startled me from the silence of the room.

"Honey, come in here," Kathy was yelling from downstairs.

Her husband must be home. I hadn't even heard him come in. She kept calling until I realized it wasn't for Steve.

"Chris, honey, come down here."

I shoved the journal down the back of my pants and walked down the stairs.

Kathy stood in the doorway of the kitchen, a bottle of wine in each hand.

"Which one would you like better?"

TWENTY-SIX

It was the Monday after Halloween. Ethan turned himself in as promised.

I was going back to Sociology. This time was different. The back of that head had a name.

Heather.

Spending more time on my appearance than the first day of class, I went through four different shirts before deciding on a dark gray one with thin black vertical stripes. Jeans, of course. Stan, waking up to poison the room with his morning masturbation funk, gave his approval on my looks.

"You're starting to look less like a 'tard," he said.

At least that's what I took as his approval.

My plan was to run into Heather before class. I'd get an invite to sit next to her. Her perfume would cling to my jacket. I'd be breaking the seating chart rule, but Professor Talking Mop Head wouldn't even notice.

All I would have to say is "Hi." That's what I told myself. The rest would take care of itself. The best relationships require the least maintenance. She did call me "cute."

Twenty minutes before class. I lit a smoke and waited. The campus was dead, except for a few lost souls bee-lining from one building to the next. I studied them all looking for her.

Stuffed backpacks and travel coffee mugs. Library to the Liberal Arts hall. Performing Arts Center to the Union. Franco Shade and Avirex. Union to science building. Once second silence, and the next chaos.

Building doors exploded open with students pouring out. One hour of classes let out and there were ten minutes before the next one began. The crisscrossing sidewalks melted into one massive flow of students. Traffic lanes headed one way as students bumped into each other where the lines intersected. No one set foot on the grass. It was the first time I actually watched it.

The North Face and Columbia.

Old Navy and Banana Republic.

They all looked the same. None were Heather.

I lit another cigarette.

The flow of moving bodies kept the doors behind me open. People stood in between the inner and outer doors as the congestion caught up with them. Some heading in, others heading out. Bodies bumbling. No door was designated as the entrance or exit. Faces of frustration as a funnel formed at front of every building.

Without instruction, there is only confusion.

"Chris."

That voice, I recognized.

"Chris."

I looked around.

There was Ethan, trying to hail my attention as he made a direct line towards me, cutting through rank-and-file lines of students as he strutted across the lawn. No one was stepping on the grass.

No one but Ethan.

"What the hell are you doing here?" I asked as he came up to me. He was supposed to be at the police station. Maybe jail.

"I told you I'd take care of it," he said.

He went to the police station and was charged with obstruction of justice. One charge. It's the same one you get if you give the cops someone else's name. Running from the cops was a misdemeanor. Ethan wouldn't even miss a class.

"They squeezed me into morning court," he said. "The judge gave me pretrial release. Musta' been a defense attorney before taking the bench."

Pretrial release. No posting bond. No more jail. Just pass go and show up on this date. The cops spent all night looking for him and a judge let him go.

"I just wish I could see that cop's expression when he hears that," Ethan smirked.

My friggin' hero.

"Hey guys."

There was another voice I remember.

On the tail end of the herd, Heather bounced up to us. She panted and half-smile, showing she power-walked her way across campus. She stopped just short of me, closer to Ethan.

"Hey, you're alright," she said to him, a little out of breath.

"Pretrial."

"I can't thank you enough," she said. "My parents would have freaked if I got busted."

"Hi Heather," I said, getting a quick "hello" before she turned back to him.

"I owe you one," she said.

Ethan said he was going to get coffee. After a buzz-kill morning like that, he said he needed some stimulants. Heather said she'd join him. Ethan invited me.

"But we've got class," I said flustered, looking at Heather.

That's what I said. My golden opportunity and I was thinking about some jerk-off class. I wanted that perfume stuck to my jacket. I wanted her next to me. Just us. And about a hundred other people, but us together.

I looked at Ethan.

"It's nothing we can't skip," she said.

"Nah, you don't want to start skipping already," Ethan said. "Besides, we can all go another time."

Heather insisted. She tugged slightly on Ethan's jacket. She was buying.

She was almost begging.

Ethan didn't look like he was resisting.

"I'm not going."

Why I said that, I don't know. Then or now. Still, the mentality of doing what I'm supposed to do — so Mommy and Daddy can talk to their friends about how proud of me they are — was so far ingrained in me that I couldn't even shirk one class. Or maybe I wasn't happy with the whole arrangement. So I didn't have my perfect, pre-planned mechanism, but something is always better than nothing. Not for me. Give me what I want or I'll pout.

Backing down, that's a defense mechanism.

Ethan looked a little uneasy. Go ahead, I told him.

"We'll all catch up later," Ethan assured me.

They turned and walked. I did the same in the opposite direction, into the building. I didn't look back.

Sitting in class with no back of a head to stare at or perfume to huff, I couldn't help but think of the inevitable. Sure I was in class, but what Talking Mop Head said was more foreign than it was before. I didn't write down a single word about groupthink, mob mentality or different economic theories. Karl Marx could eat dick.

"Blah, blah, blah. Rar, rar, rar," Professor Mop said.

I was there and she wasn't. I should have been drinking coffee. I shouldn't be wedged between these seats. The Abercrombie twins shouldn't have been in my line of sight.

There was no more Chris and Heather. There never was.

The rest of the details concerning that day, week or month are inconsequential. The only thing that really matters was the furtherance of the union of Ethan and Heather. The first real chance with a girl and I blew it. Somehow, I lost her to Ethan.

I can't blame her. Nor Ethan. Heather was funny, beautiful, smart. She was different from the rest of the campus bimbos. My word, no one else's.

My inaction cost me my chance at her.

Ethan succeeded where I failed.

"Are you okay with this?" Ethan asked me a few days later.

She had asked him out. A real date. Not campus coffee when she's supposed to be in class. Dinner, movie, whatever. Apparently, Ethan was more charming than I would have hoped. And she was more assertive than I expected.

"Dude, don't worry about it. I don't care," I told him.

I did care, but I got over it.

Besides, submissive girls are better.

TWENTY-SEVEN

Lying on my back.

She straddled me.

Her breasts glistened with sweat.

She bounced up and down, leaning back, forward.

Her breath was heavy in my ear.

Screw diamonds. Nothing says romance like sex in public.

It was November and I finally got laid. And, with the natural course of events in college life, everyone found out.

Don't let the movies fool you. Those groups of people hanging out on the campus lawn aren't working on homework. Sure, they're books are out, but the topic isn't cardiopulmonary rehabilitation, it's who they're humping. Who they want to be humping. Who's swapping fluids with whom. Parties. Sex. Maybe, just maybe, financial aid. Never class. Funny sexual stories get around to everyone.

Only for me, my inner circle learned this as it was happening.

This round of drunken antics was set at the overpriced loft apartments with a thousand-dollar monthly price tag view of the river. Some wannabe beatnik-types with trust funds were hosting a fund-raising wine tasting party.

Sadly, this one was invite only. Ethan secured his invitation through a fellow health clinic worker, but that welcoming didn't transcend to the rest of us.

Even this early in college, the First Prentiss reputation had preceded us. In a bad way this time.

Ethan took care of it. He told the hostess his parents agreed to donate five hundred bucks to the Cause That Is Cool This Week Fund. That's what he told her.

Ethan told me it wasn't cheating a charity because we weren't stealing. Every group that depends on donations always expects some to fall through. So, in the name of higher society, he decided we should all wear suits.

"Show a little class," he said.

That meant scouring the local thrift store. The fashion gems on the racks there were endless, so long as you didn't mind the musty smell of used Kleenexes left in jacket pockets for thirty-plus years. A three-piece suit only cost five bucks. Granted you'd have to mix and match. All of us found one that fit. By fit, I mean fully covered all skin except for a few exposed ankles. Ethan found a black and gray hound's-tooth jacket and vest to match with a pair of gray pinstripe slacks.

"I'd fuck me," Ethan said looking at himself in the mirror in my room.

I was looking quite ravishing in my brown Johnny Carson dinner jacket, matching pants, cream shirt and plaid tie. In the mirror, my eyebrows were growing back. My head was still peach fuzz blonde.

"You look man-pretty," he said to me.

And we all brought wine to share. It was going to be another night of wine in a box. Ethan's idea.

"What the hell are poor-ass college students doing having a wine tasting party anyway?" he said.

It wasn't a question. More of a statement of fact.

"Then why are we going to this?" I asked, fixing my tie after tying everyone else's.

"Because, it's something different. A chance to mix it up with people we wouldn't normally hang out with," he said.

We were greeted like the grounds crew playing a round at the golf course they maintained. Sure, we were there for a reason, but no one wanted us there.

Ethan finessed the anal-retentive girl who opened the door. She glared at our dress. He reminded her of the "donation."

So Ethan cheated a charity to get us into a party. No whales would be saved. No cancer would be researched. Oh well. Plus, it cleared us all of the twenty-dollar cover. Freedom at four times the price. Besides, we brought our own wine.

Besides, we were out of our element. The Beer Baron didn't care. He walked in without missing a beat, strutting by confidently, asking everyone how they were doing or how things were going. I walked by, holding my head down trying to avoid the stares. I was still able to pick up on a few crucial details.

No one had a single name brand on. Unless you consider the color black a label. Then, it was the coolest thing in the room.

They talked about how the right-wingers were the feces of the earth, how Russian writers were the only valid form of literature, and having children was for hicks.

This apartment with twenty-foot ceilings, a balcony, dining room and open kitchen. There were no coffee tables made of cinder blocks and plywood or kitchen tables dented from years of games of Quarters. There wasn't even a basement.

There wasn't any plastic in the kitchen. Everything was glass. Bottles, not boxes, of wine. Wine glasses, not plastic cups. With our group of friends, this just wasn't safe. If we got rowdy, we all would die at our own hands.

For the first hour, I wish the girl at the door had her way and sent us packing. I would rather have taken our boxed wine and drank it in the alleyway. At least we were dressed for the part.

These people hated everything. Well, not everything. Just anything American. The most grotesque parts of their lives were that they were born here and forced to live in this country. Almost everyone had studied abroad and couldn't shut up about it. A restaurant wasn't just a restaurant if it was in Wales. The Eiffel Tower looked best at night. It wasn't beer unless it was in Germany. Socialism can work. Scones. Frappe. Hostels.

But the one thing these pseudo-intellectuals hated the most were the drunken students that populated American universities.

Us.

That was before their fifth glass of wine.

It was a tasting, but they didn't spit out anything. They stopped smelling the wine, swirling it around in the glass and discussing what region of France it came from. Sooner than later, there was less talk about what woods, berries or what kind of potting soil they could taste in it. They started guzzling pinot and merlot like prohibition began in an hour.

Slowly, the void between beatnik and drunk narrowed. With every sip, the stern faces loosened. Their arms uncrossed. Their noses came out of the air. After enough booze, these wannabe aristocrats became people. Real people. Their attempts to maintain their upper-crust facades failed.

The social lubricant worked way too well on these people.

Except one. Thomas. Not Tom, Thomas. Pronounced "Tho-mass." How artistic. Or he had a hard-on for phonetic pronunciation. Whatever.

We settled in, and began mingling, Thomas kept his nose up. We were nothing but drunken white trash in his eyes. Worse yet, white trash that didn't know its place. Not picking up on this vibe was impossible.

The guy was a dick.

Still Ethan tried to loosen him up by talking to him. Thomas hammered Ethan for his suit, his hair, everything. Then he started lacing into him for his lack of originality. The bastard called Ethan a cliché.

"It costs a lot to be authentic," I overhead Thomas say from across the room. "And you can't be stingy with these things because the more authentic you are, the more you resemble what you've dreamed of being."

Ethan was right a long time ago. A wine buzz is different. This time I was in a lot more control than the Riesling incident at homecoming. I walked over to him. Me, the reserved little pouter, was going to start something. With a complete stranger. I must have been hammered.

Hooray liquid courage.

Wrath.

I interrupted their conversation.

"Wait, wait, wait."

Ethan looked at me like he'd never met me before.

And I continued.

"You just loosely quoted — or should I say stole — a line from a movie to make a point on originality. That's a little ironic, isn't it?" I rhetorically asked Tho-mass. "Dude, that was from *All About My Mother*. It won an Oscar in the late nineties."

Tho-mass reeled a bit and shot back. "Settle down, *dude*. This doesn't concern you. Don't get so excited," he said.

This guy straightened his black skin-tight sweater. He scoffed and said, "Anger is an impulse. You can't rationalize it."

And I laughed. "You did it again. That's from *The Sea Inside*. Besides, in that scene Rosa was talking about *love* not *anger*."

The tone and volume of my voice gathered the undivided attention of the whole loft. And judging by their faces, people were on my side. A few people laughed. I was winning.

Go Team Me.

And you would think that would have stopped Tho-mass spouting qotes from what he thought were obscure movies no one would recognize. And you would have thought wrong.

"Look at you with your braggadocio. Your parents must be really proud," he said, sipping on his wine.

"Is that the best you have?" I said, slamming the rest of mine.

"I wish that one day you will have a son like you," he said.

Never underestimate a guy who spent too much time in a movie theater or clinging to a life provided only on DVD. Worse yet, don't try to bust out movie trivia around him. Or misquote movies you think no one has seen.

And I calmly said, "*The Barbarian Invasions*, the first Canadian film to win the Best French Film of the Year award."

Everyone laughed, but no one harder than Ethan.

Pride.

"Is that what you do, rent only from the foreign-language section at Blockbuster? *Christ!*"

Tho-mass set down his wine glass. It was obvious he was shaken and doing a bad job of trying to hide it. He made his way toward the door after getting his jacket from the closet.

"I've had enough of this childishness," he said. "I've got better things to do that spend time with these *mis*creants."

Just before Tho-mass managed to close the door behind him, I yelled, "Oh Tho-mass, don't forget: stupid is as stupid misquotes foreign films."

Again, laughter. The high from scooping up the attention of the room was incredible. I had all eyes on me and I didn't drop any books on the floor. I wasn't throwing anything up. Instead of creating a spotlight, I earned one. All that time spent renting every movie at Family Video finally paid off. Not having a life got me one.

"My boy's wicked *smaaht*," Ethan said in a horrible Boston accent to the girl next to him.

"*Good Will Hunting*," I said. "At least you got it right."

And with the one dick in the room gone, it was back to the wine, the discussions. I took a seat on the couch and quickly a small group of people gathered around me to talk film. Finally there was something I could honestly weigh in on. We talked about noir, the religious genius of Kevin Smith and how *Memento* was the greatest film ever made.

And there was this girl who kept looking at me. I've seen that look before. The smile, the stare.

The look kept coming from the girl by the kitchen counter.

Again, Ethan told me to make my move.

"She just gave you do-me-right-here-right-now eyes," he whispered in my ear.

And she was. I was still riding off my high, and I went over to talk to her. She was standing in the kitchenette and, conveniently, I needed another drink. Yeah, it was just an excuse to move, but I went with it.

"God Thomas is *such* drama," she said to me.

And it was a straight dive into the usual banter again.

"I'm Chris," I started.

Still to this day, I can't remember her name. I wasn't paying any attention when she said it. I remember she lived at the apartment.

The basic interview. Name, year, major, etc. I had absolutely no interest in what she was saying, unless it was about her ability to pull her legs back to her ears. Sure that's crass, but after my little duke-out with Tho-*mass* I was ready to start grabbing what I wanted. And this girl, the black-haired sophomore with the suitable rack and rounding butt, had something that I wanted.

Greed.

STD Stan came to mind.

I feigned interest about whatever she was saying. This girl, whose name I didn't remember. It didn't matter because I didn't plan on talking to her again. If I didn't get laid now, what was the point of talking to her again? And if I did, why would I want to date a slut who slept with a guy she just met?

Lust.

But the bullshit paid off. All the whatever I said about whatever.

Pretending to be nice is actually pretty easy. Keep a lock on her eyes, agree with whatever she says and use proper grammar. Smile a little. That's all it takes. When a girl meets you, she makes up her mind right then and there if she's going to sleep with you. I already had that.

Let the booze do the rest.

As we talked in the kitchen, the party began to die down. It was already around two in the morning.

Ethan came up behind me while the girl was refilling her glass with white zinfandel. He slipped a pill into my pants pocket. The blue diamond. Viagra. Down it went with a mouthful of merlot. Why I was given it, I didn't ask. With college freshman's libido, it was sure to help my stamina.

An hour later and these socialite wannabes were either leaving or crashing. They couldn't take it to dawn like the rest of us. They were slurring and stumbling while First Prentiss was still slugging and slamming. The cops weren't going to end a party with only fifteen people left. The numbers were on our side. These socialite wannabes were going to end it because they couldn't tolerate their own expensive wine. The boxed crap we brought remained untouched in the fridge.

The pill began working. My cock was ready to tear its way out of my slacks. If it had teeth it would have tried to eat something.

And she kept talking.

Ethan came back from his convo with the First Prentiss boys and the few remaining wine-whores.

"The boys are ready to roll," he said. He slid something into my back pocket. I reached back and felt it through my pants. The unmistakable thin rubber ring of a condom. I was this hell-bent on losing my virginity and I didn't even carry one.

Again, STD Stan came to mind.

"You want to go or are you sticking around?" Ethan asked, planting the necessary seed in the conversation.

"No," she said to me. "You should stay for a little longer."

The wine was heavy on her breath.

"Nah, you guys go ahead without me," I said to Ethan. "I'll be fine."

We were upstairs in her room in minutes. A few more and she was naked. She required no encouragement. I had the feeling I was being used, but who cared? I don't remember her name, but I remember she looked good naked. At least for what I could tell by the little light coming in from the window at the head of the bed.

Then I recalled my last sexual escapade.

Squeeze. Squirt. Skedaddle.

Please God, if you give me anything, please let me get through this without spunking in less than thirty seconds.

I prayed to fake my way through like it wasn't my first time. At least for the first five minutes. That would be long enough to make me happy. I've heard it takes most women a half-hour to get to climax. If she got off, great for her. If not, I couldn't even care if she faked it. I was here for only one reason.

Fortunately, she was a worker. There wasn't going to be any lounging on her part. No comatose laying on her back. She undressed me, tugging a little on my tie as she began kissing my lips. She started working on me right away, kissing me all over, biting in the right spots. I just mimicked what she was doing and went with her responses. When she started moaning when I bit her ears, I figured I was on to something.

Down below, you could have built a tree house on my dick.

So far so good.

And then, to spare you the details, after the warmup of licking, biting, stroking, petting and stuffing, we got around to the reason I was here. I did whatever the skin flicks told me to do.

This little thing threw me on my back. She grabbed a condom from her bedside stand, tore open the package with her teeth, and slid it on me.

She'd obviously done this before.

Still going strong.

This is where we left off. Her on top of me. Straddled.

Things to do:
- Get drunk for the first time
Check.
- Try pot
Check
For the love of God, lose your virginity
- Currently checking

Man, was she aggressive. At least I'm assuming she was. Like I had anything to compare it to.

The whole time she was pumping on top of me, her warm ass bouncing on my lap, all I could think of was that condom. It was a question of where she got it. If it was from the student clinic.

Ethan and his trusty safety pin.

I envisioned her pregnant, or worse, me catching something this girl might be carrying. I thought if STD Stan had gotten to her. Even if the condom had a hole, even if it was pointless to wear it, there was no way I was going to let her stop.

But she did.

It wasn't because I was done. I was close, but not done. The combination of the wine and power of the little blue pill had kept me from making a disappointing end for the both of us. Well, me. I didn't really care about her end.

Considering she didn't have some screaming orgasmic end like in my pornos, I figured she hadn't come. What she had done was finally opened her eyes to what was going on outside the window a foot away from our heads. I felt her clench around my hard dick. She stopped moving and kept staring straight forward, her grip still firmly on the headboard.

There was a great view into her bedroom window from the roof across the alley. These old renovated buildings were only about ten feet away. All it took for box seats was a quick climb up the ladder on the back of the building. Ethan and the guys found that out. They had *not* gone home to the dorms. I should have figured something was up considering they didn't close this party down.

There, while I was getting my cherry forcefully popped, Ethan and the guys were watching. When she started freaking out, I finally heard them. Their voices had been faint compared to her panting and moaning.

"Yeah, buddy," one voice said.

"Get some, Chris. Get some," another said, barking like a drill sergeant. I could tell it was Collin.

I would like to say this girl was less than impressed. That was an understatement. Screaming in my ear, she slid down me, her powerful clenching pulled the condom off with her.

Face down on me with her head near my chest, she tried to hide behind the headboard.

"*Your* friends are *watching* from the roof," she screeched. "*And they're doing commentary on it!*"

That's just plain funny. I don't care how little of a sense of humor you have. Trying not to—using everything I had left—I laughed a bit. Just a little. The kind of slight burp of a laugh that escapes when you watch people fall on their asses on a fresh patch of ice.

That was not a situation you want to laugh at. Especially when you're so vulnerable to attack.

All of the sudden, her embarrassed shock wore off. She glared up at me. The face that was moaning in pleasure a few seconds ago now was scrunched and scowling. Tense, the way the faces were when we first showed up that night.

"*You asshole!*" It wasn't a yelp. It wasn't a cry. But damn was it loud.

She grabbed my shoulders and jerked herself up closer to my face.

There was no way to deny it was coming, but there was nothing I could do. One of her legs came up higher than the other. And then it hit me.

I cannot describe the amount of sheer pain it is to have a shaved knee cap car-wreck into your naked testicles, the same ones that had just been preparing to dump their release valves. I felt one of them being split against my pelvis. I could feel each individual hair being ripped out.

Think of how a wood splitter works.

Think of teeing off with an egg.

That would have been the appropriate time for a puking response, but it never happened. Even as a testicle became lodged just under my left lung.

Even before the searing pain rushed at me, the tears began. Through the water and the physical and emotional paralysis, there was nothing I could do but yell. Loud. Soft. Loud. It's not like I could control it.

"Mother … of … God! Jesus-H-fucking-Christ! Sweet … *dear* … Lord!"

If there was any other way to break the Second Commandment, I would have done it.

After removing her leg from in between mine, she frantically grabbed for clothing on the ground to cover herself up as she dashed out of the room.

"Oh, what's the matter baby," one voice from the roof said.

"Don't worry honey, I'll finish you off," another said.

She slammed the bathroom door across the hall behind her. A muffled bellow came from the other side of the door.

"*Get the fuck out!*"

Any chance of getting breakfast was gone.

Still, I wallowed in her sheets for a bit, gently cradling my bruising gear. I threw a middle finger up to the window as I waited for the building pressure of the shot to the crotch to wear down. I stared down at my red and swollen member. I was checking for blood. None could be seen, but it still felt like it was gushing.

And thanks to the Viagra, I was still lugging around a telephone pole.

Once the temporary blindness wore off, and the tears from my eyes subsided, I grabbed for my clothes on the floor. It was *my* shirt that she had yanked from the communal pre-humping stripping pile. I wasn't going to ask for it back.

Dressed in what I had left, I left her apartment after grabbing the remaining boxed wine from inside the fridge. My buzz was completely gone and I needed some kind of pain reliever. I needed to whiskey-dick away the monster below. Putting on my boxers and pants was painful enough. Inching up the zipper kept me in terror. I didn't need to bump the damn thing on something.

The guys were waiting for me outside the front door and laughing like they just shaved me again.

They noticed me slowly hobbling out. They hadn't seen what had happened on the other side of that headboard. They saw her bouncing up, looking out, and then jerking down. Next thing they saw was her running out of the room. They asked where my shirt was.

That's when I told them about the shot to the sack. They all moaned in agony and continued chuckling at the same time. Collin offered to rub them for me.

"Don't worry," Ethan said. "They'll grow back."

If my balls weren't still swelling up right then, I'd think it was pretty funny, too.

With the heckling out of the way for a bit, we started on our way back to the dorms, each one of us taking turns pulling off the box of wine.

Ethan put his arm around me in consolation.

"You did good champ," he said.

"I figure nothing can be as bad as this," I said, my voice a little higher than normal.

"Nope," he said. "Unless she cuts it off."

That's not as comforting as I would have liked him to be.

"I'm joining the *fucking* priesthood first thing tomorrow."

And the boys laughed more.

As we walked down the middle of the now abandoned streets, dressed like hobos and drinking like them too, I realized I'd have to tell this story a million times. Actually, it'd probably be told for me anytime we met someone new. Or just whenever someone felt like it. I didn't care. Somehow I knew I could count on Ethan to make sure it would never be mentioned this was my first time. Technically. I didn't even get to finish so I didn't know if it counted.

There with the guys, a select few of us belonging in a story that would come up anytime anyone mentioned sex, I finally felt like I belonged. No longer was I just scenery. Telling off Tho-mass, getting the girl—granted, who would eventually knee me in the sack — that was all my own doing.

Ethan had helped me along this far. I could lean on him less.

But, as for right there and then, there was no greater feeling than what was going on. School was meaningless. There was no bullshit there with the guys. We laughed at it all. Ethan, me and the boys, alone in the streets without a care to be had.

Except for my balls.

Yeah, they still hurt.

TWENTY-EIGHT

Ethan and Heather continued seeing each other.

Theirs was a good relationship, at least from my perspective. This was only based on what I saw—he never talked much about her. Maybe he realized what he did.

Maybe I felt a little better about the whole thing because he didn't just fuck her and run. Maybe it was because he seemed to genuinely share something with her. Maybe it was because I felt bad about his last relationship. The abortion. The breakup. Maybe that's why. Or, just maybe, it was a way of teaching myself a lesson. You snooze. You lose. Maybe.

Ethan and Heather.

They weren't hard to miss on campus. They weren't one of those campus couples that nauseatingly depended on each other for their own self-worth. They were together and they weren't.

They'd have lunch, lounge around and study together. But Ethan promised one thing to me: they would never plan to party together. If they both accidentally end up at the same house, so be it. But never would it be planned.

If you really wanted to see them together, you couldn't plan it. They rarely made plans, but always seemed to find each other. They ran into each other after class, but it was never routine. It was finding each other in the caf, but without regularity. Or at least they made it seem that way.

It was their spontaneity that kept it fresh. They were two best friends that acted like they hadn't seen each other in years. They met, got acquainted with, and fell in love every time they saw each other. The rest of us were not forced, but rather fortunate enough to witness it.

And for a long time, Ethan was good on his promises.

Heather was kept separate from his friends. There was time with her and time with us. He'd guaranteed to keep them apart. You'd have to know otherwise, to know that Ethan was dating anyone. His party calendar stayed filled, me tagging along for the ride. Weekends were still all about the boys.

Bros before hos.

It wasn't long before their names turned into one term, EthanandHeather. It started sounding like a venereal disease spreading through campus.

"I have EthanandHeathers. What do I do about this rash?"

Go to the clinic and find Ethan. He'll get you something.

At least now you could trust the prophylactics from there. Since he'd started dating Heather, he'd stopped poking holes in all of the condoms. Asked why, he just said it was getting old. I figured something else was up.

EthanandHeather were so deep in the honeymoon phase of their relationship that it made me jealous. Not a visible argument was had.

I can genuinely say they made a good couple. Their bliss was one to be envied and copied. Believe me, I tried. It never worked out. EthanandHeather had a relationship that couldn't be replicated. It was even harder to explain how it had happened so quickly.

Still, a part of me wanted to be a part of them. Their chemistry was undeniable. A cool guy everyone liked and a girl you couldn't help but fall in love with. It's a shame I didn't have the guts to snag her when I had my chance.

She smiled. He smiled. They both were dumb-happy with each other.

At points it was so sweet it made my teeth hurt. But I couldn't help but watch. Okay, it was closer to staring.

The way she rested her head against his chest and laughed with her whole body. The way she bowed her head when she pulled the loose strands of her hair behind her ear with a slightly-bent middle finger. The way she smelt like lilacs or vanilla. The way she called him "baby."

Even the sex sounded like it was great.

Her soft moans turned to spectacular orgasmic explosions through Ethan's door. It's not that they were annoyingly loud, but you couldn't help noticing them. You couldn't help but get a mental image of Heather's gorgeous body sprawled out naked on the bed every time you saw her. You couldn't.

Envy.

As usual, I was jealous of him. It was not always because of their relationship, but how they tried to include me in it. Sometimes it was retarded, other times it was nice to have Ethan rescue me from my weekday boredom. They always made sure to stop by and invite me to whatever they were going to do. It started out slightly awkwardly between the three of us. Heather didn't catch on at first. She'd be blissfully ignorant of the situation, but Ethan knew. He knew where to tread lightly until I was more and more accepting of EthanandHeather. More often than not, it felt like walking on broken glass.

In the beginning, I went out with them. Played the third wheel. That was my status in life. I'm sure I could hear people saying, "There is EthanandHeather. And that other guy."

Even a few times, I brought a date with me. For a while it was with Kristi, the roommate that was at the Halloween party. The two couples —and I use that term loosely with Kristi and I — kept separated like at a junior high dance. Guys on one side, girls on the other.

Next time I brought a girl I knew loosely through parties. Nice, but nothing worth getting into. She was quickly, though unintentionally, alienated. Three people who knew each other and a fourth wheel. There's nothing worse than going out on a double date when three-fourths of the people are all friends. The remaining part of the equation is always left out of the conversation. Maybe if I tried harder to include her she wouldn't have felt so left out.

It never worked. Without exception. Still, I was trying to copy the other couple. I wanted what they had. I wanted it all.

In watching them, I looked at myself further. Ethan could only bring me so far before I could realize my inaction cost me what I wanted. I needed to succeed where I had previously failed.

Ethan was the pattern for my life. My savior.

But, in the interest of full disclosure, they did piss me off at times. Best handled in small doses. That's why I went back to spending those hours in my room with my nose in a book. An excuse was always available if asked if I wanted to go out with them. Homework, tired, group meeting, too cold out. Whatever.

Despite the increasing amount of time he was spending with Heather, I still considered Ethan my best friend. When we did do something, we had a blast. It's like the old times never went away. I say "like" for a reason.

Every time you start one relationship another suffers.

There was still First Prentiss to consider.

The camaraderie of First Prentiss—bonded by sharing a class, partying or killing mutual boredom—began wearing thin halfway through winter. With our time recovering from the night before, trying to reconstruct what the hell happened, grievances with each other were amazingly seldom, but still present. Roommates who knew each other before college were the worst. Nothing but constant drama. The quirks that had prompted mild annoyance before, all of sudden started sparking hate-strewn screaming matches.

It's impossible to keep dozens of guys locked inside without some kind of incident. Think of the power structure with prison inmates. If you're the bitch the first day, plan on being that for the rest of your stay. Working your way up is as challenging as maintaining alpha status is to the top dog.

The same goes for a dorm-full of eighteen- and nineteen-year-olds.

We lived together, ate together and partied together. We were all doomed to kill each other. We thought maybe one at a time. We'd all gang up on the kid that couldn't keep his opinion of everyone's lives to himself. That stupid kid who always told us what he would do in a situation he wasn't in. The one spewing out advice no one wanted. Killing the parasite would have been for the greater good of the host.

With fifty-some guys living in close quarters, there was an ever-present chance for bloodshed. Winter was upon us. The cold and snow outside our windows were relentless reminders that we were stuck inside. The white snowdrifts were as good as prison bars.

That's when the first brawl ensued.

What started as a bitching match between Bubba and Aaron erupted into the hallway two doors down from me. Lord knows what they were arguing about. Everyone poured into the hallway as their yelling grew louder. Some of us were waiting for the blows to begin. Others were telling the two high school buddies to shut the fuck up.

Instead it was a shoving match. Aaron pushed Bubba, or the other way around, and someone tried to break it up. Gage, maybe. Or Nick. I'm not sure.

And then more were involved. One of the Bens was the first. Could have been. Pretty soon all of us were pushing, shoving and wrestling each other melee style. People trying to walk through the mess in the cramped hallway had no choice but to join in.

Bodies were slammed against the floor, which was nothing more than outdoor carpet covering concrete. Grunts, expletives and the sounds of flesh slapping was the soundtrack to the evening.

These are the future police officers, U.S. Congressmen, CEOs, newspaper editors and college professors of America.

It was an angry mob, like the way you think of street riots. It was a frustration expression. No one wanted to be inside. No one wanted to start classes again after Christmas break ended.

Too much testosterone in too little an area. Everyone wanted to hit someone. It wasn't entirely about each other. It was bloody and friendly at the same time.

This was the second time I punched Ethan. This time he hit me back. His face looked pissed, as I'm sure mine did too. It might have kept going if Collin hadn't grabbed my shoulders from behind and yanked me into a separate pile of kicking legs and flailing arms on the floor. Ethan dove into another pile.

Despite the yelling and noise, security never bothered us. Who was going to call them anyway? Everyone was tied up in the fight.

About half an hour later, the survivors were left panting and wheezing on the ground. There were a few black eyes and one bloody nose. We all smiled. Everyone laughed like bastards. It was the most fun thing we'd had in awhile. That's saying a lot considering how much we partied.

That doesn't mean it killed off all the pissiness in the place. Nope. That would come back real soon.

Fast forward to late spring. Almost summer. That time between midterms and finals. When the good spirits pick up with the mercury. My eyebrows and hair had long since grown back from my homecoming shaving.

Ethan had been working as the Beer Baron for almost the entire year. While he charged handling fees for those he didn't know, he never took a cent above cost from friends. He figured it was either that or they didn't get booze.

"That's just plain inexcusable," he would say.

Bros before everyone.

Every week, before he made his Friday night run, he'd stop by the room of anyone on First Prentiss he considered a friend. That meant knocking on about twenty-five doors, writing everything down, getting a hold of one of his dozen contacts, going to the liquor store, grabbing everything, loading it up into the car, and smuggling it back into the dorms without security catching on.

With this daunting task, he'd still repeatedly ask the people who routinely didn't want anything. They'd always say no, but he'd always ask. Well, almost always.

Despite any of this—any of the feeling of being stuck in our cages and the need to beat each other's asses—there was that friendship. We'd do anything for each other. Ethan especially. That was until he got tired of the Beer Baron business. He said it was getting old.

"I'll finish out the year and then I'm done with getting booze for everyone," he said.

"What about me?" I asked.

"Oh, don't worry about us," he responded. "I won't leave you hanging."

With all of my Friday classes in the bag, I got my paper for Dynamic Earth done for next week, and finished my laundry. I was free from any obligation over the weekend and damned relieved for that. At one point, there was literally nothing to do.

Then it was onto the normal crap we did every week to kill time before going out and killing brain cells. Go get dinner, wait around, shower, get changed, wait, drink it up in the dorms, gather everyone up and get the hell out of there. This Friday, I hadn't seen Ethan all day. No response from numerous text messages. Still, a twelve-pack was in my fridge and I was drinking it with STD Stan.

Yes, I know what you're thinking. In my defense, I couldn't find Ethan and damned if I was going to drink alone on a Friday afternoon. Besides, it was a good way to keep him from jacking off on my bed.

Later, however, I overheard some argument next door. Something about alcohol and the word "fuck" came up a lot.

Apparently, the one time Ethan didn't ask my neighbors if they wanted alcohol—the ones who *never* drank—well, they wanted some. A year as Lobby Lizards, playing cards and shit-talking about us, and they wanted in to "our lifestyle," as they so cutely put it.

The planets aligned correctly in their universe and they felt it was time to relax. And when Ethan failed to meet their needs, they bitched him out. He was on his way to my room when they summoned him into theirs. The yelling went on for ten minutes before he came into my room. It was the first time I had ever seen someone slam a door *open*. He looked uncharacteristically pissed and started screaming at me with a long speech.

"*What* in the *fuck* was *that*? Jesus-fucking-Christ. I swear to God all of the shit I do for these guys; go out of my way to ask them if they want booze and the one time I skip them and it's Armageddon. They've got the balls to yell at me because I didn't ask them. All they ever do is sit in their room on the fucking computer. How the hell was I supposed to know they were going to become humans today? Fucking Lobby Lizards."

He paced around the room, yelling at inanimate objects and throwing his arms in the air. I sat at my desk, as usual, wondering how much of this was directed towards me. STD Stan listened in too.

Ethan continued venting. His usually-reserved demeanor had been shut off. His reaction was how parents react to their pregnant teenage daughters. This was how Moses reacted to the Egyptians.

Then his rant went off from my neighbors and on to everyone else.

"Nothing's ever good enough. They bitch at each other all of the time over the most stupid shit. '*I want to go to this party*,' '*No, I want to go to this party*,' and then it goes on like that for hours. Planning their relaxation comes in painstaking detail. Fuck *all* of them. You would think some things they could just let roll off. But *nooo*. Everything, every trivial little thing on the face of the earth has to be treated with the greatest of importance."

The main point I gathered from his rant was that Ethan was through playing housemother.

"Let them do whatever they want, without my help," he said. "From now on, all I'm worrying about is myself."

Our leader was abandoning us. He was the one who kept a strong sense of family with our friends. He kept us together through all of it. He calmed the aftermath of the brawls, making sure no one took anything personally. He'd make sure no one was left behind in the dorms on a Saturday. Or at a party. He *had* been a housemother.

Now, he was ready to give up. He wanted the year to end and be done with it. He'd already signed a lease to live off campus next year.

Ethan stopped yelling and leaned up against the edge of the sink. He stared at his shoes. Still huffing, I thought he was done. He breathed in deep, attempting to collect himself.

"You all right?" I asked quietly, looking at him and then STD Stan.

"Yeah," he said, standing upright.

He looked collected. Looked, only for a second.

His arm sprung from his shoulder as he punched the concrete wall next to the mirror. I could hear the crunching from where I sat on the other side of the room. You could see the deformed bone under his skin.

"I'm fine," he said.

He left, slamming the door behind him.

Wrath.

Stan looked at me and laughed.

"Dude, your friend is *fucked* in the head," he said, returning to his usual dufus manner. "You might think about getting him some clinical help."

"Thanks for the input, Stan," I sarcastically said back.

"No, I'm serious. Pay attention to that stuff. It's obvious there's more going on with him than you know," he continued. "Shit like that's going to make him implode."

"Mind your own fucking business, Stan!" I yelled, as I left the room.

Wrath: The Sequel.

Ethan stood in the hallway, leaning up against the wall. I couldn't tell if the blood on the carpet was fresh from his knuckles or from our previous episode of communal aggression expression. He said he didn't want to talk about it.

All he said was, "I don't think I'll ever understand people."

It was obvious he broke part of his hand. He just clutched it close to his body, walked out the door and went outside. I didn't follow.

Instead, Stan and I finished the beer and got high in our room.

It was Friday after all, and we were going out.

I wouldn't see Ethan until the next week.

And even less for the rest of the year.

TWENTY-NINE

I am trapped in this dazed euphoria. Not asleep but constantly in a dream. There is no possibility this can be happening. My hand is being forced. My choices were made before I was born. Not destiny but devastation. I can't say how I feel. Compare and contrast, constant judgment without a prerequisite. There is no way they could understand. They wouldn't care. I just can't bring myself to tell them.

If they could only see inside and not what is reflected on the exterior. People come by and offer a friendly nod, but nothing is shared. I know I am accepted but there is a part that won't allow it. They know nothing. I don't feel a connection even though I feign one. There are moments where I am alone. I am not just sitting alone, but I am alone.

My social stigmas won't allow me to turn into what people see. No one knows the truth. We're all too doped up to realize more exists beyond our plastic cup politics and the jingling noises of change in our pockets. There must be more.

What if it was all different? It couldn't be, not now, not ever. Nothing matters. Nothing can take this emptiness away. I wish something could. My addictions give me a temporary smile as I forget. For a few moments, I am just like them and I've convinced myself I'm happy with it.

Then that feeling escapes and I'm left where I am now.

Times change. People don't. There are those who will not grow out of the shells they have become so at home in. It would seem an atrocity to believe that they might be able to do something different from the norm. It takes an insurmountable amount of energy to convince them to do something other than the weekly routine. I know I sound self-righteous in this, but I now believe that broadening ones horizons is the only way to allow for growth.

One must possess the drive to pursue change. To have the willingness to accept it.

THIRTY

The door to the basement was just outside the kitchen.

I politely left Kathy to preparing dinner.

"If you don't mind, I'm going to poke around a little more," I said in a cheery tone.

"No dear, you go right ahead," she said, not looking up from the pots on the stove. "Dinner will be ready in a half-hour."

I opened the door and walked down the stairs. Kathy didn't see me and I didn't want her to.

There wasn't a slice of my being that wanted anything to do with the basement. I knew what happened down there. There was nothing else that Ethan's mom, the cops or anyone else would have found. Still, my legs carried me. The better side of me knew I owed Ethan at least a look.

Down the wooden steps the smell of cleaning solvents still hung in the air. The crime scene cleanup crew had tried to cover up the acidic smell of their cleansers by running a few loads of dryer sheets. It didn't work completely, but you'd have to know what happened to notice the contrasting smells.

A newer washer and dryer combo sat spotless at the bottom of the step. There were no drops of spilled liquid laundry detergent like at campus or at my parents' house. A drawstring laundry bag I recognized as Ethan's rested next to the washer, the top tied in a neat knot. I wondered if it had been left there on purpose.

To my right, a room was filled with boxes and totes marked "Xmas," "Photos" and "Ethan's Baby Things." The limbs of an artificial Christmas tree poked from a box with mashed edges. A set of golf clubs was piled in with the mess of outdated lamps and stored fishing tackle. A garden hose and lawn chairs hung from two-by-four beams.

It was everything you expected to find in a quiet suburban home.

In another room on the other side of the basement, there was nothing. Unfinished walls and floor. No windows or boxes. Not a speck of dirt or dust anywhere. Cobwebs like in the other rooms of the basement had recently been removed. Lines from scrubbing the floor circled around a certain part of the room where the cold floor and wall met. A small patch in the wall looked like it had been filled in recently.

That must have been where it happened. It was where Ethan put a gun in his mouth and splattered himself all over the wall.

It's not suicide. It's Art Deco.

I stared at the spot for what seemed like an hour.

The swirling pattern was loose at the ends, growing tighter as it centered. Someone scrubbed the shit out of the floor and walls. More blood meant more scrubbing. Getting bits of Ethan out of the tiny holes and cracks of the floor was easier than getting him out of my mind.

You had to stare hard to even imagine a tint of pink in the concrete.

The memories I had been replaying over the last few days shot through my brain at a rapid speed. Our meeting. The abortion conversation. Homecoming. Fighting in the hallway. Heather. Campus terrorism. Beer Baron. The clinic. Drink Day. The last time we talked.

Still, I couldn't force myself to cry. I had tried. I wanted to feel the usual emotions you're supposed to feel when a good friend dies.

Commits suicide.

Say it.

Normal people cry. Almost everyone else did when I gave them the news. You're supposed to be sad. I told myself I was. But, I couldn't feel it.

Confusion. There's that emotion again.

And I sat where he sat.

Despite the humid warmness of the basement, the floor was cold against my stocking feet and my fingertips.

I tucked my knees close to my chest. I put my head between my knees and tucked into a ball. A familiar nauseating feeling came over me as I sat hunched against the wall, my hand skimming over the smooth floor.

Nothing.

I stretched my legs out in front of me and rested my head against the wall. The filled-in patch right behind me.

My eyes closed themselves.

Nothing.

I can't tell you what I expected from sitting there. I imagined Ethan steadily putting a gun in his mouth and pulling the trigger. A last second regret jerked his head to the side, leaving him bleeding for hours. Or maybe he did it in drenching tears. I had never seen Ethan cry, so the later scenario seemed unimaginable.

I took out Ethan's journal and read more, attempting to connect them to moments of his life.

I am trapped in this dazed euphoria. Not asleep but constantly in a dream. There is no possibility this can be happening. My hand is being forced.

Page after page, and for some reason I couldn't cheat and read the last section first. All I wanted were answers and I was still avoiding them. I studied his writing intensely. Word choice, penmanship. I tried putting every minute I spent in Psych 105 to good use. ·

Nothing.

There is clarity in intoxication. It rids the mind of all rationality. It is under that fake cloud of irrational bliss that the mind clears itself of all barriers.

And then I heard the footsteps down the stairs. The break in the silence startled me.

Quietly, I closed the cover and jammed the journal back down the back of my pants.

"Honey," Kathy said, stopping halfway down the stairs.

"Uh, yes ma'am?" I quietly said back, hoping she wouldn't hear me.

"Oh, I told you, call me Kathy," she said in a correcting tone.

"Yes, Kathy?"

"Honey, get changed and be ready for supper. It's almost finished."

"Yes ma'am…I mean Kathy. I'll be right up."

"That's a good boy," she said.

Her footsteps went back upstairs.

THIRTY-ONE

Sophomore year.

We'd never be called freshmen again. It was kind of sad.

Everyone we considered to belong to First Prentiss came back. No one had yet dropped out, but only a few returned to living on campus. Most took over houses spread all over town. Eric definitely had the best one for parties.

Ethan had signed a lease for the upper half of a two-story house four blocks from campus. He needed a roommate and asked me to sign up. When I half-jokingly suggested EthanandHeather get their own apartment, Ethan said they weren't even close to being there yet.

"Don't worry," he told me. "Heather won't be living there. I promise."

He had still been good on his first promise: He'd never bring her to a party. They had met up a couple of times, but as always unplanned and he still hung out with us. For the most part.

Ethan and I weren't like we were before, but I figured we'd spend more time with each other if we lived together. Things might go a little back to the way they were freshman year, right when we met. Drinking, getting high, terrorism. I could fix it.

When EthanandHeather continued over the summer and into the next year, Ethan kept promising she wouldn't live at the apartment. The last thing I wanted was to live with a couple. They'd take up the living room, the kitchen and the shower. They'd be an undeniable force anywhere they went. There's a reason the worst hurricanes have girls' names.

Ethan kept saying it wouldn't happen.

Ethan stayed in town over the summer, sub-letting an apartment. I went back home and had to explain why I didn't make Dean's list second semester. Maybe it was the partying, but I just said my PR classes were tougher than I expected. By then I had chosen that as my major. Ethan still didn't have one.

We met up again once on the first of June when our lease started and my dad helped me move my stuff in. We didn't spend the night. Ethan stayed there and when I moved in a few weeks before classes started, everything was set up. Ethan had turned it into a decent place.

For the first few days, things did return to normal. We'd play video games, watch movies, and meet up with the guys. We had nothing to do and the time to kill. Heather hadn't moved back yet and neither of us mentioned her.

But, no matter how hard I tried to recreate the same feeling of returning to our college home, some things just weren't the same.

Then freshmen week came, the second time around.

We pre-partied at each other's houses most of the time and trucked it to our old stomping grounds again. It wasn't the same. The party houses we spent the majority of freshmen year at seemed to lose their attraction. The same people at the same places seemed tired. The friendships that had formed on First Prentiss were beginning to wear. It was no longer about going out, but where and why.

We were all starting to build histories with one another. We were no longer of herd of partiers, but friends with arguments, differences and back-stories. All that included a steaming pile of bullshit. Our hallway fights couldn't cure everything.

Freedom House was filled with assholes. The Pink Taco was a shit-hole. The party Meccas were losing their hold on us the second year around. A night of drinking became repetitive. Been there, done that. Still, we had nothing better to do. So we searched for something new, attempting to discover in our freshman counterparts, something it seemed we had lost.

We'd stand in the corners of these basements together and retell the stories of earlier days even though they were only a year old. The fishpond diving experience. The tarnishing of the clock. Getting busted in the dorms. The knee to my balls. That always came up. So did my shaving. We'd rehash every funny memory we had.

In these same basements around the same campus where we made the memories, we'd be swapping them like we were long-removed alums. It was about our stories. Our memories.

The problem was that we weren't making any new ones.

When those ran out, there'd be awkward silences.

Our friendship seemed to be escaping into our past.

That could only last for so long.

Eric always wanted to stay at his house. Collin didn't feel like sweating it out in another basement. One of the Bens never went out any more, the other was pickier than shit over where to go. Aaron, Nick and Zach had jobs. Gage and Bubba hadn't changed and still wanted to get drunk and deflower freshman girls.

Still, despite our growing differences, we got each other out.

The guys, the First Prentiss boys, teased Ethan, asking him where Heather was. They talked about "how he's wrapped up in his chick" or "I've never seen anyone more pussy-whipped." Those few weeks before Heather arrived, Ethan couldn't hang out with us without someone mimicking the cracking noise of a whip.

He'd give an uncomfortable laugh and then shrug it off.

Then a voice would come out of him, a voice I hadn't heard in a while.

The voice of the old Ethan. The one where no one could get the best of him.

"It's not my fault you guys can't keep a girl's interest for more than an hour," he said, pulling off a bottle of beer on a couch at Gage's house. "Besides, if I hung out with you all the time, you'd just call me a fag."

Everyone laughed.

Not me.

THIRTY-TWO

The dining room table remained set for three.

A layover at O'Hare ensured there were only two of us at the table.

"You know, Ethan mentioned you all of the time," Kathy said. "Well, whenever *he decided* to talk to me."

Her tone was bitter. Their disconnection was his fault.

No response from me, other than complimenting her on the garlic mashed potatoes accompanying the lamb, string beans and butter rolls.

My search for answers why he was dead had not ended with his journal. I asked what Ethan was like as a kid.

"Oh, he was a such a good boy growing up. It wasn't until high school that he became such a difficult young man," she said, sipping on her glass of wine.

Kathy had changed for dinner, wearing a slim black dress and a string of pearls. I pulled a button up shirt from my bag and put it over the same T-shirt I'd worn for the past two days.

Ethan was the result of a New Year's Eve party as the world was welcoming in 1986. Steve Costello's sperm came careening up the birth canal after a night of twenty-five cent taps at, strangely enough, a corner bar called *Steve's*.

Certain details I wished she would have spared, but she was telling me everything like TV cameras were rolling. Like she'd been practicing in front of the mirror preparing for tomorrow's funeral.

Nine months later, he was the Dead Baby Ethan. She explained it the same way Ethan did the day I met him.

Not breathing. Go-get-'em doc. Even after being dead for a few minutes, Ethan was fine.

"The fist time I held him, I couldn't stop staring at his eyes," she said. "They sparkled like diamonds, just like his grandfather's."

His was a normal childhood, as normal as growing up as a product of Steve and Kathy Costello could be.

Good grades in school. He took a shine to English and art. His dad coached his T-ball team. Mom and dad went to all of his flag football games. They went fishing, golfing and to hockey tournaments together. It was just Ethan, mom and dad. The Cleaver's didn't have shit on them. On the surface.

"You couldn't force the smile off that boy's face," his mom said.

And he grew up the way any kid from a middle-class family pretending to be upper crust would be raised. The expensive foreign cars, the house in the suburbs, the name-brand everything. But dad's job as middle management at a tractor manufacturer wasn't cutting it for Kathy, the homemaker.

To keep the bill collectors at bay, Ethan's dad took up a job buying land so oil companies could install pipelines from Alaska. He turned large chunks of the Canadian wilderness into dollar signs for billionaire oil moguls. And because of that, Steve Costello's family got a bigger house. Mom got a Mercedes convertible. Ethan could go to college.

By the end of elementary school, dad was on the road twenty-eight days out of the month. I thought of Tho-*mass* and how he tried playing me like I had daddy issues. No wonder Ethan didn't say anything.

"I don't think Steve was around as much as Ethan would have liked, but all those hours were for his family," she said. "He's a hard-working man."

Yeah, I thought, working when his son's getting his suit fitted for his funeral. Because half of Ethan's face was missing, it was going to be closed-casket. Still, Kathy thought it was necessary to make sure he was dressed well.

Even as Ethan started his "troublesome phase" in junior high, even as his usually perfect grades started slipping, his parents saw no correlation between that and his absentee father. The ribbons in his room, along with his nerd books, were from long before Ethan became the Ethan I knew.

His first arrest came at sixteen. The cops said he and some friends vandalized a playground. Despite Ethan's protest that the damage to the teeter-totter was an accident from just jumping on it too hard, his parents paid his fine and bought the school new plastic equipment.

Then it was getting caught smoking at school. And "mouthing off" to his parents. The tag on the hand basket Ethan sat in said "To Hell." That was his parents' view.

That same year, he ran away from home after mom blew up on him. He left a note saying he might not come back, but he was only gone a matter of hours before he called. His dad, who was actually home at the time, came and picked him up at the mall. He called when he got bored and needed a ride home.

The waiting sheriff's deputies at the Costello home served the commitment papers. His parents had signed them when Ethan was gone, but they didn't tell him when Steve went to pick him up. They didn't believe him when he said he wasn't suicidal. There's being sold out, then there's that.

He spent three days in an upstate mental hospital where they take your belt, shoelaces or anything else you can use to kill yourself. Steve went to work. Kathy tried visiting, but Ethan wouldn't talk.

"He was just *so* difficult," she said, taking another gulp from her glass.

Steve and Kathy had their son tested for learning disorders, mental problems and whatever they could diagnose him with up there. He saw a therapist and a psychiatrist. He was prescribed Ritalin and Prozac.

They thought pills could fix it. That's Kathy's approach.

All through high school, he was forced to cram thousands of milligrams down his throat to cure him of being nothing more than a teenager who wanted to hang out with his dad. The same stuff he would later swipe from the campus clinic. The pills that once held his mind prisoner he later gave out to set others free.

A picture of Ethan's real life was starting to come into focus.

Steve's portion of the parenting came from angry shouting emanating from a speaker phone while he was on the road. Often, he mentioned, "I work hard and this is how you repay me?" and "Do you know what my friends are saying?" Slipping grades, lackluster athletic performance, trips to the principal's office. It didn't matter. Nothing was good enough any more. The words "disappointment" and "failure" came up a lot.

Kathy took another drink. The strap of her dress slid off her shoulder, further exposing her already prominent cleavage.

When he was home, and not locked in his office, all Steve showed his son was how disgusted he was with him. Before it could get better, it had to get worse. Ethan scrapped both hockey and baseball.

"Steve didn't understand what was the matter with him. Neither did I," she said. "He just didn't want to be a part of anything any more."

Senior year. Free from all connections to anything resembling a club or sport, Ethan took up the golf team. Never picking up a club before, his parents were completely enthralled with the idea. He'd hit the range in the morning before school and play a round afterwards.

"I always heard from my friends what a gentleman he was on the course," Kathy said. "Steve was pleased too."

This connection I made on my own: out on the course, Ethan was by himself. Sure there was a coach, but during a match, it was just him and the ball. It was him versus himself. He kept his own score.

He never told me any of this. Then again, I never asked.

Along with golf, he returned his attention to school. That brought higher grades, but because of years of slacking off, Ethan's grades were barely good enough to get him into most colleges. With Ethan's improving performance on the course, there was talk of a golf scholarship, but he wasn't interested.

His guidance counselor told him and his parents he'd never make it in a four-year school and should consider community college. Ethan took that as a challenge. Someone told him he couldn't do something.

When Ethan hit college, the phone calls home were infrequent. I knew his hometown and family carried less importance than what was in front of him.

I was finally starting to get it.

But there was plenty Kathy didn't know. A lot I didn't either. Where his knowledge of getting out of underage drinking charges came from. How he knew how to handle himself in a group of people he didn't know. How he knew how to spot the newest campus wuss and turn him into a reckless partier. There was plenty we didn't know.

"You don't think it was *my* fault, do you?" Kathy asked me.

Her big doe eyes stared at me. Looking prim and proper, yet on the verge of breaking down at any moment, she was still a MILF. A hot mom just short of wigging out.

Yes, Kathy. It's your fault. All of it.

The way you kept the house the image of perfection. The way his dad was never home. The way you wanted me to pretend to be your son for a few days. It was easy to draw some conclusions. It was a luxury I so wanted to afford myself.

And Kathy needed to know what those were.

It's all your fault. You, and only you, are to blame.

You couldn't see that Ethan didn't care about the crap you did? His dad made him hate money. Everything he did was a cry for attention. You treated his problems like they were inconveniences, like you were scared the neighbors might find out.

By the time he came to college, he perfected the art of keeping that exterior up. Sure, there were a lot of unknown problems underneath, but he learned to not let them out. You taught him to be scared of being himself. You taught him having any sort of imperfection was rewarded by a psychoanalytical couch ride followed by a heavy regimen of pills.

By showing his weaknesses, he was rewarded with numbness.

But, I didn't say any of this. I couldn't. It would have been cheating, not any kind of answer. Only Ethan got the easy way out.

She wanted to know if it was her fault.

There was no way to answer that question. I still couldn't find anyone to blame, although it would have been nice. My mouth was agape. No sound would come out.

And she chuckled a bit, in sad, desperate sort of way. She took the last sip off her wine, cautiously setting the glass down.

That's when she started crying. She just burst into tears. I had yet to be able to do that.

Envy.

She tried collecting herself. She tried laughing again, but it was useless. The woman had just lost it and I had a front row seat.

"How was I supposed to know," she bellowed, sucking back snot inside her rhinoplasty-perfect nose. "I thought I was a good mother. I gave him everything he needed."

"None of us knew," I told her.

Ethan made sure of that. He hid everything from us. Whatever was bothering him, he did a fantastic job from keeping out of public view. He came to college searching for a new family. For a while, he had one. The boys and all of us were inseparable. He ruined that himself. Him and no other. It certainly wasn't my fault.

If you go into any relationship in pieces, you'll come out in ruins.

Ethan taught me that.

If he only knew.

Abruptly, Kathy stopped crying. She composed herself, wiping her eyes with her white cloth napkin.

Her emotionless face stared at me.

Pushing her chair out from behind her, she said, "Will you excuse me?"

She walked into the kitchen with her wine glass in hand. Her high heels clacked loudly against the ceramic tile. Otherwise, the house was silent. Next was the unmistakable sound of pills rattling in a plastic bottle. It was a noise I've made myself a few times.

Crush up a few Ritalin. Snort them up. Party for hours.

I bet she was going for Percoset or Vicodin. Or maybe the prescription for Prozac she'd kept refilling even though Ethan had stopped taking it years ago. That'd hit the spot right now.

Her head jerked back once quickly, a second followed by a long pull from her refilled glass. After letting out a long, slow sigh, she walked back into the dining room.

"I'm going to bed," she said as she stuck her chest out. That wasn't on accident.

Down the hallway she sauntered with her legs close together, wine glass in hand as her shapely ass swung from side-to-side. Slowly she unzipped the back of her dress, revealing her toned back muscles. She turned and went up the stairs.

"You can join me if you like," her voice came from the stairs. "Steve won't be back until tomorrow afternoon."

When we'd be throwing Ethan away.

Her hand extended from the top of the banister. Her dress floated to the ground when she released it from her loose grip.

All night I had imagined what was underneath it.

She leaned over the top of the banister, only wearing a black lace bra. This early in my sexual career, I knew that meant she hoped she'd be getting laid tonight. That's the only reason women wear their best underwear.

"Are you coming up?" she said to me.

Frozen at the table, I responded, "Yes, ma'am."

"Kathy," she said, walking up the rest of the stairs.

"Kathy," I said to myself.

For a second I was right behind her. The chance to bang a pent-up emotional wreck of a torrid exurbanite housewife was appealing. The chance to hate fuck the woman who tore my best friend up since birth would have been a trip.

I'd slam her into the headboard hard enough to drive a nail into a concrete wall. I'd tell everyone.

I stood up and took five steps toward the stairs.

"*Jesus*, what's the matter with you," I said to myself shaking my head in disgust. "It's Ethan's mom."

Ethan, who committed suicide just a floor below where I was standing. The guy who I just found out was more messed up that I had ever imagined. The way I considered plowing his mom like an Iowa cornfield was appalling.

That, and a few hours ago she wanted me to pretend I was her son.

Hello, nausea.

I couldn't spend another second in that nuthouse. Grabbing my bag, I got the hell out of there.

What a mind-fuck, I thought, slowly closing the door behind me. I was careful to do it quietly as to not bring Kathy out for a screaming match on the lawn. After that, God knows what she was capable of.

Outside, I looked back at the house. It looked the same as every other one. A long line of perfectly kept American dream homes. I wondered if everything going on in the rest of them was as fucked up as what went on in Ethan's house.

Where was that hotel? I didn't care how far I had to walk. Just as long as every step was away from that house. The first step was the easiest to take. Walking in a town where I had no idea where to go, I wanted to do the only thing I knew how: get blazingly wasted.

I picked my phone out of my bag and saw the guys had been texting me all night. They were on their way.

Forget it all.

A drink would help.

THIRTY-THREE

Homecoming had once again arrived.

This time around I was keeping my guard up to prevent the random acts of shaving. Losing your eyebrows is something you'll laugh about later. But only once. If it happens a second time, you're just an ass.

The plans were kegs and eggs at Aaron's, followed by parade, followed by the beer pong tournament to end all beer pong tournaments at Eric's. And no, paddles were not used. We went free hand. Sure, some pong purists would say that defeated the whole point, but our way got more beer into us quicker.

For the few days beforehand, Ethan had been non-existent. I hadn't seen him at the apartment. He didn't answer his cell phone or return the messages. He was never online to get an instant message. No one had any clue where he was. The guy had vanished.

The boys and I wanted our old friend back. The way he used to be. The partier, the prankster, the anarchist. The one who talked about ripping norms apart, keeping life interesting to defeat death. Sadly, when I said "the guys," it included Ethan less and less each day. We'd all hang out together, but it was without the person who had united us. We became our own sect without him. He chose it. He chose her over us.

Despite the fact he'd slowly been slipping out of our social circle, the Ethan Costello I knew would never forsake a day as holy as Homecoming.

Our Father, who art in heaven, Heineken be thy name. Thy kingdom come, thy beer bong be done.

Still, I kept leaving him messages so he knew about the plans. Still I heard nothing. Every message I was getting more hostile. This wasn't like him. Something had to be up.

The morning of, I finally gave up. It was clear Ethan would not be part of the homecoming festivities. It was eight o'clock and it was time to start drinking. Ethan hadn't slept in the apartment in two nights.

There were kegs and there were eggs. Gage made an omelet with Guinness and Jell-O shots. That was possibly the worst thing I have ever heard of, but, surprisingly, with some red hot fire sauce, it wasn't that bad.

No word from Ethan.

Then it was on to the parade. Nothing but a line of college students curing hangovers with more booze. Again, the bladder strapped to the stomach was used. This year, with some forward planning, we saved bladders from previous parties and filled them with whatever we wanted. I opted for Jack and Coke.

Me and the boys yelled at cheerleaders, catcalled at anything attractive that walked by, and booed the Role Playing Game Club. Geeks.

No sign of Ethan. No missed calls.

At Eric's, we began creating our own homecoming traditions. It wasn't anything far from what was going on at any other house on campus, but these were ours. We lived off campus. We ran the show.

Eric, Nick, Zach and Collin got a house on Fourth Street, just a few blocks away from the Attic House. When they moved in, it was recently refurnished. By early October, we had already put a kitchen chair through the ceiling, torn down the banister and scuffed up every wall with shoe prints and beer funk. It was small, but it was just enough room to cram a few hundred people in there.

Sitting on a couch on the front lawn, we hollered at a passing alumni float. We raised our beers and told them they ruled. They rolled by, pulled around and partied with us.

They drank our beer. They used our beer bong. One of them admitted he was now on the university alumni association board. I still have a photo of him throwing down a pitcher of beer via a nine-foot beer bong in about fifteen seconds. I'm sure it will come in handy someday.

Despite our differences, the alums were surprisingly pretty cool. But did they suck at beer pong. Only one of the dozen that stuck around knew how to play.

"My son taught me. He goes to school here now," he said.

That put this guy at about forty, that's assuming he was a decent guy and didn't knock up some girl in high school.

The tournament started with around one hundred contestants on four tables. Six hours, two kegs of beer and twelve delivered pizzas later, six remained. The all-star alumni team was pitted against Eric, Nick and I.

No sign of Ethan.

It was to be a Battle Royale of Beer Pong. Best of seven. Defense allowed only on the bounce. This time one rule changed: slam full beers. The cup stays half empty until a ball lands in there, then it's filled up all the way.

And we weren't playing with any of that pussy three-two crap beer. We were pouring out of forties by this time. Seven-percent alcohol. That was sure to put a few alumni on their asses.

If the game went down to the wire to the seventh round, each player would end up putting down a case of beer each. If it was a one-way slaughter each member of the losing team would have to chug the equivalent of a twelve-pack.

It had never been attempted on this campus before, as far as we knew. The alumni said they were up to the challenge.

After winning the coin toss, I was first up. I set the tone of the game by sinking a score with the first ball. The eighty-one grad who's now in real estate, did not.

"Do you realize when you graduated college, I wasn't even born yet," I said to him, knowing that was enough to make the game personal.

Remember kids: In beer pong, there is no such thing as good sportsmanship. Throwing of cups, spitting of beer and insulting the other team is encouraged. It's called good defense. Some rules afford for extra points based on unruly behavior.

First Prentiss took the first round.

Finally, Ethan called back. Nine voicemails and thirteen text messages later and he decided he still talked to me. Why would he talk to me? I'm just his fucking roommate.

"Where the fuck are you?"

That's how you say hello to someone who goes AWOL on homecoming.

"Upstairs," he said.

"Get your ass down here," I yelled into the phone. "We're waxing these fogies."

I looked up at the three-member alumni team, gave them a wink and I closed my phone.

Back to the game. The alums had to sit in chairs in between their turns, while the rest of us were barely fazed.

Ethan walked down the stairs hand-in-hand with Heather, a case of beer in the other hand.

I was speechless, but no one seemed to notice.

The beer was nothing more than a buy-out. Some cheap peace offering.

"Ethaaaan!" the guys yelled, obviously tanked.

I said nothing.

Ethan promised a lot of things. He promised Heather would never be brought to a party.

Promise broken.

It used to be bros. Now it's all about the ho.

"How's the game going?" Ethan asked, poking me in the ribs like nothing mattered.

"Fine," I said to him and looked back at the saggy-faced alumn. "We're about to waste these fools."

"Hi, Chris," Heather said to me.

"Hi," I responded in a barely-audible tone. I didn't look at her.

And the game resumed as Ethan stood close to me, but closer to Heather.

Yeah, I was yelling, screaming and going through the motions after each shot. Yeah, I played one helluva game, but it didn't matter.

We closed the game down in the fifth round with two shutouts. To a thirty- or forty-something, there's no celebration uglier than a bunch of drunken middle-American college students dancing, jumping up in the air and chest-bumping each other. It was similar to a World Series celebration, but our only test of our physical ability was the hardness of our livers.

Yippee.

My celebration wasn't of happiness. The win, sinking these country club fucks, only worsened my anger with Ethan's absence and Heather's presence.

How could he shirk *us* on Homecoming and then think it was okay to bring *the skirt* with?

The rest of the guys didn't care.

Once hecklers, they'd turned into a crowd that loved Heather. They thought Heather was cool and hot, but it didn't matter. When they gave Ethan shit about her, it was only an excuse to give him shit. They meant nothing by it.

Everyone was occupied by Heather, hitting on her and trying to get her to call some of her friends. At this point in the day, the best looking girls had left or passed out.

I pulled Ethan aside.

"What the fuck dude," I sprayed at him.

"What?" he asked. His surprise bothered me.

"What do you mean, what? What's with bringing her here?"

"The guys seem to like her." He pointed over to Collin and Gage laughing with Heather as she held a beer. Their smiles were enormous. I had forgot how beautiful she looked when she smiled. They were still bugging her to call her friends.

EthanandHeather had infected what was now *my* circle. There was guy time, and then there was chick time.

Screw Team Us.

There was no Team Us anymore.

Ethan ceased to exist.

There was only EthanandHeather left.

"Fuck the guys. You said you'd never bring her to a party. *You* promised *me*," I said, poking him in the chest, then pointing to myself.

"That was *a year* ago. Things change."

"Apparently," I spit back before turning around and walking away.

Ethan grabbed my shoulder, stopping me in my tracks.

"Let me make it up to you," Ethan said from behind me.

"How can you?" I asked over my shoulder.

Walking in front of me, Ethan yelled, "Everyone! Hey! Guys!"

Everyone stopped what they were doing. The whole house. This removed from the partying routine and Ethan had the presence to captivate a house of drunkards. Even at five o'clock on Homecoming.

"It has been brought to my attention that I have not been as good as a friend to those who have so good to me," he began.

I said nothing as the guys gave a murmur. They weren't agreeing with him, but they weren't disagreeing either.

"In honor of this glorious day, and to make up to my friends, I hereby declare a day where there is nothing but good times and high times. A day with no parades, no football games. A day only of drinking."

"Isn't that what we're doing right now?" Nick asked.

"Yes," Ethan said. "But homecoming is a day for everyone, drunks or not. I will create a holiday so great only those with the strongest livers will be able to tolerate it."

Everyone laughed. I didn't.

"When?" I asked.

Ethan looked up at the ceiling, thinking.

"Uh … to pick a date … the last Saturday in February. It's a nice middle point between New Year's and St. Patty's Day. It shall be known as Drink Day."

Again everyone in the room raised their glasses and cheered. I couldn't help but smile. Ethan turned to me, putting his hands on my shoulders. Those gray eyes.

"Trust me, it's going to be great. I owe you. You're right, I've been out for a while, but this will make up for it, I promise."

I said nothing.

"You're my best friend. My brother. Forgive me."

"Don't get all soft on me," I said. "Let's drink."

THIRTY-FOUR

I always feel like I am being watched, but who would care enough to actually watch my average day-to-day stupid life? I am not being looked at. I am being glanced at and filed away as nothing. I am being ignored.

I am a disappointment to all that I know. My parents started the cycle and now I have ended it with myself. I don't even like who I am. I want to be someone else who has everything, but I have become this beast without a purpose. I am hideous to all. When I'm ignored, I'm happy. I want to be accepted, yet I don't. I wish I had something to offer her, but who I am is not enough. I have nothing to offer. I am not funny, good-looking, smart or brave. I only pretend I am. I wish I could say, after all of this, that I am the only one that understands me. I am the person that understands me the least. Some people have an idea of who I am, while I am the only person that knows all what I do. I lie and hide from others. They only know me by who I appear to be at that moment. That is who I decide to be just then.

Nothing is real. I live in a world where nothing really comes together but everything just decides to fall apart before me. I have the chances, but decide to fail, against my own judgment, because I decide not to get hurt or get involved. If I decide to do something, I will find a way to wither out because of the consequences that may come. I am scared of what may happen.

There is nothing that can come too fast or too soon. If someone could just give me something more to feed the happiness that I crave, I could sleep.

People are scared of me. I am seen as a normal person with different sides that are thrown away. One side is embraced … the smile. Everyone loves a clown. One side is disregarded … me. Who would want the person I am? There are a few. They do not want me for who I am, but for rather what I have become. I became someone who is superficial with little moral value.

THIRTY-FIVE

The first promise Ethan broke was about bringing the woman to parties.

But I can't be too angry about it. If he hadn't, we wouldn't have Drink Day. Bringing Heather to a party meant Ethan was creating a day for the boys. For every action, there is an equal and opposite reaction.

Immediately, he set to task. This wasn't just scrounging up sixty bucks for a keg. This was trying to rally campus together. Creating unity. Getting everyone together for a series of parties all over town.

Establishing a holiday is no easy task. Even with four months to plan for it. But the name spoke for itself. Drink Day.

Ethan used every party connection he had. He contacted The Dealer from freshman year to make sure the pot supply would be ample enough to meet the need. Ethan took up his formerly abandoned leadership position again. The Beer Baron was back in full force. Resurrected.

He levied every liquor store clerk to get the owners to run specials for the day.

"We're going to need to make sure there's at least forty kegs available," Ethan told me one night as he hammered away on a list at our apartment's coffee table.

"*Forty*," I said spitting out a mouthful of Ramen noodles in his direction.

"You think we need more?"

"Uh … who's going to drink forty kegs?"

"This baby's going to be a big deal, you just watch," he said.

Ethan even got fake IDs made up for the seven closest friends from First Prentiss. He wanted us all to save them until then. It would be my first time at a bar.

While Ethan was planning how to rectify breaking his first promise to me, he was breaking the second. I don't think he even noticed it. I sure as hell did.

He promised Heather wouldn't live at our apartment.

She had a toothbrush there before the first snowflake hit the ground. Then it was razors in the shower and a box of tampons under the sink. It was bad enough she brought all her she-products into the place, but then she followed that up with herself. It used to be him and me. Now it was her.

The sappy-happy couple would be lounging on the couch when I'd get home from class. They'd make dinner as their incessant chatter could be heard through my door. Their happiness only pissed me off more. I couldn't turn my stereo up loud enough for them to get the point.

Ethan had once rescued me from being a prisoner in my own room. Now he making me one.

Still, I said nothing. I kept quiet, knowing Drink Day was fast approaching.

We'd have so much fun that day Ethan would be Ethan again.

The only established rule for Drink Day was simple: You have to drink.

There was no standing around with a bottle of water, saying you wanted to come out but you still have a paper due. There was no having a few and stopping. To be at a party, you had to be continuously drinking. The peer pressure was going to be outstanding. This would make all those old after-school specials, where the social outcast gives in to the cliché cool kids, look like Saturday Morning Cartoons.

Bottles of gin, whiskey, tequila and whatever else began piling up in cupboards of the houses surrounding campus. They'd all been marked "Do not open until Drink Day." All of the First Prentiss boys were taking this as seriously as Ethan.

He planned for months. He'd still study, spend hours in the library, work at the clinic and such, but when not doing those things, he was getting the word out on Drink Day. The campaign was mostly word-of-mouth, but he employed other tactics. Posters, repeated mass-university wide e-mails, and the like.

The few times he went out with the guys, when *she* wasn't in the equation, it was like using a steel brush to clean him off. He was calmer, more relaxed. He drank less. He'd just chill and not want to get into the hardcore action. No beer bongs. No bongs. No upside down shots. No more pharmaceuticals.

The guys and I would be razzing each other. He would just smile and laugh. His taming was pathetic.

Staying quiet could only last so long.

And then there was Heather.

The razor, the shampoo, the tampons.

That was bad enough. Then she started coming over when Ethan wasn't there. She waited around for him. She tried idle talk with me, but I usually just grunted back at her. I sure as hell wasn't pleased to have to baby-sit his lost puppy.

But I said nothing about her presence. I played it off. I said I didn't care she was there. The first time I did say something I played it off like a joke.

"So we've got another roommate," I said, not looking up from the TV.

"Things haven't changed," Ethan protested, "I've just got one more thing in my life."

One more. Her. One less. Me.

It was how children of divorced parents feel when everyone remarries. The new always takes precedence over the old.

The disconnection between us caused by this chick was appalling. Just seeing her made me want to put cigarettes out in her eyes. Okay, that's a little harsh, but at times that's how I felt. In my better moods, when things were going my way, I made an effort to talk to Heather. We'd talk about nothing in particular, mostly what was on TV or classes. Other times, I just said nothing at all.

Still, I was uncomfortable around them together. The more they turned the apartment into a gooey, mushy love nest, the more I went out.

Drinking four days a week freshman year was nothing. I was up to about six on average now. Weekdays turned into sitting around with Nick and Bubba with a few beers, turned into party-hopping, turned into more Ritalin, turned into coke.

It's not like I had a problem. Gage first turned me on to it near the tail end of Christmas break. That much time to waste so I figured, why not? One call to The Dealer and we snorted our way through a hundred buck's worth. It burned more than he said it would. A gram later and it was dawn.

We started partying around noon. It was just that one time.

It was February and Drink Day was only three weeks away. Months of a fake ID burning a hole in my pocket. I studied it regularly.

Nathan Goodson

DOB: 6/26/79

A lush with a fake would only last so long. I wasn't bursting my bar cherry on Drink Day. Ethan wanted us all to save them for then, but he still owed me.

Eric was the only one willing to use Ethan's gift a little early. Besides, the fakes weren't great, but we had to test them out. Like college bars actually try to keep minors out. If you believe that, then you deserve the beating coming to you.

The bar was called Rascals, I think. No guy at the door, just a cute bartender with a nice rack but an oversized ass. She barely passed for twenty-one herself. And I—being the king shit I am—did everything you shouldn't do. I looked around like a mope. I acted like I was about to get busted. I had no idea what to order. My newbie status was disgusting. I lit a smoke to keep me busy while Eric handled the situation like a pro. He sat down, ordered two Long Island Ice Teas in pint glasses, and immediately looked bored.

The bartender gave half a glance at our IDs and put down our drinks in front of us. I still had my tick that whenever I got nervous I buried myself in my drink. Sip. Smoke. Sip. Smoke.

After my fourth drink in an hour, I started leaking it out that I was only twenty. After long enough, Eric couldn't help but repeatedly smack me on the back of my head. We went to another bar the next night. And the next. And the next. Everything went on my "emergency" credit card. Having a fake and no money constituted an emergency in my eyes.

With my running tabs, the ATM fees were racking up, which called for repeated answers to mommy and daddy to explain why. My dad was so anal-retentive about the thing that he checked the balance online. Daily.

I guess four hundred dollars a week would raise some suspicion.

They bought whatever excuse I gave them.

Books. Supplies for a project. Groceries. Clothes.

Dumbasses.

By the time I'd stumble into the apartment around two in the morning, the light in Ethan's room was off. Her jacket and backpack were always slumped over the arm of the couch. The weeks coming up to Drink Day, we barely saw each other. We had gone from best friends to mere roommates. Barely even that, more like guys who lived in the same place. "Roommates" implies some kind of connection.

The extent of our conversations had become minimal exchanges about rent or whose turn it was to do the dishes. Before he was the only person I wanted to hang out with. Now when he came to the apartment, his "what's up" would be followed with "nuthin'," if anything at all.

Then I stopped answering all together. Then he stopped asking.

He stayed in. I went out.

I had the guys. He had Heather.

The more I was drinking the less I wanted to have our little chitchats with Heather. When she'd come over before Ethan was back from class, I'd explain how hung over I was and what color and consistency my shit was that day. Black. Nothing solid. "Butt pee," was how I think I phrased it. She'd just go into Ethan's room and leave me to my movie or video games or whatever.

Stay in there.

Keep the door shut.

This is my apartment.

You don't pay the rent.

I don't see your name on the fucking lease.

Persona non grata.

But silent I remained.

Drink Day was on its way.

Drink Day: The Cure for the Common Sobriety. That was the headline of the story in the campus newspaper. The buzz caught the nose of the only person on the campus newspaper staff with a life. Or sense of humor. They interviewed Ethan. He said he created it to "force everyone to ease up and relax for one day. Kick back, have a beer." It irked me he didn't give the real reason: *I broke a promise to my best friend.* Whatever. I was just impressed it made the front page.

My idea of Ethan and Heather seemed to be lightening up. Everyone seemed to like them, so I figured it was just a matter of time. Besides, Drink Day was only a few days away. It was all anyone I knew was talking about.

Then there was the hair.

Her long brown hairs were everywhere. After sitting on the couch, I'd have to pull them off my shoulders. They'd be on my jacket after tossing it on the chair. I'd come to terms with all of those things. I'd expected Ethan's bitch to shed.

Then one morning I saw these little brown strands clumped on the wall of the shower. The swirling wad of excrement from Heather's head had been slapped on the stall, obviously when she had stayed the night. That tight coil ate at me the whole time I showered.

The razors, the shampoo, and the fruity-smelling lotions I had grudgingly come to accept. It took a while, but soon they were just part of the scenery of the apartment. Then there were the hairs.

She did it on purpose. Maybe she was trying to make a point.

This was our apartment. Ethan's and mine. That was it. No more.

I don't care how happy they looked together. What people said about how cute of a couple they were was making me sick. Not my normal puking fit sick—the kind of sick you can't shower off. The shower filled with coiled baby Heathers spawning on the wall.

No, silence is not fucking golden.

THIRTY-SIX

Drink Day.

The Saturdays had rolled off the calendar and the last one in February was here. I hadn't seen Ethan that much in the past few weeks, but evidence of his planning was around.

His list had been left on the kitchen counter, the coffee table. It listed the party houses and the number of kegs. With about fifteen to twenty houses, those forty kegs he talked about were going to be gone quickly.

Everyone was talking about it. Even the kids who sat around doing nothing. I overheard the former Lobby Lizards talking about it in the student union one day. A year of sitting around on Friday and Saturday nights had managed to loosen them up by sophomore year.

The Goths. The Preppies. The Emos. The Jocks. The Hippies.

They'd all be at their own respective parties, but hell, Ethan's little holiday was poised to be a hit with everyone. I still couldn't help but be jealous of him.

Drink Day, the day of days, was upon us.

I awoke early that morning. Not college early, *real* early. By seven in the morning, I was dressed and ready to get drinking.

Steve Madden shoes. Jeans from The Gap. T-shirt and button-up collared shirt from Abercrombie. Tweed two-button sport coat from Express. Boxers and matching socks from Calvin Klein.

I had been learning image is everything. It takes away half the work of getting laid. If you look put together, then everyone assumes you are. *American Psycho*'s main character, Patrick Bateman, taught me that, I think.

None of Heather's things were anywhere in the apartment. No jacket, no bag. All her crap was still in the bathroom—including her coiled wads of hair—but there was no evidence she spent the night. There was also none that Ethan had.

After doing my hair and spraying myself with Armani cologne, I called

Collin.

"Hey, where are you?" he asked me. "We've already started."

"Who's 'we'?"

"The guys. Me, Aaron, Zach, Eric, Gage, Nick, Ethan and Bubba."

"Ethan's there?" I asked.

"Yeah, man. He showed up like a half-hour ago."

"I'll be right over."

At the house, the guys were playing Presidents and Assholes at the kitchen table while others were in the living room watching a porno. They started their morning with bloody marys and mimosas. With my shirt and jacket combo, I was overdressed, but the dozen or so girls there took notice right away. Ethan was at the kitchen table with a decent hand of cards. Two twos. Three jacks, a few pair and no real low cards. He saw me come in and heard the corresponding yelling.

Nothing makes you all warm and tingly inside when your best friends yell your name when you walk through the door. Ethan yelled too. He was in one of those great partying moods that I hadn't seen in a while. Heather was nowhere to be seen.

"What's up brother," Ethan said, slapping my hand.

"How's the day lookin'?" I asked.

"Good, good," he said, nodding his head. He threw down his three Jacks as everyone around the table took a drink. "After this, we're going for breakfast at Heather's."

"What?" I asked, a little pissed, but more intrigued.

"Yeah, her, Kristi and a few other girls are making us all pancakes and whatever before we go party-hopping."

"*Fuc-king pan-cakes!*" the other guys growled, getting some laughs from the freshman girls around the table.

Ethan's phone rang as he lobbed down the rest of his cards, round after round. He was declared President as he talked into his phone about something to do with the keg supply at Third Street Liquor.

"No, no, no, don't worry. Jerry said he's got about twelve on hand. If not, there's always the one a few blocks away on Fifth Street," Ethan said into his phone. "No, I got it taken care of. Just tell him I sent you and everything'll be fine."

I grabbed a beer from the fridge as Ethan closed his phone, got up from the table and came over to me.

"This is your day, baby. It's going to kick ass."

Any feelings of resentment I had immediately melted away.

Freshman Ethan was back.

A few hours later, we all walked four blocks down to Heather's place.

In our walk, we saw herds of students, the same amount you'd see freshman week, walking in every direction. One group would yell to the next, "Merry Drink Day."

Hers was a one-story nothing buried deep in the no-college-students section surrounding campus. She shared the house with Kristi, who for the record, managed to completely gain the Freshman Fifteen and then some. STD Stan was right. Sophomores only. So you can see how the fat hits them. In her case, not too well. Heather was the exact opposite, getting better looking every day.

The food was nearly ready when we arrived. These two girls had prepared pancakes, French Toast, sausage, eggs, hash browns and cut up fresh fruit for roughly ten of us.

The guys and I tore through the food, already getting the drunken munchies after only three hours of drinking. It was going to be a long-ass day.

Heather and Kristi stayed behind to clean up our mess. Good girls.

After breakfast, we went to Sixty-Six. Their plans were to have a lawn beanbag tournament, even though it was only forty degrees out and there was still snow on the ground. Screw Mother Nature. This was Drink Day, damn it.

But there were few girls and barely anyone else there that early. The guys who lived there — Scotty, Clint and the others — stayed and played in the snow, but we took off for elsewhere, seeking something more entertaining.

We stopped by the Freedom House around noon after Ethan told us they were grilling out. Drinking keg beer — Busch Light, maybe — and eating Wisconsin-style brats, we hung out in the cold basement playing Quarters on their bar. About forty other kids were there, slamming beer bongs and blue Jell-O shots, screaming and yelling. It was a good mood. Everyone was taking to the new holiday well.

Ethan had been on and off his phone all morning, securing plans for everyone else. Still, he was drinking and partying like nothing ever changed. He just kept smiling and laughing. I was no different.

After about three hits on a bong, Aaron tried conking out—yawning like a bitch and sitting in an armchair while it didn't phase the rest of us. His eyes were red from the weed and glazed from the booze. We hassled the crap out of him until he started playing Quarters with us. Still, he was *Night of the Living Dead* the way he bounced the coin on the table.

The most beautiful part of Drink Day, the part that set it off for us, was that if a party flat-out sucked, you could just high-tail it to another one. This time we got smart and made Ethan make some phone calls first.

The King Street house looked like it was going, so we walked over there.

The cold air and forced movement seemed to wake Aaron up. The herds of students on the sidewalks grew larger. Some would bump into each other and talk about where they were going and what parities were dying out. By two, some of the early morning ones were cashed.

On our way, we stopped by a dingy corner bar. It was the kind with a screen door that scared the crap out of you when it slammed closed. The ten of us wobbled in with fake IDs in hand. A stern-faced couple looked up from the bar as a fifty-something guy propped up his John Deere hat. Besides them, there was no one else in the place.

All eyes were on us as we sat at the long bar, which looked like it'd been carved out of a Redwood. Gage attempted to get the bartender's attention away from the fishing show on the television above his head.

"Three pitchers of your cheapest beer," Gage said.

The thick-fingered bartender, aware of what was asked, barely flinched. He said, "We don't serve college students."

It's a song and dance we've heard before. Not those exact words, but it's the same as going to a restaurant and watching our drinks sit empty for a half hour while waitresses stand in the back, waiting for us to get the hint. It's the rolling of the eyes at the gas station. It's the huffing we get when we ask a Big Box employee where's the toilet paper.

These townies. The college was here before they were born. Deal with it.

After enough silence as the bartender watched a guy yank a bass into his boat, I yell, "Fuck you townie! We've got more money among us than you'll make all month. Serve … us … the … fucking … beer!"

Ethan had already stood up with the rest of the guys. He put one arm on my shoulder and pulled me away.

"Let it go," he said.

"No, fuck this asshole and the white trash with him!"

The bartender wasn't even phased. He'd heard this all before. Calmly he picked up the phone and pointed to a sign behind him. We reserve the right to refuse service to anyone, the sign said.

"Leave or I'm calling the cops," the bartender said to the TV.

We all left, slamming the screen behind us. I was fuming while the rest of the guys laughed.

"Dude, that was *awe*some," Bubba said.

"Enough of that crap, let's go to King," Zach said.

It had been a while since I'd been to the King Street house—even longer with Ethan. More than a year after we had first partied there and not a thing had changed. The same songs could be heard from outside the house as when I first stepped inside as a measly little freshman. The sights and smells hadn't changed either. The air was thick with the familiar smells of flat beer and cigarette smoke, with an occasional whiff of weed added in.

Some things were different.

Ethan was the first one in the door, everyone at the kitchen table yelling, "Ethaaaaan!" The other guys went in behind him, slapping and shaking hands with the regulars. "Chriiiiiiis!" they yelled as I came in. I knew almost everyone there from somewhere, mostly other party houses, and most recently, the bars.

Some things were the same.

Ethan handed me a red plastic cup. Since it was *his* holiday, and he was orchestrating it from behind the scenes, he sure-as-shit wasn't paying for anything. We could hear everyone downstairs, but our gracious hosts blessed us with a pitcher and sent me downstairs to fill it. I lit a cigarette and went down the creaky wooden stairs.

If a fire broke out, all of these kids would be dead.

Again, the crowd moved in unison. I moved through them avoiding the splashing of beer everyone else was wearing. I made my way to the keg, which was surrounded by beer-greedy freshmen. One guy on the outside noticed me.

"I'll get that, man," he said, grabbing the plastic pitcher and hoisting above his head. "House pitcher!"

This skinny blonde-haired kid passed back the full pitcher, his cup still empty. He reminded me of myself at my first time at that house. He held his cup out to me.

"Fill me up bud?" he asked.

With my cigarette in my mouth, I looked right him with squinted eyes. "Fuck yourself freshman," I said. "You have to earn it."

I walked through the horde and back upstairs.

The guys weren't in the kitchen. I looked around as Jim, one of the guys renting the house, pointed with his thumb to the living room. There, the guys were stretched out over the chairs and couches, their feet up on the wood and cinder block coffee table. Ethan sat next to Heather. It was a sight I'd like to be appalled by, but it was half-expected she'd show up sooner or later. Kristi sat next to Heather. An open seat was next to her. I filled my beer, sat the pitcher down and sat next to Kristi.

Aaron looked like he was about to pass out before Collin slapped him across the face. He woke up and tried to slap him back, but his groggy motions were pitiful. Everyone laughed, even the girls. Heather and Kristi downed their beers as Heather went back downstairs with the pitcher.

Okay, for a girl who took my best friend away from me, she wasn't half-bad. She did make us breakfast and fetched us beer. Besides, Drink Day wasn't supposed to be a day of drama. We could save that for another time.

Hours went by, along with daylight, and we kept latched on to the King house. All of us kept bouncing between the living room, basement, bathroom and kitchen. The Dealer even showed up, passing around some herb brownies he made for the occasion. It was on the house considering how well his business was going that day—thanks to Ethan. Rarely will you ever find a drug dealer to *ever* show gratitude, no matter how good you are in his graces. He came up to me in the basement.

"Diet Coke?" he asked, flashing a small bag of pills in his hand.

"Uh…yeah. I'm out."

For twenty bucks, I got four. It's a lot more expensive if you don't have a prescription or a hookup at the student health clinic. The Dealer gave me a little something extra for free. These pills I recognized. Vicodin. I shoved them all in my pocket and waited for the opportune moment.

EthanandHeather weren't always together, so I wasn't getting my nauseous feeling. Freshmen kept coming up to Ethan, introducing themselves and thanking him for Drink Day. These little worshippers treated Ethan like God. He had projected his savior-like abilities onto them just by getting everyone together for parties.

I was waiting in line for the bathroom, half-cocked, when Kristi came up behind me. She started with whatever bullshit banter to keep from us having to stand together in silence. After the silence returned, she dropped into something I wish she wouldn't have. It wasn't hard to tell she'd been drinking all day.

"I think it's pretty cool how well you took the whole thing."

"What *whole thing*?" I asked.

"The EthanandHeather thing."

"What the *hell* are you talking about?"

"The way they started dating and you were cool with it."

"Why wouldn't I be?"

"Oh, come on. It was obvious how much you liked her."

I pounded on the bathroom door to make my point clear, but she just kept talking.

"The way you stared at her in class. The way we went out with them when they first started dating. And even now, the way you act all pissy around her. She knows you don't hate her, despite how hard you try to make it look that way."

She was being a pushy little cunt right then, but I was still contemplating boning her.

"What in *God's name* is taking so long in there," I yell at the door.

"Admit it, you don't hate her," Kristi said. "You kind of like her … in your own way."

The bathroom door opened at the perfect moment. Some hefty football-looking bastard came out and wasn't too impressed with my impatience, but with only a mean look, he passed by Kristi and me.

I closed the door in her face and took the most refreshing piss in the history of pisses. On the sink, I crushed up two Ritalin and snorted the lines with a rolled-up dollar bill and washed down a Vicodin with my beer. My mind instantly cleared and that great calming feeling from the painkillers would visit me in another twenty minutes. A gentle knock came from the other side of the door.

I unlocked it and Kristi stared at me.

"Admit it," she said.

"Admit *what*?"

"Admit you secretly like Heather," she said, her drunkenness even more obvious. She leaned in on me, putting one arm in the doorway to stop me from getting by.

"Why is this such a big deal to you? Let it go," I said.

"Because," Kristi said, looking ungodly desperate and sad. "I want to know what makes her so special? Tell me."

Ethan was right. Every college girl secretly hates any friend that gets more attention. Heather and Kristi say they love each other in the sorority kind of way, but it was all bullshit. Loyalty in college is in short supply, especially among roommates.

I was starting to get pissed. All I wanted was the warm feeling of the mixing stimulants, depressants and whatever was left of the weed to wash over me.

Deliver me, oh Vin Vin Vin.

To Kristi, I said, "Whatever. What-*the-fuck*-ever. What do you want?"

"God, you are dense sometimes," she said.

She grabbed me by my shirt and started licking the inside of my mouth. At first I kissed back to keep her from talking, but I caught on to where this was heading. We left the party together without telling anyone and went for my place because it was close. The whole time half of her footsteps were sideways on the snowy sidewalks. I half-carried her up the stairs. The Vicodin began working well with the Ritalin.

We started stripping each other in the living room. I had her shirt and jeans off when she whispered in my ear, "The shower."

The room began steaming up as we climbed in. It was then I realized that fucking in a shower takes a certain level of acrobatic strength that neither of us had. It takes even more ability with a fat chick.

I bent her over as she grabbed a hold of the faucet. The water hit her back and rolled down the crack of her ass and onto my dick. She began moaning immediately. I tried not to touch her chubby thighs.

The razor. The fruity shampoo.

I pushed harder. Kristi yelled "Travis" and I didn't even care.

The tight little coiled piles of hair stuck to the walls. I shoved myself in her, harder each time. Her head hit the wall and she let out a different kind of moan. Her head kept making a thumping noise, but I didn't care.

I grabbed the hair off the wall and stuck it to Kristi's back before the water washed it down the drain. I wasn't wearing a condom because she never told me to and I didn't care.

"You … better pull out … before you … come," she said between moans and pants.

Harder. Her head hit the wall again before I finished and purposely sprayed her back. She might have had an orgasm, but I didn't care. I stepped out of the shower, wrapped myself in a towel and went to the kitchen for a beer.

Kristi came out of the bathroom as I sat on the couch watching TV. Another towel barely covered her grotesquely huge body.

"You can go now," I said to her.

She said something back.

I didn't care.

THIRTY-SEVEN

There are plenty of things Ethan's suicide taught me.

If a young guy kills himself, you can search for his motivation all you want and you probably won't find it.

There's always someone to blame.

Ethan's obit hitting the paper on St. Patrick's Day pretty much guaranteed an Irish wake. That and his mom's maiden name is O'Leary.

At that particular Irish bar, in that particular small town, on that sacred day, you can be sure no one will get turned away. I passed the doorman my fake ID, but he was so blasted on Guinness and Irish Car Bombs that it wouldn't matter if a school bus of second-graders wanted in. He handed it back after the quickest of glances and returned to his glass of whiskey.

It wasn't really an authentic Irish pub. It looked like a former sports bar that had been slapped with a fresh coat of paint, a few Irish flags on the wall and some four-leaf clovers on the coasters. It was dark, but on this auspicious of evenings it was alive with fun-loving people.

After the dealings with mommy dearest, the walk and the remaining journal pages I had yet to read burning a hole in my jacket pocket, I could have used a couple of unknown grinning faces.

I sat on the bar stool surrounded by plastic green hat-wearing jackasses.

I pulled the journal from my pocket went back to where I had been in the basement. I digested everything. Judging by the way Kathy was drinking, popping pills and attempting to seduce her dead son's friend, I didn't think she'd miss what Ethan was writing about. The way she asked me if it was her fault, I didn't think she really wanted to learn anything more than she already knew.

Page after page, I continued trying to connect the entries to specific occurrences. Lord knows when the damned thing even began or when he wrote the last one. I feared I knew that answer, but I didn't skip to the end. My cell phone kept buzzing with text messages from First Prentiss.

Inside, Ethan had this bitter loathing for himself. Somehow he'd got it into his head that striving to be his best wasn't good enough—perfection was necessary. He found solace in what he wrote. It was an attempt to discover who he was at that moment.

My phone rang. Aaron had just got into town and wanted to know where I was.

Ethan wanted to have life figured out right now. He didn't want to wait. Bubba was in town. "Big Willie McGinty's," I told him over the phone.

Somehow Ethan felt this force around him telling him he was a failure. He couldn't see what he had and what he threw away. His writing showed me he was confused as any of us. I felt better knowing that not even Ethan knew who Ethan was.

As Aaron walked in the door, I closed the journal, quickly stuffing it back into my pocket. I had more to read, and I wasn't interested in answering any questions about it yet. Bubba, Collin and Gage followed Aaron in.

It wasn't long before people overheard Ethan's name in our conversation. I wasn't surprised how many people in there knew him. At least this crowd knew who he was. The death aficionados shrouded in black on campus came back in mind.

Steve Costello's son?

"The local boy who died recently? How'd that happen anyway?" one fat drunk man asked. He didn't know Ethan. He just wanted to quell his curiosity after scouring the listed dead on page A5.

"He gave a Beretta a blow job," I said rather bluntly and a little drunk. I glared at the fat man.

"Oh," he said realizing he touched a nerve. "Betcha that must'a been messy."

He was trying to make a joke. Use humor when it's awkward, that was his defense mechanism. Not funny.

"Yeah, we still can't find his ear," I said back, still glaring.

The guy ducked his head and walked away. He bought our next round.

There were high school friends. People who remembered Ethan from junior high were there. Old friends from odd jobs, people who knew his parents. It was that group that never left town that knew Ethan the best. The people he vowed never to become.

I think I even met the abortion girl. This cute little blonde with nipples poking through her green T-shirt. She came up to us saying, she dated him until he left for college. I was the only one of us who knew about her significance in Ethan's life. Slyly, at least I thought it was, I asked her why she didn't go to college.

"There's no way my parents could afford it," she said. "Ethan was the lucky one who got out of here."

I remembered her scholarship. The reason Ethan told me she didn't want to have the kid.

"What about scholarships?" I pressed loudly over some Irish music and drunken idiots.

"No, no way. My grades were never good enough for that."

She said little else and before I knew it, she had returned to her boyfriend.

Great. Add that to the list of things I thought I knew about my best friend. Things I was wrong about.

Me and the rest of First Prentiss that showed up, we talked about everything. We shared the same memories again, the same we did when we were together when Ethan was alive. The circumstances of each event seemed to gain exaggerated details every time we told it.

In death, Ethan became a god. The same way I viewed him when I first met him. The parties were bigger. The pranks were more elaborate. The girls' boobs were bigger. We talked about everything.

What wasn't mentioned were the last words I had with him. That's mostly because I was the one telling the stories. I still managed to keep my PR face on when it came to his death. I was still in control of what people knew. I was the filter.

And the night went on. And on. We kept pumping money into the jukebox. Mainly we wanted to keep the sad songs from coming on. When you're trying to get smashed in your friend's memory, you don't want songs that are going to make people start crying. A bar full of grown men pouting over their dead friend is such a buzz-kill.

And in the tradition of Irish wakes and St. Patty's Day, we got rowdy. We were throwing ice cubes, jigging like idiots and rumbling on the floor. As Collin and I were rolling around, my head hit a barstool. It was hard enough for the guys to ask if I was alright, but it barely phased me. I went to the bathroom to snort some Ritalin.

It was a nice way of ignoring everything. Our jackass nature was a nice distraction. Alcohol created the numbness we all needed.

Get drunk, that was my defense mechanism.

Even with our usual antics, there was still the knowledge that Ethan was dead. More drinking lead to more thinking. No one doubted how good a guy he was, but it was about time for someone to tell everyone. Someone had to make a speech about the twenty-year-old man we were putting in the ground tomorrow. It wasn't my idea, but I was the obvious choice. Volunteer, I did not.

"Dude, you were his fucking roommate," Zach said.

"Yeah," Eric chimed in. "He liked you the best."

After enough shoving from the now eight or nine guys from school now there, I stepped up on a stool and hopped up on the bar. Why, I don't know. It seemed to fit.

"What can I say about Ethan Costello?" I said.

All of the faces in the bar were at my attention. The bartender had switched off the music.

"What can I say?"

Thinking about him was something I didn't want to do. I thought of the first day I met him. His words of advice. The way he helped me start the downfall that was my undoing.

I thought of his pill-popping nymphomaniac mother. I thought of this teenage kid who wanted nothing more than to hang out with his dad. The way he never talked about any of it. That was also in my head.

The way he was always calm under pressure. The fact that everyone knew and liked him. The way he could control a party. The way he spent endless hours in the library preparing for a future he no longer had. The image of himself he kept in his head. The ideas of who he felt he should be.

Ethan was dead and everyone wanted me to say something about him.

What would you say about your savior? The person who delivered you from all that was boring? The person who was exactly what you needed at precisely the right time?

A churchgoer could go on for hours about Christ, but at this moment I couldn't say a damn thing about Ethan Costello. I didn't know him. None of us did. We all knew him from different places. Places where he felt he had to be someone else to be accepted.

Ethan didn't know himself.

Here was this person who I had thought I had figured out. I know now he had tried to change his life by getting out of the stupor I stayed in every night. He tried grabbing at something better and I wouldn't tolerate it. I wanted him to stay the way I met him. I had introduced myself as a naïve kid who thought the best of life was to come from getting plastered all the time. Now that I do, I miss who I had been. I don't miss my social stammering, the kind I was doing now as I stood silent on the bar.

I missed the way everything was new to me. I missed Ethan. I wished he was there at that time, egging me on as I searched for the right thing to say about him. The guy who had helped me gain confidence and I was too dumbstruck to spew out a word in his favor.

The closest person to me died and I felt nothing. I wanted to cry like a normal person would.

With all eyes on me, I finally got it. I realized something that should have been clear long before. I wasn't more confident. I was an asshole. Booze was my self-esteem. It was all I knew. I was in a perpetual hangover hooked on liquid courage. I wasn't addicted the way alcoholics were, alcohol had just become the crutch I had leaned on more every day. At first it was Ethan. Then my other friends took his place.

Sam Adams, Evan Williams, Jack Daniels, Johnny Walker, Michael Collins, Jose Cuervo, Johnny Love and Jim Beam.

Getting drunk was all I knew. If it weren't for parties, drinking games or shots, I'd return to the sniveling piss ant I was before. Wednesday, Thursday, Friday, Saturday. These were the only days I felt like I was alive. It wasn't because that's when I had fun. It's the only time when I felt I was able to relax.

Repetition was all I knew.

Ethan wanted something else. I killed him because of it.

And finally I started talking.

"Ethan Costello was dead before he was alive. We all could have been better to him considering how good he was to all of us. None of us should aspire to live our lives like him."

The faces in the bar scrunched. Some looked pissed, some looked confused. That really wasn't the tone they were looking to hear, but it was true. I think they were expecting something about how much he loved life, how he'll be sorely missed by all, and how we'll get tattoos in his memory.

"We should all want to be the way he wanted, the way we saw him. We all thought we had him figured out, but we were all wrong."

The crowd still wasn't content.

They wanted their post-suicide clichés, but I wasn't going to give them any. They all would have been a lie anyway. Like they usually are.

"Ethan spent his entire life trying to fool people. And he did that well. We had him pegged as something. We envied his confidence."

And I paused, looking in my glass, the ice cubes jingling. I sighed.

"He was faking it all. He figured if he could pretend hard enough, he'd convince himself. He finally realized it wasn't going to happen."

That's no way to talk about your dead friend. That's what their faces were saying. I was looking right at First Prentiss.

"We … all of his friends … we were his family. We betrayed him. We abandoned him when he reached for better things. This is all our fault."

There's that blame again. Someone needs to take the fall. I finally got smart and made sure everyone did. I'm not going down alone.

"Don't make a martyr out of him."

The faces were not even close to happy. With that many people looking at me, there was no way I was ending this public speaking event comparing Ethan to a fucking saint. Yeah, I owed him a lot, but not that much.

I drew from my extensive mental bank of drinking toasts and movie lines. I smiled and raised my glass in the air. Everyone else slowly followed.

"May your glass be ever full. May the roof over your head be always strong. And we should all pray Ethan made it to heaven before the devil knew he was dead."

The devil always knew he was coming.

"Cheers."

The toast was tainted from my lingering profession of how Ethan's should haunt us all for the rest of our lives.

Hopping off the bar, I threw my glass behind me. Jack and Coke went everywhere. The glass shattered in front of the bar. How fitting.

I pushed my way out the door, past First Prentiss, past the doorman who tried snagging my arm to pay for the glass. I didn't care what was going around me or what the guys thought of my little performance. All I knew is that I didn't want to hang out and talk about my dead best friend any more.

Walking to my hotel, nothing was going through my head. I got what I wanted.

Up to this point, I've done everything I needed to do. I've searched for answers and in my quest, I discovered what I didn't want to know. I would have been better off keeping up the charade. Somewhere, something went wrong. Somehow, I stopped caring.

I just wanted to return to my blissfully stupid ways.

Now I was back in a place I didn't want to be — dumb, drunk and alone.

Until now, I had never realized it.

Blame was put on everyone. Everyone but me. We all knew that it was Ethan's fault. There are just a couple of us that were more culpable than the others.

A few of us could have prevented it.

THIRTY-EIGHT

Hanging has been one of the most infamous forms of execution for those who didn't want to die, but their governments said they should. During the 1800s in England, ironically, if you failed to do the job yourself, your punishment was to be hung.

Fortunately, for you, it's still a stylish way to die.

The key to making your hanging death as quick and painless as possible is all about supports. You want to find a sturdy one at least ten feet above the ground. If you use the over-publicized "standing on a chair and kicking it out from underneath you" method, you'll spend up to five minutes dangling, spinning and kicking at the end of a rope. If you're discovered and saved, you'll probably be a vegetable for the rest of your life. That, and as your body invokes every natural spasm to prevent its ultimate demise, you'll piss yourself in the process.

The secret to hanging, besides the sturdy support, is how far you have to drop. The lighter you are, the farther you need to fall. If you're around two hundred pounds, eight feet will do. If you're a one-hundred pound sickling, nothing less than ten feet or it's asphyxiation. You don't want that. Talk about painful.

The rope has to be sturdy and long enough to support your weight multiplied by the deceleration of your falling body.

Rope = Lbs. × Decel. = Success!

Then there's the self-poisoning technique that's popular with the ladies. Unfortunately, it's also the creator of the most botched suicides ever. Knocking back a handful of Tylenol, Advil or Aleve won't do it. It'll just get you high and leave you with a nasty hangover. Oh yeah, and possible liver or brain damage.

Over-the-counter drugs aren't it. If you drink bleach, you'll just have a long painful puking match. Your body has a natural instinct to protect itself from anything stupid you want to do with it. That's why you'll end up throwing up most of whatever you ingested.

You could just go out like a rock star and cook up an extra large batch of heroin, but that stuff's impossible to find when you're actually looking for it.

But, if you want the man's way of dying to preserving honor—unlike other girly ways of suicide—there's Seppuku, the Japanese ritual method of suicide practiced with regularity in medieval times.

Dress up in ceremonial garb, write a death poem, open your kimono and shove a razor-sharp tantō into your stomach. Cut left to right and then upward. On the second slice, your attendant—and yes, you have to have a friend for this one—would perform a daki-kubi. Basically, he would all but decapitate you. Since your friend will most likely get charged with your murder, he better be a really good friend.

During the Sixteenth Century, the Chinese ate a pound of salt to commit suicide.

A .22-caliber shot to the temple won't work. If you aim wrong the bullet will ricochet off your skull and ruin your hairline. If you do it right, the bullet will go in your skull, but won't have enough force to get out. It'll bounced around inside, tearing everything to shreds.

A Florida man was charged with murder after his suicide attempt. He surprised his ex-girlfriend and her husband in their home, put the gun to his chin and pulled the trigger. The bullet skipped off his teeth, out his cheek and into the husband's head. He died almost instantly.

Almost without fail, a shotgun in the mouth is a money shot. Point that baby at the back of your brain. One hand on the trigger, one on the barrel. If you don't hold on up top, your flinch moves the blast to the side of your mouth. You'll be laying there on the floor, staring at the pieces of your jaw on the wall. The gunshot will summon onlookers, who will help you out of your pathetic failure.

Imagine living with only half a face. And you thought your were ridiculed before.

A Lithuanian man wanted to shoot himself but didn't have a gun. But he had a bullet. Putting it in a pan on the hot stove, he held his head over the bullet for what must have been an eternity. And he waited. And he fell asleep. With his mouth open. He awoke to a bang as the trick worked, but sent the bullet through his cheek. Afterwards, he said he was lucky to be alive.

An exit wound out the cheek isn't from stupidity. It's from jerking on a last-second guess. That flinch is your heart changing. After feeling your finger or toe easing the trigger back, you decide you don't really want to die.

But that comes too late.

There's self-immolation, if being burned alive is your thing. You'll be able to feel your blood boil inside your skin, which I've heard is fun. Great if you're making a point in the middle of Times Square, but there's a chance some hero will throw a coat over you to put out your broiling ass. Visit a burn unit and look what happens to the survivors.

Suicide bombing, suicide by cop and jumping in front of cars. Just don't do it. Just because you want to die doesn't give you the right to take unwilling participants with you.

Fuck those school shooters. The ones who gun down their unarmed classmates. Eric and Dylan felt like everyone at Columbine needed to pay for their ridicule. The Virginia Tech massacre was the same thing. Getting picked on doesn't give you the right to go on a rampage. You just prove everyone right — you're a little pussy. Having a gun doesn't change a thing.

Some Illinois asshole tried committing suicide by asphyxiation. He filled his apartment with natural gas but it blew. Three other people died and he was taken into federal custody. At court hearings, he never looked at the families of those he killed.

Be private about it. Go quietly. Stop being such a bother.

Unless you can find a cult the feds are going after.

If you recall the mass-suicide of Jonestown in 1978, a punch bowl filled with cyanide and Flavor Aide works well for groups. More than nine-hundred died. They all drank the magical punch or shot themselves. Many wanted to after listening to Jimmy Jones, the pedophilic, drug-addicted leader.

Why die alone, right?

But don't go because someone tells you to. We're told what to do since birth. Why commit suicide the same way?

If you're going to die, do it because you want to.

Find an isolated place so no one can come in and try to rescue you. If you're serious about killing yourself, this is important. If you just want to fake one, just so you can get attention, you want to make sure there's going to be someone around to step in and make you change your mind. That's if they care enough to make you stop. They could just want a front row seat to your death.

But, if you're not serious about throwing everything away and taking the easy way out, don't go messing around. Don't fuck with death. It has no sense of humor.

Becoming a martyr or trying to get back at someone is just a myth purported by suicide enthusiasts. Do you think someone is worth dying over, especially just to ruin her day? Didn't think so.

Those who spend all day long talking and thinking about suicide want you to believe suicide is the only way to die.

Suicide as a fashion statement.

For the cult of death aficionados, death is the "in" thing. Don't let them convince you they're experts at suicide. They don't know shit. They're still alive.

Suicide is unnatural. No other species besides homo sapiens does it. Except lemmings, but those glorified rats are too stupid know what they're doing when they follow each other in line to their deaths.

The elderly people who use death doctors, they're sure they want to die. They make an appointment and pay someone to kill them. They've thought about it, not wanting to continue with what's left of their life as they die of some horrible disease that's excruciatingly painful. They've told people about their decision. They've said their goodbyes.

They've spent their whole lives working to become strong people and after a while they're helpless, dependent on everyone else to feed them, change their diapers, and wipe the white crusty stuff from the corners of their mouths. The whole while, their kids are spending what's left of their retirement account like they've been dead for years.

When life is like that, death is a vacation.

Then some merchant of death comes in with a lethal cocktail to send searing through their veins. He double-checks, making sure all the witnesses in the room are positive the near-dead are ready to go.

They go to sleep. They don't wake up. In the last fleeting of moments of life, while so wasted from the chemicals, finally the pain is gone. They smile. The disease dies with them.

That's not suicide. That's just dying with dignity.

It's been going on forever. The ancient Britons euthanized themselves by jumping off cliffs. If you were too sick or old, you likely got a helpful shove from someone.

The Kevorkian family tree is deeply rooted.

Doctors are sixty percent more likely to kill themselves than the rate for women. Psychologists kill themselves twice as often as their patients.

Assuming you get out clean, and your suicide is quick, painless and successful, you still have hell to look forward to.

That's only if you believe in that sort of thing.

Risking eternal damnation because your girlfriend broke up with you doesn't sound like a good idea to me. Besides, you want to be around while she gets fat. They always do.

But you really don't want to die. You just think you do.

There's nothing out there worth dying over. No one.

Screw your parents. Screw your ex. Screw everyone that says you can't do something. If you really want to piss people off, stay alive. If you blow your face off because you can't handle it, they win. You're dead and not annoying them anymore. Stick around just to get under their skin. I guarantee in your adventures of annoying the crap out of people while you're still kicking around this plane of existence, you'll find another reason to live.

Some British guy's wife left him. He wanted to die. Three months and seven tries later, he hadn't got it just right. He survived overdoses. He wrapped himself in raw electrical wire and plugged himself in while sitting in the tub. The fuse blew. They always do. Due to modern wiring, just like the Brit, you'll end up with some electrical burns and smelling like beef soup.

Hanging himself with the wire didn't work either. Lighting a smashed gas pipe in his place just blew the whole thing up. He survived with flash burns. After all of this, scarred flesh included, he ended up on speaking terms with his wife.

Go figure.

Thirty-nine

The line of people waiting to get into the funeral home extended out the front door.

Their faces reflected their hangovers after a night of green beer and cabbage. Or maybe that's what people are supposed to look like at funerals. I don't know. This was my first one. My parents had successfully shielded me from the deaths of any great-grandparents or long-lost uncles. Until this point in my life, death was nothing I had to deal with.

Ethan was the right age to ensure maximum funeral attendance. Just outside of high school, deep into college, hundreds of people would show. Everyone had fresh memories of him. With him. He was half a century away from when reading the newspaper only meant checking the obits for your friends. Too many people were around to remember him as a baby.

Parents should never have to bury their children. Unfortunately, Steve and Kathy Costello did. And unlike a car accident or homicide, Ethan's young death didn't come with an easy person to blame. No other driver or gunman. Suicide just left a lot of questions.

No one had any answers just yet and there was still a funeral before they could put him in the ground. There's still that need to have the public showing of grief. There's this room of people where no one wants to talk about the reasons that brought them all here. In small conversations in back rooms, people talk about who should have known and how they failed to help the newly departed.

Casting blame is all we know.

I tried avoiding everyone by purposely showing up late. It was bad enough I couldn't get the wrinkles out of my pin-striped suit using my hotel room's iron. Apparently suits don't travel well stuffed into duffle bags.

Then there were the newfound enemies I had made at the bar the night before. Putting someone's death on others' shoulders wasn't what they wanted to hear, but it was something I needed to say. Still, I was the killjoy.

And then Kathy. Ethan's nympho mom.

Heather. Outside of our short conversation on campus, I had successfully shirked her. I hoped to continue that here.

Disobeying the rank-and-file of the mourners dressed in their best black clothes, I went in the front door and right into the viewing room. Kathy was inside, greeting everyone as they processed in.

Underneath her black sun hat, her little black dress wrapped around that tight body. The dress was small enough to show her underwear lines. That is, if she would have been wearing any. Spotting me trying to sneak by, she grabbed me by the arm and pulled me close to her.

"Steve won't be here. He had a last minute meeting in St. Louis," she whispered into my ear. The brim of her hat poked the bruise on my forehead from the barstool the night before.

"He won't be home for *two days*."

The First Prentiss guys hovered over the table of hors d'oeuvres. None of them saw me go through the room. Or, they completely ignored me.

There in the throngs of people — some old, most my age — I couldn't see one person who understood Ethan. There was no way anyone could have gotten him. Or who he pretended to be.

Ethan had us all fooled. Except himself.

He was stuck somewhere between the conformity that he despised and the independence he longed for. He learned to shed his skin. His journal, the one in my jacket pocket, showed me this much. One minute he was the partier. Next, he was the clown. The thinker. The good son. The best friend. Being his friend taught me this.

Searching for one mindset, Ethan found no happiness.

The line of friends and family weaved around to look at the photos displayed on the tan coffin, kept closed because of his injuries.

All the king's horses and all the king's men couldn't put Ethan's face back together again.

Bumping into arms and shoulders of those who had a view of Ethan different from the next, I could hear proposed explanations for the suicide. All of them wrong. It wasn't answers they were searching for. They wanted someone, something to take responsibility. They wanted to find a word to sum everything up so they could categorically dismiss it.

Depression. Attachment issues. Failure of acceptance. School pressures. Uncertainty of his future.

It was nothing short of casting him out in hopes to keep themselves away from the stigma of suicide. It wouldn't work.

We were all to blame. We all failed him. We all fail each other.

Ethan's exit was a message to all of us. There is no way to protect ourselves from our view of everyone we knew. He put a gun blast in the face of everything we thought we knew about the person standing next to us.

If someone like Ethan could do this, who's next?

There was no single answer. Nothing would be explained. We would get no comforting closure so we could wash our hands of Ethan's blood.

Only Ethan had the answer and he took it with him.

Still, I wanted one. I, too, felt as if I was owed something. My investment in his life should come with a payback.

Closer to the casket, I saw all of the photos lined up. Ethan playing T-ball. Holding a bass he caught when hot pink shorts were acceptable. His grandfather giving him a whisker rub, Ethan's face lit up in adolescent agony.

I couldn't help but smile.

Up until this week, it was hard to realize that someone with such authority in my life actually came from somewhere. He was someone before the day I met him. He had memories outside the ones I knew about.

All of the aunts, uncles, cousins, grandparents, neighbors and friends looked at me. It wasn't my wrinkled suit or bruised forehead. It wasn't my toast from the night before. It wasn't my cutting in line. They all knew something I didn't.

Finally, Ethan seemed human. Before his death, before Heather even told me her name, there were no faults. He was the golden calf I had built up in my mind.

The pictures showed me that he too was scared at one point. He had been alone. He had felt the walls closing in. His room told me. Kathy told me. In his journal, Ethan told me.

I just didn't see it was happening right before me. He fooled me.

It was supposed to me that panicked. I was the insecure one. Run from trouble. That was me. It was me that was supposed to be in that coffin, although I probably would have slashed my wrists. Less messy, easy to clean up. A slow gradual decline. Nothing too drastic.

No, Ethan and I weren't truly different. In essence, we were the same person. The only difference was I was honest with myself. I admitted my weaknesses. I'd grown from them instead of hiding from them.

His downfall was trying to convince everybody he was just like them and unique at the same time. Ethan tried playing chameleon. He was an actor, forever playing a role to deceive us all. He had us all fooled, but not himself.

In all of the photos he was smiling. It now seems odd that a person torturing himself could fake happiness long enough for the flash to go off. Maybe he was happy at times, but I couldn't figure out when.

As the line of mourners progressed, so did Ethan's age in all of the photos. At the end of the line, everything post-high school was tacked up on poster board. A huddle formed around it. I nudged my way into the center, eyeing the collage.

Ethan and I at homecoming. Me and him in front of the dorm flashing our fake First Prentiss gang signs. He and I the night we met Heather. The cops in the background.

Me holding his feet on a keg stand. What kind of parent puts that photo up for a funeral?

Me and Ethan. Ethan and I. Out of all the people this college socialite knew, I was the only one in the photos. His mom said he talked about me, but to what extent, I didn't know. This guy knew everyone. Everyone knew him, yet all these photos told me and everyone else that I was his only real friend.

I was the only person who should have known.

I was the one.

I was the one to blame.

My best friend killed himself. I didn't save him the way he saved me. I chose not to.

My savior, he's dead.

I failed him.

Me. I was to blame.

Looking around, all eyes remained on me. Everyone wanted someone to feel the guilt and it was me. The pictures told the story.

One person knew Ethan the best. He did nothing. He went out drinking.

The faces were angry. A few were sad. None were sympathetic to me. Their eyes told me they had it figured out the way I had.

Everyone stared.

The only sound was a bagpiper's version of *Amazing Grace* playing over the speakers.

How sweet the sound.

Only one thing could make it worse. And it did.

Without notice, I threw up.

Chris will puke.

Before Ethan was dead, it had been a while since my last random barfing fest. I had managed to control it. Not anymore.

The upheaval projected out of my mouth and slapped all over the poster board. All over the pictures of Ethan and I and everyone near it. It was everything I drank the night before.

An anonymous communal moan was heard. People pulled their hands, arms and legs away from me in disgust.

There was no lower feeling than this.

Now it was obvious. *Everyone* was staring.

Save a wretch like me.

Standing there with some of Ethan's family wearing my stomach contents, I had only two choices. I could have stood there and defended myself. I could have tried to blame everyone else. It was their fault, too. I wasn't the only one. I could have stayed and stood my ground.

Instead, I chose flight.

I pushed my way out of the crowd, stumbling at the start until my body took over for me. It was telling me to get the hell out of there. Out the doors, past the parking lot, my legs carried me as my arms swung with them.

Blocks went by and I kept going.

The possible signs screamed through my mind. The abortion, his rebellion, every piece of advice, our last conversation, our friends. Campus terrorism. Homecoming. Drink Day. Hours in the library. They were all I had now. Left to dissect in my brain.

Stories. Memories. The rest was waste.

Heather stuck out the most.

I kept doing the only things I knew how to do. Panic. Run.

It wasn't until I passed an aging diner, down the hill, past my hotel and the movie theater that I stopped. There was nowhere else to go once I hit the river's edge. Ten blocks later was I was stuck.

There was no going back.

I once was lost.

I hope I'm never found.

FORTY

Weeks had passed since Drink Day.

I thought the cure for the common sobriety had cured all ills between Ethan and I. I thought I had him back. I was wrong. It wasn't the first time.

"Your bitch is shedding."

The hair. The little clumps of Heather left in the shower.

That's how I said hello when I heard the front door of our apartment close. I knew it was Ethan because Heather had learned to close it quietly and try to hide her entrance. Good dog.

"What the hell did you say?"

That was how Ethan said hello.

"Your… bitch… is… shedding." I repeated it slower, not looking up from my video game. I had just smoked a chick on the sidewalk with a sawed-off shotgun.

It was March 14. Shit between Ethan and I had been silently brewing, even as he and Heather spent less time at the apartment. Silence would no longer be the status quo with me.

Ethan stood in front of the TV. You don't want to do that to a guy playing such a violent video game. Not a good idea. I told him to move, but he didn't.

"Alright, I'm sick of this. What's your problem with her?" he said.

His tone was that he finally wanted to say something. Or hear it.

"Oh, besides her constant presence in this apartment?"

Let me think. The hair in the shower. Homecoming. The extinction of the former you. EthanandHeather. No Chris and Ethan.

"She doesn't fucking live here!" I yelled at him after jumping up from the couch. I stood right in his face.

"And while were on the subject, let's not forget how *you* follow her around like you're the bitch. This chick has changed you," I said poking him in the chest. "You're *not* the same person."

"Neither are you. Look at you. You don't do anything anymore but go out. Partying has become your life. You're like those dicks you always used to hate. You've become STD Stan."

In some ways, I'll admit now, he was right, but he could only blame himself. I followed his lead. He made me. He never taught me about pacing myself.

And some of this I told him. "Looks like you fucked up, pal."

I was yelling the way you yell at the kicker who missed the game-winning field goal in the Super Bowl. The way you yell at the dog when it pissed on the carpet and you've already had a bad day.

I wasn't the one in the wrong.

"Besides, I like who I am," I continued. "*I've* got friends, *I'm* not boring. You notice how none of the guys call you anymore? I'm living the life you *used* to have, while now you're out playing Clark Griswold with Heather."

Pride.

And it went on. There was more about Homecoming. The broken promises. The way he stopped hanging out with us. The way he all of a sudden thought he was better than all of us. The way he abandoned me.

We paced around the room.

"Is this really about her and me or is there more here?" Ethan yelled back. "This has nothing to do with Heather, does it?"

Finally, I had pissed him off. He was yelling the way you'd yell at your boss if you didn't care about getting fired. The way you yell while stuck in traffic.

"I guess I can only blame myself," I said, throwing my hands in the air, "because I'm the only reason you know her."

The sarcasm ended there.

"Go on," Ethan said.

"*You stole her from me,*" I spat at him.

There I said it.

The fucker stole her from me.

The one girl who noticed me. The girl who smiled. The first girl to ever show genuine interest in me. Yeah, I had said I failed with her. I failed to tell Ethan to back the hell off.

My best friend. What friend?

Then he tried using my words against me.

"You told me you didn't care if I saw her," he said as his anger faded.

"I *lied,* asshole. How could I not care? I'd been staring at her in class all year. I told you about her. You *cock*-blocked me."

I was still plenty pissed. The way baseball coach fathers are pissed when their kids strike out. Their failures projected on others.

It was getting worse.

Wrath.

"Hey man," he said.

Somehow, he was trying to settle me down. It's the last thing I wanted. Holding all of this in, I wanted his reaction to be equal. I was sick of him being the calm one. I wanted him to feel what I felt.

Still, he wouldn't return the anger I spewed at him.

"I'm sorry, I know that was a asshole thing to do, but it was so long ago. Besides, I love her," he said. "She loves me. We're talking about a future together."

Panting in anger, I said it.

"You *love* her? *You* love *her*? *I* love *her*."

There's no way to know how those words passed my lips. The rage had lubed them out of my mouth.

I love her. It was impossible not to. Her laugh was gorgeous. There was the way she'd lift just her eyes and do a slow blink when she was nervous. She'd come into the apartment and leave her smell on everything. No matter how much everything else pissed me off, I couldn't help but breathe her in.

She was Heather. God creating Eve was just practice.

When those two met, I lost everything I had. She went away and so did Ethan. I escaped the best way I knew how.

Ignore everything, that was my defense mechanism.

All I got out of it was her hair stuck on the shower wall.

Ethan stood there. I stood there. We just stood there, inches away from each other and yet miles apart. He couldn't hide his shame.

I started yelling again. "*React* motherfucker! Say something."

There was nothing he could say, he told me.

"I'm sorry," he said, those gray eyes pointed down at the floor. His indignity was pitiful.

Finally, I stopped yelling. I ran my hands back through my hair and took a deep breath.

"What's done is done," I said. "I just want you to know the only reason I hadn't said anything until now was because I needed you. I needed you to get me connected, teach me what I needed to know."

Drink Day topped it all off. It was the proving point that I didn't need Ethan anymore. I had my friends. I knew the right party houses. I dressed well. The Dealer was my dealer. Girls threw themselves at me.

Now was time to let Ethan know.

"I never *fucking* liked you, you arrogant prick. Mr. I'm-So-Cool, I know everything. You're so full of shit. Look at you, you couldn't even decide on a major."

This is how Judas would have talked to Christ.

Outraged is how I'd like to describe the look on his face, but despair would fit better. It's how a kid would react to watching a brand new fluffy puppy get tossed in the microwave and set to Popcorn.

That's the reaction I wanted.

Ethan just found out someone who seemed to worship him, someone he genuinely thought he was helping, comes around to shove a spear in his side.

My savior.

It felt good. Hurt those who hurt you. That's another defense mechanism.

And it was working. He tried shrugging it off, but I could tell it cut him, especially when he saw me smiling after I said it.

He was finally the one stuck saying nothing. He went into his room, stuffed things into a laundry bag and headed for the front door. He held a leather book in his hand.

Ethan said he would go home for the weekend and let things chill.

"Good, run away," I yelled.

But I was still pissed.

The door clicked shut.

"Don't fucking come back. *You're dead to me anyway!*"

Little did I know Ethan, would be found dead in his parent's basement less than twenty-four hours later. I left the apartment to do the only thing I knew — get drunk. It was the hangover I'd awake to the next morning.

The morning of the phone call.

The gut-wrenching feeling I had on the bathroom floor.

The throwing up.

I deserved it all.

FORTY-ONE

My lungs burned. My legs ached.

It was at a park on the river's edge where I finally couldn't go another step. I nearly collapsed on a bench. The cold winds guaranteed there wouldn't be anyone else around. I was alone.

I wanted to run farther. I wanted to run until I felt nothing. Physical and emotional numbness was what I craved. But my body, completely out of shape from too much beer and deep-fried food, told me it was time to stop.

Catching my breath, I watched as a crowd of ducks plucked at the barren grass. In the hundred or so green and gray birds, there was a single white one with an orange beak. The little bastard gawked at me as the rest pecked at the ground for food. They all stood around or walked in circles. The white one looked at me. I glared back.

I didn't know whether to feel sorry for the sole white bird because he didn't fit in, or be jealous because he wasn't like the rest. Sure. there were others like him somewhere else, but in his social circle, he shone like the sun. And he kept staring at me.

That's when I finally got it.

I put that gun in Ethan's mouth.

The second I figured the voice on the other side of the phone was Ethan's mom, I knew things were totally fucked. That's what I get for letting Ethan give her my number in case of emergency.

That sigh of relief when I realized Ethan hadn't called was just to make sure no one would find out. To make sure questions wouldn't immediately fall on me.

Sure, I turned against him. The guilt over the Heather situation, arguably the best thing in his life, was my doing.

Still, there was Ethan that I knew—who he thought he had to be—and who Ethan was before. He was as confused as I was when we first met, but too scared to admit it. His two sides were at war.

Pit a guy against himself and he'll always lose.

Then to top it all off, his best friend tells him he was used through their entire friendship. And his last words to him were "you're dead to me anyway."

The guy never stood a chance against himself.

If we only knew.

We didn't.

Finally, I cried. There on a park bench, sweaty and covered in my own puke, I cried. It's the reaction you're supposed to have when your friend kills himself.

I couldn't pull my head out of my hands. Slumped over with every sobbing breath I pulled more of the rancid smell of the vomit into my mouth. I didn't care.

Maybe everyone from the funeral home was right. Maybe I was the one who should have known. Maybe it was my lack of action that killed Ethan. We had been friends for years, yet I never suspected anything. His journal, the one I kept in my jacket pocket, told me everything.

Ethan hated himself. He felt he couldn't create the change in himself, but he never realized he did. He loathed the world he lived in and the hatred that fueled it. The bickering and the self-centeredness. The egos, the brand recognition. Status symbols. His own apathy.

No.

It was his inability to accept himself when so many others did. If he would have just looked for a second, let his guard down and taken that stupid mask off, he would have realized. If he could have just seen everything, everyone who loved him, everyone who worshiped him, he would have been fine.

I'd like to think all of this crossed his mind that last second before the bullet did. With a pull of the trigger, he found something out.

Maybe he flinched.

He paused.

He jerked.

He moved.

He must have.

The second before the pressure from the shell expanded in his mouth, maybe he realized he wanted to live.

For what reason, I don't know. I'll never know and neither will anyone else. We can only speculate. That why I'm now the enemy. That's where we are now.

I can only guess at the details. There's no real concrete proof that this is what happened, but at least thinking about it helps.

We had our argument. Ethan felt he had long betrayed me. Then he discovered it was I that had used him. Me, the only person he thought was a real friend. He was sick of faking everything. He longed to feel something real, even though he was too dumb to see what he had before him.

He went home planning to kill himself. I can only explain that by the fact he left his sweatshirt. He never would have left that otherwise. He had intent when I last talked to him.

Ethan had intent the whole time I knew him.

He went home. Maybe he was looking for a reason not to. Maybe he could move back home, forget who he pretended to be at school. His family would understand.

They didn't. As usual, his dad probably ragged on him and his mom questioned his every move. The boa was wrapping tighter around his neck. His options were cut off. His mom and dad had left him sitting in front of the TV. They had no reason to suspect anything was wrong. They had their date planned for a month.

Now alone in the house, he went into his dad's office. He removed the 9mm Beretta from the glass case. He loaded the clip, cocked it and headed for the basement.

Again, I am speculating, but I can only say he went down there because it would be easier to clean up. Maybe he didn't want to be found. Maybe he didn't want the neighbors to hear, knowing the house's foundation would muffle the gunshot. Maybe he knew he wouldn't spoil his parents' evening by just going away to a remote spot in the house.

It could have been worse. Ethan could have gone out to the middle of the woods where his body wouldn't have been found for weeks or months. Then they would need to pull his dental records because animals would have eaten the flesh off him. I don't think he wanted to be that much trouble.

Screw what the cops call it. That's not a "clean" suicide. It's better to know right away than hold onto hope that someone's alive.

Hope will kill you. Especially when you lose it.

Maybe he went to the basement because that's where he felt the most comfortable. Partying in basements was where I'd seem him the most alive.

Sitting down, he propped himself up against a wall. He might have fidgeted for a while trying to make sure he'd be able to hold the gun securely enough and where to point it. Maybe he didn't because he already knew.

Maybe he knew the head is a natural silencer.

He pulled the trigger. He jerked slightly at the last moment.

It wasn't enough.

The bullet tore through his head, leaving him just alive enough to lie there thinking.

What was it about? What was that one thing that made him think twice? Was it Heather? Was it me? It probably wasn't either of us.

Little did Ethan know his own strength until he found out that even a gunshot to the head couldn't kill him right away. It took about an hour to bleed out. It happened just about the time Kathy was getting her salmon and Steve his steak.

But I can't blame them. I can only blame myself.

My hands were covered in Ethan's blood. In God's eyes, it's just like I pulled the trigger.

Honestly, I'm really not a bad guy.

All I got out of it was a journal in one pocket telling me I was clueless to who my friend was, memories of who he pretended to be, and a funeral home full of friends and family that wanted my head for not knowing the difference.

It's a lonely place. There's only one way out of it now.

But my tears weren't for Ethan. They were for myself. They were for who I was and what I've become. Ethan's suicide told me I was just another drunken idiot college student. Not the good kind, either.

Trying to convince myself Ethan was culpable, I finally realized this was not his doing. I did it to myself, but still I put it on someone else. Blame was all I knew.

Enough of this crap. Enough waiting. I wanted to know why. Damn it, I was owed at least that much. I pulled out his journal, flipped past the pages I had already read, and jumped to the last entry. I started reading.

Now in the winter of my lifetime, I make a declaration while in sound mind.

Ethan wrote as an act of contrition. I read for absolution.

I read the full entry and put the journal back into my pocket. I stopped crying.

As I stood up, wiping my eyes with the sleeves of my suit jacket, a car horn blasted from the nearby street. It honked again, with a familiar voice calling my name.

"Chris," she yelled.

It was Heather. I avoided calling her after I had found out. I dodged her on campus. I didn't even notice her at the funeral home. She was the last person I wanted to talk to, yet the only one I wanted to be with now.

"What are you *doing*?" she yelled. "Get in the car!"

As I got in, she just started talking.

"We're all taking this hard, but there was no reason to avoid me," she said. "No one's blaming you for anything. Ethan did something foolish."

She talked in clichés. Suicide is the permanent solution to a temporary problem, she said. She didn't know what that problem was.

Up until where we were now, Ethan still talked about me. He wondered what it was that he did to upset me. He wanted a way to bring everything back to the way it was. That's why he worked so hard at Drink Day.

"He worried about you. He didn't understand how you changed so drastically in such a short while."

At a time when I should have been the one explaining things to her, when the girl Ethan loved should have been getting the answers, Heather couldn't help but console me. She was trying to make me feel better. She was being sweet to me. It was the only thing she knew.

"You were his best friend," she said. "At times, I think he loved you more than he loved me. But it was apparent you broke his heart."

Ethan felt like he couldn't talk to me anymore, she said.

Now would have been the appropriate time to tell her about our fight, about everything. In pain, full disclosure carries the most healing power. This was when I should have told her we fought over her. I should have told her it was my fault.

But my confession would have served no purpose other than to cleanse myself. It was something I didn't deserve. Nothing was all I said. There was no given answer to these circumstances. I thought my newly-structured self could handle it, but I was wrong. Still, all I wondered was what Ethan would have done in this situation. Which Ethan? The one we knew or the one he saw himself as.

"Ethan wasn't the person we thought he was," she told me.

She knew.

She just stared at the steering wheel. There was no way to judge if she actually knew this fact or it was just something she had to deal with. Maybe it something she was proud of. She wasn't looking at me at all.

She explained everything.

"There was always something about him that seemed wrong," Heather said. "There were these moments where he had that look in his eyes that he didn't know what to do next. Then in a flash, that look would be gone."

"I think that's what I loved about him the most, those moments," she continued. "It wasn't when he was running around with you or when he was being a sweetheart. It was when he looked like he was about to just lose it all. Those moments were only when he was being honest with himself."

But Ethan wouldn't say anything if questioned. He'd always brush it off as nothing, she said.

Somewhere Ethan got the idea he had to be somebody else. We didn't know where that image came from. Maybe it was early in high school. Maybe it was from mimicking his dad.

Always in the back of his mind, Ethan realized he was a faker. A fraud. An imposter. A pretender. A phony.

Maybe he knew it wouldn't last. Maybe he knew it would all catch up with him. Someone would find out and it would all be over. His charade would come crashing down in one failed moment.

Until the day he died, Ethan did everything to insulate all of us from finding out things about him. Even from our first conversation, he could have said something about how much we had in common—the clubs, the sports, the anything—but he didn't. There was something in his past that scared him. Maybe it was his normalcy that terrified him. Or becoming his dad.

You can only lie to yourself for so long.

With a family like his, I can see why he wouldn't want to parade them around. Mom the nympho. Dad the judgmental workaholic. It's amazing, growing up around that shit, that he didn't have more congenital personality defects. He tried. He failed. The farce could only go so far.

It was self-destruction from the beginning.

And our fight told him all the people he loved were now against him. I told him—in essence—he had no reason to live. With my twenty-twenty hindsight, I could give him countless reasons.

The girl in the driver's seat would be number one on that list.

Lately, I wouldn't have put myself near the top, if anywhere on the list.

Staying inside the car, Heather and I finally began to talk. We had our first conversation. The one we should have had with that first cup of coffee. Instead, I went to class and now we're burying Ethan. Mostly we talked about Ethan when he was alive, but she also confronted me about my animosity towards her.

I blamed the hair, the shampoo, and the tampons. It was anything but my feelings for her. It was not the fact I loved her. It was the hair in the shower. It was not wanting to live with a couple.

It was anything but the truth.

I looked at her. Her brown hair pulled into a ponytail. With the freckles. With the eyes red from days of crying. Her with the blank look of acceptance. I didn't even want to know what I looked like.

And we kept talking. Then it was time to stop.

It was time to go back.

We needed to say good-bye to a friend.

A best friend. A boyfriend. The one we barely knew.

FORTY-TWO

Now in the winter of my lifetime, I make a declaration while in sound mind.

Some time ago, someone wrote something different for me. What that was, I am unsure. There's no hint to what could be done, but there's soot on my hands and dirt underneath my fingernails that cannot simply be washed away. There are those who have gone before me that might have the answers, but I have failed to learn from the wisdom they left for me.

Somewhere, something went wrong in so many ways that I am left with nothing but remorse that has taken over a place once filled with shallow happiness. Someone wanted bigger things for me, but all that is left is the hollow person writing these words. There used to be dreams, hopes and ambitions, but it has all been replaced by fear.

I wish for nothing more than for lights to guide me home.

With clear vision all I can see is a future dominated by dread. I have let in that which is killing me and everyone I love. It is for them that I must do that which is necessary. My only hope is that they realize that I wasn't the person I presented myself to be.

There is a reason I am here, the x-point in the plotted path that is my life. The road is diverging and all I want to do is continue driving straight forward. I am attempting to take the unavoidable option. That means I must ultimately admit defeat. I have denied it for too long. I lost. I am lost.

There is no way to reverse the steps I have taken to this place. The closer I get to admitting these words to be true, the closer I become to clearing those around me of any wrongdoing. My bed has been made for me long ago. All I dream of is sleep. A sleep no longer haunted by the mistakes I have made. A sleep that can only come after all past sins have been atoned for. All hope for a pure personal absolution is lost.

My hand is forced only by the actions that cannot be changed. I have failed. There is nothing for me here.

FORTY-THREE

The funeral procession of cars drove past us on our way to the cemetery. Heather knew where she was going.

We meandered through the winding road looking for the site. Huge statues of angels, Mary and Joseph lined the path of the cemetery. Ethan's grave was near the back.

Out of sight, out of mind, I guess.

A middle-aged man was already there, ready to cover Ethan's casket. A small bulldozer-like machine was already parked there as the worker pulled what remained of flower arrangements off the casket. Heather parked the car and we walked up to the grave. All the other mourners were gone.

Seeing us standing there, the man walked up slowly and handed a red rose to Heather. She said thank you.

"Give us a minute, would ya' pal," I said to the man.

I glared at the headstone. It was a Celtic cross. There was an inscription below his name and the birth and death dates.

There, but for the Grace of God, go I.

Ethan, the guy who died at birth and questioned if God existed. Still, his mom thought after committing a mortal sin, her son would be whisked away in God's arms.

His soul would be tortured for all eternity. He thought life on Earth was bad. As I stood there, Ethan was probably burning in hell.

"Save me a spot in heaven," I whispered just loud enough so Heather would hear.

There was nothing else for me to say. It would have been just the same if the gun was in my hand.

"I'm sorry buddy," I mumbled. "Please forgive me."

Heather looked over at me, tears coming down her face. I wiped one off her check.

"Chris … eventually, you'll have to stop blaming yourself," she said.

The apology wasn't for what I had done or for what I failed to do. It wasn't. I was sorry for finally rationalizing everything in my head. I shouldn't have been worrying about how I could come out on top, in one piece.

Ignore it and it will all go away.

I was never looking for why Ethan committed suicide, but somehow, in all the possibilities, that I was not the reason he decided to do it. I wanted someone, something else to be cast as a traitor. It was the first thing I had done when I found out about it. It was my initial reaction and the right one.

Once I could clear my name of his death, I would have stopped looking.

Heather didn't blame me. That was good enough.

Call me Brutus.

Ethan was nothing special. I put all of my stock in him because he was a means to an end. He could get me to where I needed to be—the parties, the friends, the drugs, the girl. To his credit, I wouldn't have done it on my own. He was my ticket in.

It's what I had told Ethan before he left. It wasn't just to piss him off. I meant every word.

We create our saviors.

That's what I did. From our first cigarette together, I knew I wanted to be Ethan, or who he was pretending to be. I wanted his calm demeanor under pressure, his way to unite people and the way he always had answer for everything. I wanted his life experiences.

But he was a fake.

It was obvious when he punched my wall freshman year. I watched as he tried to keep everything together and then sprang out in anger. Immediately, he became calm again, trying to keep his exterior up. I knew what was going on.

Still, I didn't care, unless it could get me into a party.

Ethan's downfall was that he couldn't see how well he had us all fooled. It was working, but then he had to go and ruin it. If you play pretend long enough, it becomes reality. A reality you create.

My tears weren't even real. Not anymore.

Bless me, Ethan, for I have sinned.

The cemetery worker looked at us. After burying probably hundreds of people, he still managed to look like he was sad. I wondered if it was sincere or if he learned to fake it, too. I gave a nod and he began filling in the grave. He started with a shovel, maybe just for show. The dirt made a thumping noise when it hit the aluminum casket lid.

Heather grabbed my hand. I was playing the part of the grieving friend and it was working. I was getting what I wanted. She looked at me, her eyes soggy with smearing black mascara rings around them. She squeezed my hand and gave me a comforting look.

"Let's go," she said softly to me as she turned back toward the car. She dropped her grip of my hand.

"Yeah," I said, wiping my sleeve across my face.

It was the last tear I would shed for him.

The future for me was clear. I'd remain pretending to grieve Ethan's death. Heather and I would continue to ponder what went wrong. I'd use her devastation and grief to my advantage.

We all do it.

Before long, she'd forget about Ethan, or just use me as his replacement. She'd begin looking at me the way the way she did him. She'd love me back.

But, before any of this could happen, there was one more thing I had to do.

I watched as Heather walked away, far enough so I knew she wouldn't see. I pulled the journal from by pocket, my fingers sliding over the smooth leather cover. I tossed it in with the dirt as Heather's back was turned.

I guaranteed Ethan's suicide would remain the mystery it needed to be.

As far as I knew, I was the only one to see the journal and I wasn't telling anyone. No one would have any idea where I could have stepped in to save him.

No one would ever know what he was really thinking.

No one knew of my involvement.

Everyone could remain dumb to the details. Only I knew the truth. I had control.

A fake reality works beautifully.

And God thinks He has all the power.

Envy. Greed. Gluttony.

Sure, I'll end up throwing on the mask Ethan wore. I'll be playing roles over and over to get what I want. We all do it. Some are just better than others.

Bless me Ethan. It has been seven years since my last *real* confession.

If you would ask me, I would say I didn't want Ethan dead. He was my best friend. My corruptor. My savior.

Was. He was what I needed when I met him. Then I outgrew him.

My guilt over his suicide has subsided. It's come and gone. My hands have been washed clean. His death is not my fault. He failed himself. He failed me.

Just because he's dead doesn't mean I can't get something out of it.

Every time someone dies, someone else profits. Insurance benefits, promotions, property acquisition, power. It's the paycheck of other's weakness.

The demise of others is good for business. Without others ahead of us ending up as spectacular failures, we'd all be stuck at the bottom.

Good-bye my friend. It's forward now I go.

It's in the ground with you.

I am sorry for my sins. They are lust, pride, gluttony, greed, wrath, sloth and envy. I'd finally gotten through all seven. I got what I wanted and I was still alive.

Ethan killed himself every day he couldn't admit to himself that he wasn't the person he saw in the mirror. His death began the day he started lying to himself. If he would have been as smart as he pretended to be, he would have seen everything that he had. Fuck him for missing it.

By now, taking Ethan's path of self-denial, I run the risk of the same outcome. I don't care. I'll get what I want. It would be a means to an end.

The girl would surely be mine. I'd have friends. I'd be the life of the party. I'd succeed where Ethan failed.

People do it every day. We put on makeup to mask our imperfections. We wear name brands to prove how much money we have when we really don't have shit. We say what's socially acceptable instead of what we feel. We PR ourselves to death.

We create our saviors.

Then we quickly destroy them.

Ethan tried creating a savior inside himself. It didn't work out.

We can't be God so we settle for telling ourselves we can. We hope people will think the personas we keep are who we really are.

Little white lies are fashionable. The Seven Deadly Sins are in this season.

All of us lie all of the time. We lie to everyone. Mostly, we lie to ourselves, perpetuating the train wrecks that are our lives.

I'm no different.

But at least I admit it.

Acknowledgements

The author would like to thank his mother and father for the support, and sacrifices they always made for their children. For my sister and brother, for always watching out for me.

Special thanks go to Shawn Eldridge, a great motivator, editor and designer. May his payment in karma come to him ten-fold.

Thanks to Matt Meenan for proofreading in a pinch.

Other thanks go to good friends and the faculty of Winona State University, everyone at SkateChurch and Copia Martini & Wine, The Rock Island Argus/The (Moline) Dispatch.
Also to Meredith, Barb, Tony, Melissa and Aiden.
Thanks, everyone, for believing in me.